The Accessory

James G Hutchison

The Accessory
Published by James G Hutchison

This is a work of fiction. Names, characters, places, and
incidents either are the product of the author's imagination,
or are used fictitiously.

Any resemblance to actual persons, living or dead, events,
or locales is entirely coincidental.

ISBN 978-0-9812343-0-4

Typesetting: Helen Moss

To my wife Moira

Acknowledgements

There are a few people that deserve much credit for their help in creating this novel. Firstly, my wife Moira who was an invaluable sounding board throughout the initial plot development, as well as my first draft editor. Rene Labreque: thanks for going over the trial portion. May you rest in peace my friend. My sister Helen for the final edit: your sharp eye has left your mark on just about every page – thanks sis! Ken Bell: you caught typos and spelling errors no one else did. Many thanks. Stephen Haigh: for your insights, suggestions, encouragement, and most of all, friendship.

James Hutchison
Burnstown, Canada

Prologue

It's the morning of the big day. Prepping his old firearm means using liquid gun blue to protect the exterior of his .22 caliber rifle. He hates rust... makes his Remington look old. Well, it is old, but this gun kit keeps it shining. And thanks to a few drops of light oil here and there, it looks and handles as if it were brand new. As he savors the results of his efforts, the orange glint of the early morning sunrise off the scope's lens gives him pause. A new day. *Servants of Satan must be punished for all to see* he thinks to himself. But, daily devotions come first. His prayer time will help him focus, and distract him from the reality of today's mission.

The ride into town is a little different than usual; he doesn't normally drive this early Monday mornings, so traffic is sparse. "We should have this job done well before work starts," he says to his passenger. Today, they will exact judgment on a murderer of innocent life, and their reward is knowing that divine justice will be channeled through them.

The clinic door is locked. The frightened girl sits on the concrete steps, butting out her second cigarette since arriving ten minutes ago. She rarely smokes this heavily, but this morning is an exception. Her nervousness almost gets the better of her – she is just about to desert her appointment when two vehicles pull into the parking lot, one after the other. The first steers towards the sign that reads "Doctor" and the other over to a sign that reads "Employees". With a sense of relief also comes a fear of the unknown. *Will this hurt?*

A few hundred yards away sits an idling half-ton truck, with the passenger side window rolled half-way down, and a beanbag strangely perched on the edge of the glass… it's supporting the tip of a Remington .22 caliber rifle if you look close enough. "Why didn't he listen!" he whispers, peering through the scope. Letter after letter, the doctor was warned by an anonymous group to stop these pro-bono abortions on young girls – heck, they're not even in college yet. No money or medical coverage, and parents that won't listen, this doctor figures he is doing them and society a service. Why bring unwanted babies into the world?

The nurse waves at the young girl, walks to the back of her car, opens the trunk, and begins unloading the audio-visual equipment from last night's family planning seminar. Her presentations are an attempt to lobby for minors that need access to abortion without parental consent. "Equal access for all." That is her mission. Her daydreaming is interrupted…

BLAM! The shot is precise. The .22 caliber jacketed hollow-point flies down the barrel at 1,750 feet per second, and instantly finds its way to the doctor's cerebellum. Stepping out of his SUV with briefcase in one hand and clinic keys in the other, he had no idea what hit him.

The nurse's back is turned, but she hears the crack of the rifle, tires squealing, and from the doctor's vehicle – a tinkling sound. What catches her eye is someone running a couple of blocks away, then a set of keys skidding across the parking lot, stopping in front of her back left tire. She turns her head, and shock overtakes her perception of reality. *WHAT? Can I believe what I'm seeing right now?*

She runs to his side, watching literally quarts of blood cover the pavement, his arms and legs jerking as if a puppeteer was having a bad day. Hands shaking, it is all she can do to press the numbers on her mobile phone… 9-1-1. As she yells out the clinic's address, the doctor slips into unconsciousness.

The shocked young girl has never seen this much blood before – knees shaking, she frees herself from the shock of disbelief and bolts towards the doctor, removes her hoodie, handing it to the nurse.

"Nurse – here's a pillow for the doctor – can I help?"… the nurse slowly looks up, tears streaming down her cheeks… "Thanks sweetheart, but I think it's too late."

In the dimly-lit basement of a large industrial building, a small group of men are standing around a massive oval-shaped wooden table. Light from torches and candles barely illuminate the gargoyles and other night creatures carved into the large twisted pedestal leg. This table is considered sacred to these men, who seem to be a little nervous at this present time… A figure from the shadows approaches the Group.

"For you, sir" he says, handing someone a mobile phone. The group leader quickly places the cell phone to his ear…

"Yes – yes – OK. No witnesses? I see… I'll pass that on. Well done, son."

He clears his throat, and in a low, booming voice exclaims:

"Gentlemen, it is done. We have conquered evil again. Our identities are safe. Brother Michael, please pour the wine."

"Yes, sir." Brother Michael walks around the table, pouring wine into everyone's chalice, then returns to his spot.

The leader raises his cup in the air as the others follow his lead.

"Death to evil!"

"Death to evil!" they all respond in unison, their voices echoing off the concrete wall.

Part One
Chapter 1

Deforestation of the Amazon is not of particular concern to Peter G. Underbridge. What does interest him, and his company's shareholders, is the readily available gold just under the surface of the area's weak and fragile soil. *I've made a few bucks from this place,* he reflects. And so have the *garimpeiros* – the local gold miners. They use powerful water cannons connected to nearby rivers to blast away vegetation and soil, creating open pits so the collectors can dig and pan for their daily quota.

Underbridge knows his time in Brazil is short – the central government is beginning to enforce their border controls and export restrictions. Still, he has a month more than any other mining operation. He'll miss that ambassador he's had in his back pocket since opening operations in the state of Roraima two years ago.

Venezuela is next. No such restrictions like Brazil. *Yet.* His trip today to Valencia will galvanize a deal with a mining operator who doesn't want the investment risks anymore – just a cut. Outsourcing the expertise to the locals is Underbridge's way of minimizing cost, reducing risk to employees, and staying at arm's length from day-to-day operations. They're paid to produce, not whine about being so far from home.

"Sir, another drink?" The flight attendant catches his attention.
"Yes. But no ice please."

Walking away, he eyes her calf muscles. *She must run*, he thinks. *I need to get back to the gym.*

He returns to his report. He takes note of the key players in Valencia: the politicians for and against open-pit mining, the tree-huggers from California that have set up permanent camp, the other mining operations already in full swing. His research assistant back in New York has done his job in spades, and he knows he'll miss important details by not reading it cover to cover. That's his way. Hire the best and pay them the best, otherwise the competition will nab them.

I wonder why this is...? Underbridge murmurs under his breath. What others may pass off as a minor detail, he knows from experience that every fact is of vital importance. He lifts the phone from the cradle in front of him and dials a number. Three rings and someone answers.

"Hello, this is Clark. How may I help you?"

"Clark, it's Peter. You holding down the fort OK?"

"Oh hey Mr. Underbridge, how are you? You sound like you're still in the air. Let me guess... you're reading my report and you have a question."

"You're telepathic! Yes, I've a question about the tree-huggers, specifically the ring leader. Any more word from L.A.? I'm concerned that they may be up to something unusual; you know, different this time."

"Funny you ask. I was confirming the details and was going to email your Blackberry. Our source in L.A. has some new information on our Miss "Change-the-world-with-eco-terrorism" chickadee you'll want to know. You won't need to write this down... just listen to this!"

Underbridge covers his other ear...

"Go on."

While Underbridge listens intently, his flying partner takes note of his changed demeanor, and half-cocks her head. *Something's up* she ponders.

Underbridge and his research assistant exchange a few more words, closing off with...

"Thanks Clark, keep your ears to the ground and call if you hear anything more. Thanks."

With that, he returns the receiver to its cradle and makes an expression at his assistant Maria, as if to say *I got it under control.*

What little Spanish he knows can get him around OK, but not well enough for business. Hence the need for Maria. Originally from Brazil, her folks emigrated to Los Angeles when she was six. A graduate of Berkeley with specialties in business and foreign communications, she is also trained in protocol. She's been the perfect travel partner for these stays south of the equator. Her quick tongue and good looks keep Underbridge moving swiftly through customs, car rental arrangements, and – most importantly – business negotiations.

"You look a bit concerned. Everything OK?"

"Ah, we'll be fine. I'll fill you in later."

He returns to his report, opening it to the middle where he has underlined someone's name.

"Maria – this politician – Jose Alverez… did he confirm?"

"Yes – it's in your day timer and your Blackberry."

"Thanks. Did I mention I don't pay you enough?"

"I remind you all the time." She smirks.

Underbridge is cordial, even kind to the people he surrounds himself with. But if someone gets in his way or they mess up, they're the first to know. Sipping on his rye and coke, he looks calm, but in his mind he's like a hawk circling its prey. He loves the adrenaline rush of starting a new mining operation; each location has its specific challenges, both technically and logistically. Like a master conductor, he doesn't play anyone's instrument – well, at first anyways. He'll be both strategist and tactician when first presented with a new set of challenges, a new set of politicians to analyze, a new group of protesters. He gets his hands dirty when he has to, and will always use the lessons he learns to teach the people that work with him… "You saw how that went. I shouldn't have to see it happen again, right?"

Yes sir, Mr. Underbridge.

Once the place is spinning like a top, he moves on to the next gold mine.

———————————

The Hawker 800 jet touches down smoothly on the airport tarmac. While they unbuckle their seatbelts, the flight attendant informs Maria and Underbridge they are just behind a *Spanair* A320 that will be out of the way shortly. Looking out his window, Underbridge spots what looks like their limo a quarter mile away. *You have eyes like an eagle*, his doctor told him long ago. While his friends in the army reserves tried to convince him he'd be a great sniper, he learned soon enough that the pen was indeed mightier than the sword.

Through customs and baggage claim in thirty minutes, they find the limo and give the driver an address. He whisks the pair off to a luxury condo just north of the airport. Maria has the keys in her purse; her assistant made the arrangements weeks ago.

Once up the elevator to the third floor, Maria opens up the large double doors, and they immediately scout out the 2,000-square-foot luxury apartment.

"Nice place. There's even food in the cupboards – look at this."

Underbridge is admiring the view of Casupo Mountain – he turns his head – "So, you cooking?"

"You wouldn't want to eat what I cook. *Dogs* don't want to eat what I cook…"

"Hm. Something you're not good at. Interesting."

The driver knocks on the front door and lets himself in with their suitcases.

"Right there is good. Thanks." says Maria. "We'll be down in 20 or so minutes." The driver acknowledges with a wave of his hand.

They each claim a bedroom. Underbridge was a gentleman and had cleared the arrangements with Maria weeks ago, but he did hint at getting a one-bedroom pad. Maria was quick to stop him in his tracks.

"I guess you won't mind the couch then?"

Their banter is more fun than anything else; ulterior sexual motives don't have a place in either of their lives.

They unpack and begin changing into their business suits. Maria yells to Underbridge –

"There might be some protesters this afternoon at the contractor's. I had Gerry call the local police to tell them we were coming through."

"You're ahead of me. Good thinking. The group down here is nasty, led by some angry hippy-chick from Los Angeles. She's behind a lot of these."

"Ya, I saw the surveillance black and whites. She gets around."

"She's under investigation for environmental terrorism. I won't tell you who's behind it, but her partner's phone is tapped. I get all the intel from LAPD."

Maria walks out into the living room brushing her hair. "Well aren't you one connected guy."

"Whatever it takes," he says as he straightens his tie in the hallway mirror.

Maria asks: "Is that what the phone call was about? You mentioned you'd fill me in later."

"Indeed it was. Clark got word from the local police here via our informant at the LAPD that the tree huggers are planning something for our trip. No word what, but they warned us to be hyper vigilant. So, it was a good move to arrange for some police presence. They're already aware of them as I mentioned, so I'm sure they'll show up in droves."

Maria's face goes slightly pale. "You don't suppose they'll try anything silly like plant a bomb or anything?" Her face and voice tone give away the butterflies in her stomach.

"Listen, Maria, don't worry. I've been dodging these assholes for years. It's a bit of cat and mouse. For instance, our chauffeur – where's he from?"

"Oh dear, I forget…"

"Not *here*. Get it? I made sure he wasn't based anywhere close to Valencia where these losers could find him and bribe his ass. It happened in Venezuela when I first arrived a few years ago. The protest group found the limo company we hired and planted a stick of fake dynamite under my seat, with the words "leave or die" written in magic marker. Scared the crap out of me. Over the years I've learned most of their tactics and know what to look for."

Maria soaks in the information, and a bit of color returns to her face. "Is there anything *I* should know, or be aware of? You're kind of scaring me here. I'm not sure I signed up for this."

"Maria – please don't over react. It was fake dynamite and nothing has ever happened since. I have the confidence in the local authorities, and we're not the only ones the protesters don't like, so they keep a close eye on them." He changes the subject. "Alright – where are we going exactly?"

Maria sighs and looks up the address for their lunch meeting with Jose Alverez, the American ambassador. He's not in Valencia all that often, so they gladly changed their schedule for the meeting; this one's the most important.

Their driver knows the restaurant well. It has a back room for the elite that do not want to be engaged by the public; a perfect setting to have a meal and shake hands on deals that have no contract; agreements, but nothing is signed. "There was a gunfight there once – two years ago," the driver says. Maria looks out the window and exclaims, "Oh cute! The one day I didn't bring my Smith & Wesson" as she rolls her eyes at Underbridge. He raises his eyebrows in response, as if to say *Didn't I tell you it's all OK?*

The drive to the restaurant is quick and uneventful. The driver lets them exit the car at the front door, and hands both Underbridge and Maria a simple business card with his cell number in large bold characters. He explains...

"Call me two minutes before you need me to come back."

"Thank you."– they both respond at the same time. As they walk into the foyer of the restaurant, Maria comments:

"I like that. No middleman, no valets to tip."

"I like your taste in efficiency." responds Underbridge.

Now seated in the back room, everyone has made introductions and shaken hands. The waitress starts off the group with warm *arepas* and butter; they order wine, then begin discussing business. Mr. Alverez starts.

"Ms. Ramirez and Mr. Underbridge – I first must tell you I appreciate the generous offer you sent my wife last week. She would love to sit in the cockpit of your private jet. She has been clocking as many hours as she can for her commercial license. She fell in love with your model of aircraft in Brazil – the military have three or four of them."

"A *military* version of the 800? I'm not surprised – it's very agile. You know, our pilot will enjoy teaching her the ins and outs of the jet. It isn't the newest, but it has been upgraded since our company bought it last year. I'm sure he'll let her take the stick once or twice – pilots tell me it is an easy craft to handle. We're here for a few days, so if your wife isn't busy tomorrow, my pilot will welcome the break from his boring day."

"Yes, tomorrow is fine. Thank you."

Alverez shifts gears as the wine arrives.

"Now, I must inform you of the latest developments politically. As you know, Venezuela and Bolivia are close neighbors; they have very close ties that go back generations. There may be repercussions should America continue to dabble in Bolivia's politics; they're asking

11

Venezuela to show solidarity and expel their American ambassador
– *me* – should the situation escalate. So it's possible I may not be
around much longer."

"Interesting," says Underbridge. "I never did like politics.
What's their beef?"

"The States is accused of influencing some locals to form
a coup against Bolivia's president. The State Department denies such
things, but you know how much meddling goes on behind
the scenes."

"Will this affect mining operations? We're here to start up
a new site…"

"Yes, I realize that. You'll be safe; American dollars are always
welcome here – you employ people and stimulate the local economy.
For that, the Venezuelans are grateful."

"No export restrictions on the horizon?"

"Nothing I am aware of, and we should keep it that way.
My son goes to a private school and is friends with a boy named
Peter, same as you. His father is the minister of natural resources. It
just so happens we are having them over for cocktails and a meal
next month – I believe you will be receiving an invitation sometime
soon." He winks. Underbridge fills the ambassador's goblet with
more wine.

Maria loves watching her boss play the game. He's good at it,
and she picks up on his tactics, tucking them away for future use. *One
day I'll be doing this,* she thinks to herself. It's closer than she knows…

They chat about the so-called environmentalists who have set
up camp in Valencia.

"Yes, our local authorities have them under a very watchful
eye. There is concern that something may happen sometime soon,
though it is just conjecture."

This piques Maria's curiosity.

"Yes, exactly what do you know?" she asks.

"I do not want to alarm you unnecessarily, so please know this is only guess work at best. Two weeks ago, a construction site was vandalized, and after a quick inventory, the owner discovered that an amount of explosives were missing. Fourteen sticks of dynamite to be exact. Also, priming cord and other supplies." He holds up his finger… "Now, we *cannot* assume it is these environmental protesters, as there are other unsavory groups and individuals that would make use of such destructive materials."

"Such as…?" Underbridge chips in.

"Oh, the usual – organized crime, drug traffickers, and so on. But the unusual part of the crime is that they only took fourteen sticks. They left behind dozens more. It is as if they have a specific job in mind."

Maria's face goes flush for the second time today. Observing her reaction, Alverez handles her fear like a true politician.

"Ms. Ramirez – please do not be overly concerned, as your safety is our highest concern. I am close to the local police chief, and he assures me that his men are on high alert during the span of your visit. It would be terrible to allow such hooligans to get away with using these explosives in any way whatsoever… he tells me he has many undercover police scouring the city. He has them working on leads as we speak."

Underbridge takes control and comments as he looks at Maria, then Alverez.

"Well, I refuse to live in fear. We've been safe up to now, and I'm sure we will be for the rest of our visit. We have taken measures to be as discrete and stealthy as possible, so our where-abouts should be fairly hard to track down. We'll certainly keep an eye over our shoulders, but I'm confident we will be safe. I've lived through this in the past."

Maria interrupts – "Just the same, let's have our driver change vehicles every once in a while – like – daily!"

"Hmm. Good idea" responds Underbridge, placating Maria's fear.

With that, everyone settles back into their chairs, when Alverez holds up his wine goblet and toasts his guests.

"Peter, Maria – may your visit be prosperous, and may we all sleep like babies tonight!"

"Cheers!" they all exclaim.

The rest of the meal is taken up with the more trivial aspects of government policy, business incentives, and family. Family is everything in South America, and it rubs off on most visitors. By the time the bottle of wine is done, they're each pulling out their wallets to show off the latest pictures of their children.

"Junior baseball!"

"Debate team!"

"Theater!"

"His first tooth!"

The wine has done its job – they laugh like they've known each other for years. Underbridge orders another bottle after commenting that 750 ml isn't much for three people. Following dessert and coffee, the waitress approaches – Underbridge grabs the bill and hands her his VISA black card. Alverez raises his eyebrow.

"Is it true? Unlimited credit?"

"Urban myth. The limit is a quarter mil. I have to pay it off every month according to my bean counters, otherwise they freak. Isn't life tough?"

"Well, what I could do with such an expense account… there's a few bottles of rare wine that come to mind. You into collecting?"

Maria rolls her eyes at the waitress. *Men!*

The limo approaches a construction compound that has a large sign on the chain link fence "La Propiedad Privada. *Private Property*. Three police vehicles and a paddy wagon are close by, with a dozen officers standing around, arms folded, keeping their firearms in full view. There is a crowd of protesters in front of the gate carrying signs with words in both English and Spanish.

"Foreign Gold Miners Not Welcome"

"Stop Raping Our Land"

"We Only Have One Earth"

The group is chanting when the limo pulls up slowly, heading for the gate. A police officer blows his whistle, motioning them to allow the vehicle access. Three officers close in on the crowd; they move away from the limo. Underbridge is taken back… "How the hell did they know?" He looks at Maria. She shrugs her shoulders. Underbridge settles back in his seat, exasperated. He rants:

"Miserable people, these kids. They bitch about the commerce that makes the world go round. They complain about the system, while living off of it like leeches. They eat everything organic, then pollute themselves with hashish. The leaders are in the FBI's 'Persons of Interest' file… They piss me off."

As the limo enters the compound, people in the crowd shake their fists while yelling their slogans. The gate closes behind them as the limo heads to the main office.

"You have my number" says the driver.

"Sure do amigo. I suggest you don't leave though…"

"I wouldn't think of it! I'll see you soon."

The pair exit the limo and quickly slip into the main office's waiting area. A receptionist immediately waves to them and in broken English asks them their names. Maria takes over in Spanish and soon they are in a meeting room waiting for the company president. They both move over to a window where they can observe the group of protesters. From what they could gather, apparently someone threw a plastic water bottle at the crowd of police… someone was being escorted – quite forcefully – into the paddy wagon.

"Hold on to your hat" says Underbridge. "That may just get them going… " They're both startled by a booming voice behind them.

"Mr. Underbridge – Ms. Ramirez, welcome to our headquarters. My apologies for the crowd outside – they showed up last week."

Underbridge responds, "No problem – I'm used to their type."

The meeting room is prepped with pitchers of iced water, and off to the side, a tray with a bottle of tequila and shot glasses. *Quite the party crowd, these guys* thinks Maria. Other than the excitement of the protesters, the meeting is rather boring, and quite long. Underbridge goes over the geologist's report, talks to the surveyor with Maria as interpreter, and confirms the helicopter rental for the team's first on-site visit the next day. It takes a couple of hours to sift through details not covered by the contract, with Maria and Underbridge chatting in English in hushed tones. Maria translates to the president and his legal counsel, as they both nod their heads. They finally re-print the last draft; the secretary enters the meeting room with the laser-printed contract. Maria again interprets by scanning the Spanish wording.

"Yes, same as the English. Here's a pen."

After a few hand shakes, the company president speaks in his broken English.

"Madam and sir, we have a little custom in this company that we have been practicing for many years. When we make such a deal and shake hands, we celebrate with a drink of tequila." He looks at someone beside him – "José – *aprisa…*"

José swiftly retrieves the tray and pours everyone an ounce, then hands them out.

"Salud!"

"Salud!" responds everyone.

After the round of shooters, they shake hands again and begin to leave. Pleasantries are exchanged as Maria calls their driver, who is on the other side of the compound catching forty winks.

On their way back to the condo, Underbridge mouths the words to Maria…

"You like this driver?"

She nods *yes*.

"Then get him on retainer for whenever we're down here. I like to stick with someone steady; no surprises, you know? And – ask him to change cars every day."

"Consider it done. A good day's work." Maria then chats to the driver in articulate Spanish, instructing him of their requirements. He seems happy with his assignment.

"He's good to go. Hey – how about more drinks?"

"Are you asking me on a date, young girl?"

"Yes, but you're buying. There's a nice restaurant half a block from here. Let's walk. I need to shake off the day."

The driver pulls over at their request.

"That's it for today. We'll walk home from here – come by the condo for 8AM."

"Yes, sir. *Gracias*. Thank you, sir."

They saunter along *Avenida Bolivar* and find their destination, *Casa Valencia*.

"The place is very popular. Let's eat while we're here – their *tostones* are to die for from what I hear."

"How do you know so much about Valencia?"

"Research… and, my parents moved here from Brazil. East of here – Caracas. I'll want to see them if that's OK."

Underbridge begins saying… "For sure – and, did I mention I'm not…" she interrupts.

"*Paying* me enough? What do you plan on doing about that?"

"You're telepathic, just like my research assistant – I've something up my sleeve. I'll tell you over drinks."

Casa Valencia is a beautiful multi-tiered orange stucco building with traditional terra cotta roofing. Inside, the exposed stained beams create a rustic, yet elegant atmosphere – Underbridge is impressed.

"Good choice. Good time of day to pop in – not too many people."

They are seated in a corner booth just the way he prefers it. Back always facing the corner. As his mind wonders for a second, he catches a reflection of himself in a mirror across the room; he didn't recognize himself at first. What he did notice was the graying at his temples – it's more than it was a couple months ago. *Good thing I have black hair* he thinks… *looks distinguished*. Without opening his mouth, few locals would peg him as an outsider, or Maria for that matter, with her obvious Spanish/Mexican appearance, and Underbridge with his ruggedly handsome features and thin build.

After receiving their bottle of Merlot and appetizers, they chit chat about the new environment they'll be working in, the trips back and forth, the pain-in-the-butt protesters.

"Listen – Maria. I'm cooking up an idea for you. I think you're ready for this…"

She clears her throat – "Yes?"

"As you know, I'm always peeking into other people's business. There's a mining company that isn't doing so well on the market. I've been buying up stock. I mean damn, I thought they were going to have a fire sale last month. Eight bucks a share, down from 23 a year ago. Hard to believe for a mining corporation. Investors are nervous I suppose – remember that phony diamond mine in Nigeria? We've all taken a beating on that one. Anyways… they need new leadership. But I want the loser who's there now to stay so my stocks – well, *their* stocks keep falling. Their vice president is a damn good guy; he's worked with people I know, and I'm sure he's biting at the bit to take over from his incompetent leader."

"Why won't the board vote him out?"

"Severance. He negotiated a package that could take half the company's liquidity with him. Rat bastard. In that regard, he was smart.

"So here's my view: I can't meddle 'cause I'd likely draw suspicion. But – say you don't work for me as an employee anymore. We're done so-to-speak. We shake hands and part ways. You form your own consultancy corporation, specializing in getting companies back on their feet making a profit."

Maria swallows hard. Underbridge doesn't miss it.

"You and I become unfettered business partners. I *trust* you. There are very few people I say that to, and you know I don't bullshit."

Maria knows that for the two years by his side, she's never seen him shaft a fellow business person. He speaks his mind.

"Go on…"

"Well, I know two people on the board of this Midwest Mining Corporation, and they're desperate. You show up with your resume, and they'll hire you on the spot. Your mission is to keep the pres in place for at least a month while I buy up stock. You know, have him make a bad decision or two. Use your feminine wiles… Then get the board to boot him out. It won't matter how much the greedy prick takes with him; once he's gone, the board will look for another leader. *You* convince them the vice is their best bet. Rudman is his name."

Maria doesn't miss a beat. "Quite the mission. You think I'm up for it? You just gave me inside information. What's stopping *me* from buying, just like you?"

"*You* are. Only you can penetrate, divide, and conquer. I have to stay where I am. You'd be charged with inside trading if someone looked close enough. But Maria – there's more in this for you than making a few bucks on the market. This is about you moving on and moving up. Once their president is history and Rudman takes the helm, they'll be back on their feet by third quarter."

"Oh, you have a *schedule?*"

"Do I look stupid?"

Underbridge adds the cherry on top…

"Maria, who do you think is going to take over as vice?" He pauses to let it sink in. The light goes on.

"*No way…*"

"Yes, Maria Ramirez, Vice President of Midwest Mining Corporation."

"…and all that stock you bought?"

"I'll give you one honking big Christmas gift like you've never seen. If they rally back to – say, even just 25 a share, let's see…" He digs out a pen and does some quick math on his napkin… "That could mean – Christ – it's well over four million. How do you like the sound of say – a cool million? It'll be a bank transfer from my shadow company in Brussels after I sell some of my shares. And – you say you like boats? I'll be upgrading soon to one with a helipad. The silly thing is 227 feet long, being built as we speak. Maybe you get the keys for my old one whenever you want. Just call ahead. "

Maria's head is spinning. *Jésus Christo, this could really work*, she thinks. All this slaving away for someone else could really pay off. Her face goes red.

"And who knows what stock options you'll get once you're on the executive team. But one thing, Maria." Underbridge is very serious. "Not a single peep of a word can leave this room. I've already cut out a friend who I thought was trustworthy at first, but I caught him buying their stock."

"What did you do?"

"Don't ask and I won't tell. I trust you *because* you aren't affiliated with any old boy's club. This stuff brings out the worst in people, but I know your track record. You with me on this?"

"Totally. I'm on board. I'll have HR draw up my pink slip when we get back. Do I get a package?" she says with a wry smile. They touch glasses. "I'll owe you big time."

"Not at all. You forget two things. One – thanks to you, I'll eventually gain controlling interest in the company, essentially owning it. And two – I have you there to help Rudman make decisions that are good for everyone, me included. I say we'd be pretty well even."

Maria tries to suppress her emotions, but fails –

"Oh, and one more thing Maria."

"Yes?"

"You really have to work on that poker face of yours!"

They chuckle and touch glasses once more.

Chapter 2

Grey Falls, Utah. The small city is booming thanks to an up-swing in the local economy. Construction is mostly responsible for the growth, with mining about to be a close second – not to be unnoticed by investment prospectors from the big city looking for a quick turnaround. The town has historical architecture for the tourists, proudly maintained and promoted by the local heritage society. Their museum houses centuries-old documents that are often a draw for researchers from other state universities. Civil war buffs gawk over old black and white photographs of US postmen riding the Oregon Trail.

There's bountiful green space for young parents and their kids just by the waterfalls under the restored saw mill. Local developers thought it was an ideal place for a water park… this city appeals to many families looking for the next great place to move to. Seems the city is up for "prettiest place to visit" next year, so development loans are handed out like candy. On most Saturdays, a wedding party or two are at the waterfalls with their photographer snapping away at the bride and groom.

Not to be outdone by any larger town or city, Grey Falls is home to a sizable yacht and rowing club, and a marina owned by an elderly British gentleman who builds boats for a living. A family business established before the last century, they donated many photographs and archival documents to the local museum for posterity. The family are dyed-in-the-wool Baptists who give generously to their church, and consequently have a bit of a say when the board meets.

The expanding industrial sector keeps many locals from moving out of town after high school. Municipal statisticians say there's a family a day moving into town. With a vacancy rate hovering around one percent, the local real estate agents scramble to find housing, putting pressure on developers to build. The construction job market is booming.

The geographical center of the city is Scott's Hardware at the corner of Main and Concord, a beautiful four story stone building with a clock tower that keeps perfect time. With its third generation of owners, they're surviving quite well despite the opening of a new *Home Depot* on the outskirts of town. The downtown is filled with little boutiques, gift shops, computer and grocery stores... downtown Grey Falls is the thriving hub of a city where you can still witness friends meeting on the sidewalk, shaking hands, exchanging pleasantries – a place where one can still say "I'll meet you at the four corners", and everyone knows where you mean.

Most everyone is glad to be part of the economic benefit of unbridled growth, however the "born 'n raised here" slice of the population talk about the good old days of Grey Falls when everyone knew your name, and things weren't so hectic. But for the most part, these old timers are a good bunch, proud of their history, and even prouder of the new streets here and there bearing their family surname. Expanding as quickly as it is, Grey Falls is learning to become a big city, and there are some growing pains showing up here and there – in politics, industry, and in the personal lives of its inhabitants.

Not surprisingly, Grey Falls High School is bursting at the seams with the influx of new students. Their football team does well every year, as does women's basketball. The senior band travelled Europe two years ago and is raising funds to go to Canada this fall. The school spirit is second to none, many thanks to the various volunteer parents, the successful student body, and the strong leadership of its principal and teachers.

This particular morning is bright and crisp. A favorable weekend forecast puts WPCS's listeners at ease, despite the dew on everyone's windshields – a telltale sign autumn has arrived.

"Awesome – good weather means a good turnout," the passenger says as the non-descript minivan turns a corner, then pulls into the student parking lot. The two seniors get out with their knapsacks full of textbooks from last night's homework assignments. *I swear I could use a wheelbarrow for all this* thinks the girl. As they walk away from their vehicle towards the school, the driver turns back quickly and points the remote as if he has a Star Wars light saber in his hand. Click. "All doors are secure master." he says. She rolls her eyes. They walk together to the side entrance where the smokers usually hang out, but there's no one there; first bell is about to ring. The girl opens the door to Grey Falls High School and observes how the din in the hallway is always a little louder on a Friday morning. They have two minutes to organize themselves at their lockers before first class, which they do not attend together.

"I guess I'll see you in Social Sciences. I got math first. Hey – I'm really pumped about tonight. It's finally coming together."

"We should have called in sick. I could use the extra practice."

"You're sounding good – don't be paranoid. We have a warm-up anyways. Later Leslie!" he says walking briskly towards the south stairs.

"See ya Sean!" she replies.

Three classes later, the cafeteria lineup is particularly crowded considering the time. The tired and overworked kitchen staff, cooks, and servers are showing signs of frustration; they can't wait for the relief that is on its way. The school principal pushed through a budgetary increase that will see three new teachers, two kitchen staff, and another janitor, all none too soon. Portable classrooms have been ordered ahead of time, but they won't be ready until next semester – seems the company who won the contract is having a heck of a time finding employees. A storage room in the basement has been earmarked for a daycare facility, lessening the stress on single moms, be they staff or student.

"What a great principal he is" says Chloe, taking cash at the food line till. John Templeton, Mr. "T" as everyone calls him, is seen chatting with a small group in the far corner. Whenever he can, he'll eat lunch in the cafeteria just to hang out with his students. His habitual presence keeps order and deters any unsavory activities. Many ask about his two tours in Vietnam, and he'll respond with some story they haven't heard yet.

Two students in the food lineup are exchanging looks. One turns to the other and says -

"Why are you so insensitive? Our teacher was only trying to suggest that we perform an extra night to get more money – he wasn't busting your gonads."

Being very close in age, Leslie and Sean share some of the same classes.

"Our band is sounding real good, so if we get more gigs, I suppose that's cool," concedes Sean, not wanting to engage his cousin in public. But then he says – "Hey, you know – I don't see anyone else in our class pitching in. You should tell your friend Amanda to wash cars or something." He reaches for his plate of lasagne. "Thanks," he says, nodding to the overworked server. She did notice his kind manners, so she cracks a smile.

"Ya know, you weren't so good last night at practice," prods Leslie carefully, "...I keep telling you to lay off the weed before play-ing – it really makes you introverted."

"I *was* off, wasn't I? But – I did come up with that cool hook in the bridge!" He explains the chord change to Leslie while reaching for a small carton of chocolate milk.

Of the two cousins, Sean is the party guy with not a lot to worry about. Handsome and tall, he is a well-rounded teen with medium length shaggy brown hair, and a dimple on his chin that Leslie thinks is cute. His marks are good, and he does well on the football team as a running back – he's swift and agile on his feet. He enjoys music as Leslie does, and they jam in the garage to their favorite tunes and the odd original composition even if they're not practicing with the rest of their four-piece band. He does enjoy the occasional joint and likes how it peaces him out despite Leslie's objections. And although Sean doesn't get Leslie's dark makeup and black clothes, they *do* have fun together… they just don't show it too much in public.

Living in a town that was beginning to grow almost as fast as him, Sean found his feet very quickly. He is a natural at so many things, and enjoys every new pursuit he puts his mind to. As a boy scout, he loved the camping trips, the hiking, fishing, canoeing – anything outdoors. As he developed into adolescence, he took to active sports very naturally. Every coach wanted him on their team, from basketball, to hockey, and baseball. He preferred football, partly because of the recognition of playing for a popular high school team, but also because his coach, who also doubles as his math teacher, seems to understand and like him. This means Sean gets away with more than he should, but such is the case when an educator is blessed with a gifted student.

When his cousin Leslie moved into the house a year ago, it was strange for him at first – they only met once as toddlers. Their families lived in opposite ends of the country, and Sean's mother wasn't that close to her sister growing up, so visits were few and far between. Being teens of the same age, they were initially uneasy, but very quickly became comfortable in each other's space. At school, Les passes love notes to Sean from different girls, but he just chuckles… he isn't swayed too much by his popularity.

Leslie was fourteen when her parents were killed in an auto accident. Stopped on the I-75 north of Jacksonville, they were trying to fix a flat during a foggy night when an eighteen wheeler rear-ended them. Driver fatigue was cited as the cause. With no family around,

Les was taken in first by her grandmother, but she was too old to cope with both a teenager and a bed-ridden husband. In a month, she was with her aunt and uncle, Malcolm and Lydia, in Grey Falls, Utah. But there was turmoil here too; they were in the process of discussing how to divide up their assets, thanks to a sexual indiscretion Malcolm had with someone from the church crowd. Six months after Leslie moved to Grey Falls, Malcolm and Lydia divorced. The teens spent alternate weeks with each parent, until Leslie's behavior and school marks began to show signs of maladjustment.

A therapist advised Malcolm and Lydia to make up their minds about custody; the children needed a stable home life. After much discussion between all family members, it was a unanimous decision that the teens go with Malcolm and Marjorie. Lydia was on the way to the top in her political career and didn't have the patience for two demanding children, as well behaved as they were all things considered. Malcolm's large home in suburbia suited them better than Lydia's condo, and Malcolm's new wife was more than willing to have a larger family. The in-ground swimming pool in the back yard helped them make up their minds...

Lydia knew all along she was a hard person to live with. Driven, ambitious, popular, and a reputation for knocking a few back with the boys, she preferred the kids be raised in a conservative, stable atmosphere.

Considering her difficult past, Leslie is a well-adjusted teen, though she can have a dark and brooding side. She has taken to the Goth look somewhat, with dyed black hair and dark clothing. A stickler for detail, her fingernails are painted in very intricate patterns. Intellectually, she sees much of the writing on the wall and is bothered by the answers she *isn't* getting from her school and family, though she likes her guidance counselor. She finds comfort in music and is exceptionally talented at playing drums, Karen Carpenter being her secret idol. Owning a large DVD collection of music lessons, Leslie practices in the garage for hours on end, much to her family's annoyance. Les promises them she's close to affording a set of practice drums – all digital, all quiet. When she isn't doing homework or house chores, chances are she'll be working out some complex drumming pattern in a time signature few people have heard of.

Lunch period ends. After finishing his lasagne, Sean walks over to Leslie, who is chatting with a few of her friends; one of them whispers:

"Here comes that hunk of a cousin of yours. When are you going to hook us up for a date?"

"You're in some of his classes – why don't *you* ask him?"

"I'll pee my pants if I have to open my mouth to him – don't you remember how I flubbed up with him in chemistry?" Her hands shook so badly that day she dropped the test tube on the desk, spilling a strong caustic liquid all over Sean's notes.

"He's not into dating right now – he works part-time, we've got our band, and exams are approaching fast… but I'll put in a good word for you," she says winking.

Sean approaches – "Hey cuz – Mark is driving his van back to the gym when he gets home. He's got some help to unload, but let's be there when he shows up, OK? I have some library work to finish for Monday, but I'll meet you there at – say – 5:30?"

Leslie smiles up at her cousin – "Sure, I'll see ya then!"

Les's friend chirps in, speaking for the group – "Hey you guys, you want us to help set up? I love being a roadie! We'll have fun!"

Sean's tolerance of Amanda's constant flirting makes him even more attractive.

"Sure girls, sounds great. We really appreciate it." He digs his cell phone from his back pocket and dials home as he slowly finds a seat beside Leslie. Marj picks up.

"Hello?"

"Mom – it's Sean. Are you still bringing pizza over to the school after the concert? Great! Listen, we have a few more mouths to feed, so maybe you should make it three large – hang on…"

"What do you guys like?" he asks Leslie's friends. Everyone names their favorite toppings, Sean holding the phone up to them, then returns it to his ear.

"You get that?" – pause – "You're great! See you then."

The posters announcing their concert paid off in spades. That, plus the announcements in the paper and on TV helped as well. Sean has a knack for marketing, as well as delegating, so the band's unofficial "booster club" was more than glad to distribute posters to all the local store-front businesses, bulletin boards, anywhere a staple or piece of tape would hold up an 8 by 11 for the public to notice. Even the printing shop cut Sean a deal for the tickets, which he had custom designed. *Nothing but the best for us.*

Setting up sound and light equipment is part of the fun for Sean. Their new mixing board and powered speakers sizzle with crisp, clean sound – Sean did his research and bought the core of their sound gear from a band that had just bought it, broke up, and put it up for sale at the local music store. *What a find*, he thought, knowing what they had paid for it new.

Each band member has their area of responsibility with concert set-ups, and they're each good at finding people to help. Like clockwork, everything is ready to go within two hours of the van arriving at the gymnasium's parking lot door. Lighting is sequenced from a computer, so the operator simply clicks a mouse between songs. For sound engineering, they hire a seasoned technician from the local radio station for their gigs – a gentleman of many pasts, one of which includes running sound for a famous 1970s pop-rock glamour band. His ear is good, and he makes them sound fabulous, no matter the venue. It's really more of a hobby to him, so he doesn't charge Sean very much.

The band is on stage now – Sean requests a slight change: "Check – check – check – a little more monitor please – that's great. OK guys, let's try *Blue Blue Feelin'* ". The song is a great choice for sound check. Everything sounds good to Sean so far – there will be a few tweaks throughout the evening as he communicates with the soundman with quick head and hand movements.

The crowd slowly filters in. A hint of theatrical smoke hangs in the air as the PA system spills out top forty tunes. A small group of people chat outside, waiting till the last minute before extinguishing their cigarettes.

"It's rush seating guys, we better get in."

"Who is this band anyways? Have I heard of them?"

"Read your ticket!" a couple of people say at the same time…

"*Indigo Insight*. Hey, that's a cool name. Are they good?"

"Wait till you see – they're just high school kids, but you wouldn't know it. They're going to go places. My dad says there was a guy from Capital Records at Brownie's Jazz Bar today asking about them. "

"That would rock – imagine, a band from Grey Falls making it big."

What the concert goers don't know is the pure genius behind tonight's show. Sean and Leslie coordinated and delegated every last detail: volunteer security from the football team dressed in black suits, fedoras, and sunglasses; stage hands who knew what they were doing, two sound techs (one paid, one not), a few smoke machines borrowed from a local DJ friend. Sean even arranged to borrow two spare guitars should he break a string. That cost them a "Dino's Music Store" banner in the foyer of the high school. Their theater teacher, Mr. White, volunteered to produce their shows a couple of months ago… "Hey, I'm not a rock 'n roller, but I know live stage real well – let me help you out." He was a godsend. Normally, Sean and Leslie would man the stage, making it hard to be back stage as well. They seemed to attract everyone and everything they needed for their band's success, and Mr. White was no exception.

Most of the help they had were simply too excited to even think of asking for compensation. *Hell, pizza and beer is enough pay to be part of this… just wait till the after party!* Total bill for the show: $832. The tickets were cheap at five bucks a pop, but they'll take in over four thousand dollars if they sell out. It was an ambitious goal, and they did it.

"Ten minutes!" announces the production manager to everyone in the dressing room. Closing the door behind him, he overhears the band discussing tonight's lineup of songs.

Always last minute, he thinks to himself. "Hey guys, almost done?"

"But we ALWAYS play Momma's Bad Boy after Lone Train. We should switch it up for tonight."

"Everyone up for that?" asks Sean. "Sure," they reply.

With a magic marker, Sean scrawls the song list on a piece of paper, which then gets handed to Mr. White, who then steals away from the gym for a few minutes. At a word processing computer in his home room, he prints off four laser copies in a huge font. He is the last "staffer" seen on stage before the opening act, taping the song lists to the floor for all the band members to see from various vantage points.

"Oh, who's this?" Sean mumbles as his cell vibrates. He reads a text message from his birthmother, Lydia. "Come shopping tomorrow. I buy U clothes." Sean smirks, as his mother gets away with it once more… spoiling her son and flaunting it. You get to do that when you're the mayor of Grey Falls.

"That Lydia?" asks Les. Sean doesn't reply. Leslie is a little jealous of Sean's relationship with Lydia. Sean placates her with…

"Hey, I'll pick you up a movie or something." No one knows what's going on; it's obviously a family thing. Tucking his cell back into his pocket, he changes the subject, and bellows out – "OK, Let's do this!!!"

The night goes well, with a couple of minor hitches only the experienced and trained eye would see – ninety minutes of cover tunes and originals, all very much enjoyed by the audience. Then the "final" tune, a standing ovation, and the usual encore. Sean starts the song with a slow finger-picking intro on his Takamine acoustic/ electric, sitting on a stool, with a lone spotlight on him. *These lighting guys rock* he thinks to himself. One, then two, then three harmonies play over Sean's powerful vocals. With a deft and swift motion he switches to an electric guitar. The audience light up their Bic lighters and flip-phones, waving them above their heads. The song's finale is a crescendo of cymbals, pounding bass guitar, incredible percussion, more theatrical smoke, and a howling lead solo from Sean's Fender Stratocaster – the crowd goes nuts as he slams the last power chord. The sound tech elongates the finale with some extra reverb and a fading echo.

These guys are hot, thinks the anonymous-looking scout from Capital Records. He punches the speed dial button for the office as he walks towards the exit sign.

The band rows up and all bow at the same time. The gym is flooded with white light as they exit off to the left side behind a column of speakers, Sean with his arm over Les' shoulder. Exhausted yet exuberant, they all exchange high-fives in the dressing room.

"Damn, Mark, you rocked tonight! Your bass really filled it out."

"Thanks Sean – that extra sound tech made a huge difference – he knew exactly how much monitor I needed. And – you weren't bad yourself by the way!"

Sean usually passes off compliments.

"We'll use him for our next gig."

In the change room, they all grab another bottled water. The crowd is still a bit noisy. They decide to hang for a bit while the gym empties.

"Isn't there pizza coming?" asks Amy. "I haven't had supper – I could eat a whole one myself."

"Ya, mom is coming by in…" he checks his watch… "about 20 minutes. Can you last, or shall I check with our manager in New York to see why we have no food in our dressing room? You know, that rider you insisted on was a bit over the top…"

"Ha ha – funny. *Not!*" replies Amy.

"OK – let's go back. We're likely safe now."

In the last few concerts Indigo Insight has done, they discovered that if they hang around immediately following their performance, the groupies and all their friends would surround them – for hours it seemed. For the first few times it was flattering, but often they would play on a weeknight, so school would suffer the next day. By slipping away discreetly, they end up leaving much earlier.

Friends of the band help load up the Dodge cube van with the band's sound and lighting equipment.

"Great night guys!!! You sounded awesome." They in fact did sound tight tonight, Sean feeling particularly pleased with the standing ovation.

A friend approaches… "Sean, I have this poem I wrote for my girlfriend. Would you look at it? Maybe put a tune to it?" President of the student council and head of the yearbook committee, Josh hands him a folded up piece of paper with the words 'For Melissa' scrawled on it.

"Sure man, I'll look it over tomorrow and get back to you. Wow, you like this chick! What's her name?"

"Melissa. Melissa Young. Her mom's a cop. I used to cut her lawn a few years ago, and I thought *she* was pretty hot – then her daughter grew up… "

"You perv!" Sean says, slapping Josh's chest with the sheet of lyrics. "Call me in a week if I don't get back to you." Sean jams the paper in his back pocket. Collaborations of this kind are often requested once you get a name for yourself, yet they are seldom followed up – your friends, strangers from the audience – Sean handles it politely as usual.

Since winning "Challenge of the Bands" six months ago on a televised show out of Salt Lake, critics-turned-friends were more than eager to be their late-night roadies. They heard rumours of an A&R representative from Capital Records scoping them out. No offers yet, but this new upstart band was certainly on everyone's radar. This brought Sean and Leslie closer, as they knew what side their bread was buttered on… they started collaborating more seriously, winning cash prizes in song writing competitions around the state. Their parents were impressed and very supportive. Local radio play didn't hurt either. *Indigo Insight is on their way to the top*, Sean ponders. Just then, someone phones his cell, who in a fake voice says "Do I happen to be related to anyone who ordered three deep-dish pizzas for delivery to the GFHS gymnasium? If not, I can turn them in to the local food bank."

"Don't you DARE! We're hungry!" yells Sean. Leslie smiles, knowing who is at the other end of the call.

Chapter 3

Marjorie is every person's mother. Apple pie, roast turkey, and gingham tablecloths characterize most holiday celebrations. It was easy to live this role when she married Malcolm, with all the church socials, living in an established neighborhood, and taken care of by a husband with a well paying job. Her affair with Malcolm years ago was quickly forgotten by most who knew them; they kind of fell into each other's arms at a time when their relationships at the time were very strained.

Born Marjorie Gertrude Litvenchuck in Salt Lake City, she was raised in a strict religious home by parents who knew more of discipline than love. As a young child, she dreamed of being a mother, loving all her children to pieces. No corporal punishment. No sitting in the corner for speaking too loud during mealtime. And – no sexual abuse. At sixteen years old, she prayed "Lord, give me a husband who will love me and our children." A very shy and introverted teen, she thought her prayers were answered when Neil from her church youth group asked her out.

His father was a deacon at their church, so both parents approved. But none of them were aware of Neil's reputation for being such a lady's man. Desperate to get out from under her parents' over-bearing authority, they married and stayed that way for years. Marj went out of her way to avoid getting pregnant – something about this whole arrangement seemed temporary. Her husband's constant flirting and gambling were kept secret, but Marjorie's sensibilities told her to hang on – there would be a way out. Unknowingly expecting a child at twenty eight years old, and her husband in jail on fraud charges, her church friends did all they could to comfort the frail and broken women as she went through the difficult process of divorce.

It's Saturday morning. Breakfast is chaos, with everyone competing for the toaster, talking over each other, and generally making a mess of the kitchen. Malcolm asks Sean "So, where is your mother taking you *this* time?" Malcolm only refers to Lydia as Sean's mother when Marjorie isn't around, who tries to sleep in on weekends if there isn't too much noise. Not so this morning – she's in the laundry room folding clothes in her nightgown.

"Don't know, dad, but I'm in bad need of footwear… maybe we'll go to your uncle's store."

"Make sure you hit him up for a discount; his staff charged me full price for my last pair of tennis shoes," complains his dad.

"Hey, mom's paying, so who cares?"

His dad frowns. "Be respectful son…"

"Yes dad." Sean replies almost sarcastically.

Marjorie and Malcolm were married just three years ago, and the relationship between them and Lydia evolved into something quite tolerant and civil, considering the circumstances. They actually didn't mind bragging to the rest of the world that divorce didn't have to hurt the kids. So, Lydia would occasionally spend some time with Sean; there was a special bond one could only describe as unique. Malcolm didn't mind his ex-wife spoiling Sean occasionally – no sense coming in between such a tight bond.

A car honks its horn. Sean jumps up from the table and tells his younger step-brother – "Dude, have my waffles – you're looking hungry." Jake lifts his eyes from the comic book he's reading, pulls the mask away from his face, and says – "My name is Batman, I don't want your germs, I'm *not* hungry," he says with the bravado of an eight-year-old super hero.

"Suit yourself Bat Jerk – just remember where you get those comics from – they're worth big bucks, so don't get anything on them." Sean shoots him with an imaginary gun, one eye closed. *Blam Blam!!!*

The gunfire is returned with vengeance.

Returning to his comic book, he wipes the milk off page three. He eyes Sean's plate…

In Lydia's car, Sean comments – "Hey – nice wheels! Can I drive?"

"Not on your life, big boy – I just drove this off the lot – *I'll* be the only nut behind the wheel today." Not even finishing her sentence, she floors the gas pedal, squealing away from the house.

Inside, Malcolm rolls his eyes and mutters, "Always the wild one."

"Wow!" Sean exclaims, "Being mayor sure has its perks. Look at this thing! I love new car smell…"

Lydia's choice of vehicle leaves no expense spared. A hybrid with a perky six cylinder, this beauty has in-dash GPS, 24 valve engine, sunroof, traction control, leather bucket seats, digital sound system with a hundred gig hard drive, and power everything. Nothing but the best for Her Honor.

Sean immediately marks his territory; he pulls an MP3 player out of his shirt pocket and inserts a cable into the dash, and powers on the stereo… "Wait'll you hear this!"

Indigo Insight's latest original tune blasts from the incredible sound system, as Sean adjusts volume and equalization.

"Whoa!!! I didn't know this car could sound like *that!* Wait – is that you guys???"

"Oh yeah," says Sean, raising his eyebrows and shining his fingernails on his shirt – "This is goin' gold!"

"No shit!" exclaims Sean's biggest fan.

A few minutes pass; Lydia turns down the volume.

"So, how's school? Your team won again last night… I didn't see you on the field."

"You were there?" says Sean surprised. "I thought you knew we were playing at the school gym? … we're raising funds for a new school project. We sold out, so we're going to donate to some charities around town as well." A short pause… "Yeah, coach Smith wasn't pleased when I asked for the time off."

Sean changes the subject. "When you texted me last night, I was about to go on stage – big crowd, so I couldn't talk."

"I understand," replies his mother – "What you're doing with this class project sounds interesting, raising money and all… It's good of you. I hope you get better marks for it. What's it all about?"

Sean holds up an imaginary machine gun, shooting a number of pedestrians as they slowly turn a corner. His mother laughs and tells him to stop it… "people are *staring!* And I'm talking to you!"

Sean settles down and explains the project to Lydia. "Well mom, it goes like this: the *National Geographic Society* is running something called the Genographic Project, where any person can send in a DNA sample, and have a report written up about their ancestral heritage back as far as 60,000 years… they explain things like tribal movements over the earth, that kind of thing. Each of us will prepare a report based on our own findings. But here's the catch: the DNA kit costs some bucks, so Indigo Insight offered to pitch in some coin."

Lydia looks slightly concerned – "Just remember, DNA tests aren't always a hundred percent accurate. "

"What's the deal mom?" Sean says puzzled – "It's only to track ancestors, that's all. No big deal… it's not like we're doing some big C.S.I. thing. Why, you worried my DNA will show up in some mass murderer database?" Lydia waves her hand as if to say *get real!*

For the next few hours, Sean and his mom have a their usual good time shopping for clothes, buying CDs, and a couple of new *BluRay* releases. They enjoy lunch on the patio of a bistro just opened up on Concord Street. There are many waves and nods from people who recognize Lydia, but Sean just turns his head. He realizes their family's history has cost his mom some credibility, but Lydia is a bit of a rebel. "Screw them," she says, not too loudly. "Wait till you see the dirt I get on Mister oh-so-righteous Campbell. He thinks he'll win the next election. Humph."

Lydia has learned a lot in the past two years as Grey Fall's first female mayor. Politicians are an interesting breed, and the religious demographic made for a tough race.

Sean sips his Coke – "Hey, what was all that protesting going on down past the TV studio a few weeks ago?" asks Sean. "I saw you on the news."

"Hmm. Well, it seems our city is in the big leagues now – a couple of doctors have set up a new medical clinic on Broughton. A women's clinic, if you get my drift."

Sean knows what she means; he changes the subject.

"Hey, if I leave the tip, can I drive your car back to my place?"

"I suppose that's cheap compared to a cab," responds Lydia, "But then, who's paying for the gas?" She almost spills her glass of Chardonnay as she tosses a crumpled up napkin at his face. *"You spoiled brat!"*

Lydia Forsythe, with all the courage and determination it takes to be mayor of Grey Falls, is a sensitive, hurt, lonely woman. The daughter of a Dutch scientist with a double PhD in math and physics, she was often told growing up that children are to be seen and not heard. The oldest of three, Lydia can remember how as a young child she thought her mother was the consummate housewife, looking after her family and home with the best she could muster. But her mom was plagued with depression and alcoholism. Every few years, Lydia's father would land another teaching job in yet another university town, hoping the change of scenery would bring his wife out of the doldrums.

As the years passed, Lydia was depended upon more and more. This matured her faster than her friends, and as a first-born child, the expectations of her parents compounded her drive to be the best, do the best, and not tolerate failure. As her mother's health suffered from bad diet and decades of anti-depressants, Lydia took up the slack.

But her schooling never suffered. She often would come home with awards for best speller, fastest reader, best actor… it was then her father would coddle her, spend a bit of time with her, and tell her how proud he was of his little dumpling. Lydia lapped it up as any child would, and it solidified her determination to be as smart as she could be.

It was in high school that her mom passed away, taken by her own hand. An intentional overdose? The Medical Examiner's report was vague enough for an insurance payout. Lydia's teachers where amazed at the tenacity she displayed despite her loss. Without skipping a beat, Lydia graduated with honors, then five years later, left university with a master's in political science. *Look at me now, daddy.*

Relationships were not good to Lydia. One failed engagement, one seven-year long-distance relationship, and a failed marriage with Malcolm sealed her fate as a career woman. She has the drive, ambition, and self discipline to be where she is today, despite the loneliness and heartache. Now at 48 years old, her trim body is becoming more and more difficult to maintain, despite a daily routine on her stationary bike and treadmill. *Just another 5 pounds to go.* But she refuses to give up her two indulgences: cheesecake and Martinis. She is oblivious to her peers' envy of her lavish lifestyle, good looks, and successful career. At least once a month, she'll grab a friend and drive to another state to spend a weekend shopping and visiting nightclubs where no one knows her.

Sean is her link to something organic, real, and sacred. He grounds her in a funny way, and she cherishes any time she can get with him.

"Thanks for everything mom – you're the best. Les will appreciate the movies too. See you again soon!" A peck on both cheeks, then Sean makes his way out the driver's seat, opens the rear left passenger door and pulls out about four large retail bags, including leftovers from lunch. *Jake will love the spring rolls.*

With a wave and a honk on the horn, the mayor of Grey Falls drives away, wishing somehow things had turned out differently. *Well, at least I get to spend time with him, not like other messy divorces… I'm lucky I suppose.*

Chapter 4

The elevator of a downtown Manhattan building is filled with coffee-carrying office workers, some yawning, others reading the morning paper. The man at the back wearing a pinstripe suit and wingtip shoes patiently waits for all these worker bees to disembark at various levels… 27… 34…35…41… Finally the second-last one leaves at level 44. The doors close. Two people are left.

"What say we vie for that private elevator?"

The sharp young admin assistant knows he has spoken out of turn when the president of Midwest Mining replies without looking at him…

"Maybe when *you're* president."

Joshua Gerenberg was to be his father's prodigy. That was the natural expectation of parents having survived Dachau, then becoming millionaires ten years after arriving in America with thirty-two dollars to their names. Born with a silver spoon in his mouth, Joshua was handed every break in the book; the best of everything. Private school. Harvard. Country club membership. But all the advice from his family, the big-business mentors, and life coaches couldn't groom him to fill his father's shoes. Like a cut flower with no roots, Joshua has the appearance of success, but nothing deep inside to draw on. Nevertheless, he dresses and acts the part. The money, women, and cars are a blast. With a 4,000 square foot garage that is the envy of his friends, his collection of motorcycles and vintage cars means more to him that this energy-sucking, distracting gig as president of Midwest Mining. The board of directors saw what was coming when Gerenberg's spoiled brat son took the helm. *Run with it or I'll sink you all,* threatened his father, who at the time owned the one and only controlling interest in the company. Since his passing, the shares were dispersed to far too many relatives for anyone to have a say, including Joshua. *Good thing I run the damn place.*

His Espresso is waiting for him on his desk as he enters. Cordial "hellos" are exchanged as he heads for his hideaway. Once there, the door is closed and locked. Standard procedure, and no one dares interrupt his morning ritual. Finish my coffee. Finish my paper, noting anything of interest in the financial section. How's our stock today? Another dive? *Fuck,* he mouths, looking out his office window. *Why did that old bastard leave me here like this?* He's glad for this morning's meeting though – he has two relatives on the board, and both will actually be attending. Glenda, a middle-aged and very experienced business woman, is sticking it out for family. Her shares have dwindled to nothing, so she figures there's no way but up. Then there's Zachary, a father figure who stepped forward to help Joshua after his dad passed two months ago. Ready to retire, he has his own stash so he's in it for family as well. He and Josh's father have a lot of history, and he does with Joshua, with all the camping and fishing trips the three of them went on through the years.

Bzzz. Joshua's desk phone speaks to him: "Sir, Ms. Boyer and Mr. Hersch are here to see you."

"Thank you Liz, please send them in." He gets up to unlock his door. His guests arrive and they take a seat in his large luxurious office. There's a *Bowflex* in one corner, and a wet bar in the other. One wall is covered in brightly colored posters of Maseratis, Lamborghinis, and a shot of himself on a racing bike negotiating a sharp curve, his right knee almost touching the pavement.

"May I get anyone something to drink? Coffee? OJ?"

"We're good Josh, thanks."

As they dispense with common weather-speak and family news, Joshua's nervousness is apparent to Glenda and Zachary.

"See the paper this morning? Our stock keeps taking a dive – people are dumping their shares, but this article came to my attention."

Joshua grabs the paper and points to an article he has circled with a highlighter.

"Buyers And Sellers Draw Attention to Midwest," is all the headline says. Josh explains the gist of the article.

"You guys have your finger on the pulse of the board. I'd like to find out why I have to get this out of a bloody newspaper, and not my own staff. I'm feeling more and more alienated. I mean Christ, why are so many people buying up every last stock that our longtime investors are dumping? I feel responsible to them, and pissed at these speculators. Maybe you guys can do some digging and see if it's either legit, or someone trying to buy us through phony companies."

Glenda responds.

"Josh, you know this happen occasionally – a shark will use his or her shadow companies to buy up stock when the price is low, then reveal their identity when the share price rallies. It's shady, but I doubt it in this case honey. Hell, if you leave, half the company goes with you."

Ouch, that stings.

"Dad negotiated that – I had nothing to do with it."

"Stop being defensive, Josh. The fact is, we'd be a gamble even if your conspiracy theory were true. I'll do some research, but I know I won't find anything."

Glenda looks at Zach. "You agree?"

"Hell, who knows these days. There are crooks everywhere and our trading laws have holes in them big enough to drive a truck through. Josh, sit tight for now. And I say that, because I have someone I want you to meet."

"Here? Now?"

"Yes, if you'd take the time."

Zachary knows if Josh had been given a heads up, he would have flat-out refused.

"Josh, the board has been approached by a consultancy firm whose specialty is companies just like ours. They parachute in, whip everybody and everything into shape, and leave with ten percent of whatever profits we make in 6 months. They have a proven track record."

It didn't take much to arrange. Underbridge was able to create this so-called track record with a stroke of his pen. It's actually nothing but a vapor trail...

"Most of the board wants it Josh. We could vote."

"No no – I get it. This person's here now?"

"Yes, the president."

"Well, I can't wait," he says with a slight sarcastic tone.

Glenda motions to Joshua's admin assistant through the glass.

Maria Ramirez comes through the doorway. Her entrance commands attention and respect. The image specialist paid off; head to toe she is nothing but hard core executive material in lipstick and a skirt. Joshua's jaw drops. *Holy Christ, what planet did she just drop from? They don't breed them this perfect down here...*

Introductions are made all around. Joshua pulls a chair out for her.

"Ms. Ramirez, please have a seat."

"Thank you, Mr. Gerenberg. Please, call me Maria."

Maria's sharp instincts are correct. *He's a wimp. Rich, but a wimp.*

Putting on her best business face, she gives a quick overview of their company's strategy; their usual approach; their usual way of doing things.

"It will mean responsibilities will get shifted around, people terminated. You tell me what isn't negotiable and I'll give you our projection for the next six months, given current market trends. We're usually not out by any more than three percent. Please refer to our company's dossier – page three."

Christ, where's she been all this time, thinks Josh. It doesn't take much convincing. Maria's commanding personality and attractive looks have Joshua's IQ somewhere down in the double digits. He keeps eyeing her blouse when no one is looking. Following ten or so minutes of more propaganda, Maria knows she's in. Joshua speaks...

"You'll have our fullest cooperation. Zachary, where did you find this gem?"

Maria pretends to be modest.

"Like I said, she approached us."

"Well fine then. Ms. Ramirez, you have the full run of the place, and if anyone stands in your way, report them to me immediately. I'll have my assistant gather all our senior managers for a kick-off meeting to introduce you and your company."

Glenda and Zach steal a look with each other as if to say, "Wow – *that* was easy!"

After some strategy talk, Maria brings the meeting to a close and shakes hands with everyone. "Ms. Boyer, Mr. Hersch; and Mr. Gerenberg – it's been my pleasure meeting all of you. With this final approval, my lawyer will draw up a contract and fax it to your legal department. I look forward to working with you in the coming months."

———————————

Safely out of eye and earshot of the building, the driver makes his way to the brand new offices of *MR Business Consulting*. Maria lifts the receiver of her car phone and dials a number few people know.

"Pete here."

"Peter, it's Maria. They took it hook, line and sinker. I'm in as early as next week. That Gerenberg guy is truly a piece of work. You were right for me to pitch to those two board members. You know your shit. How's your boat coming along?"

"Almost done. Listen – you know the drill from here. Keep me up to date."

"Will do."

Maria wonders – *How did he know to pitch to Glenda and Zach? Instinct I guess.*

47

Chapter 5

"All the leaves are brown, and the sky is grey"… Malcolm hums the popular tune as his leaf blower corrals freshly fallen oak and maple leaves into a big heap. It was a busy summer at the office with too much overtime for his liking – then those annoying camping trips and church picnics. But the odd weekend he will use house chores as a kind of a therapy – a happy place to go in his mind where there are no deadlines or board meetings or family outings to worry about; where he can putter for hours and not have a clue what time of day it is.

His mind wanders to the distant past… It was at Grey Falls Baptist Church that Malcolm heard his first bible story, learned of missionaries, and sang in a choir. He remembers pastor Tony Friesen, a fire and brimstone preacher who would scare the literal hell out of any sinner from his pulpit, yet would pour love, money, and himself into any soul needing a place to stay, a square meal, and possibly some ol' time religion if they'd listen.

In the 1970s, pastor Friesen was a mentor to many, a father figure to some, and "Tony" to a select few. Malcolm earned the right to call him by his first name the day he graduated from bible college. The school was a few hours drive from Grey Falls, but that was nothing to pastor Friesen – it was his honor to bring home a member of the flock who showed so much promise.

"Thanks for the ride, Tony! I guess I'll be coming home to an empty house, with Mom and Dad in Florida."

"My pleasure Malcolm. I love this drive; it always brings back so many fond memories of my time in the same college. I'm proud of you son!" The pastor smiles and looks at Malcolm…

"Are you looking at seminary school?" he asks. Malcolm's response was understandable... "Pastor, er, Tony – I *just* graduated this afternoon. You're sounding like my father!" They both laughed, and enjoyed each other's company all the way home. The pastor kept remembering story after story of his younger years, and Malcolm loved hearing them... again.

Malcolm kept wanting to ask his mentor a question, but it never came out. Perhaps if it did, certain future events may not have unfolded. This question burned in Malcolm's heart for many years, but eventually faded after the reality of going to war, finding a career, getting married, and settling into suburbia all but smothered it.

He just remembered it again today...

The burning in his chest woke something up in Malcolm. His pupils dilated as he recalled the fervor and passion he had after graduating from bible college. These were memories long buried, but today he began to remember the many times he volunteered to canvas various neighborhoods for the church, announcing special movie nights, church plays, and generally trying to evangelize anyone who would listen. Other religions known for their door-to-door proselytizing had nothing on Malcolm Hodges – he was a whirlwind of energy who was responsible for many new converts whom pastor Tony would then teach and instruct in the ways of righteousness. *Pastor Tony's right-hand man.* It wasn't long before Malcolm was instated as part-time assistant pastor of Grey Falls Baptist Church. The role suited him well, as he now had the backing to open up a coffee house for teens, raise funds for the food bank, and begin mentoring his own followers.

Then Vietnam happened. Conscription made him a soldier, a pessimist, and quite angry at God. After all, how could he let such atrocities happen? Where was his love when napalm was wiping out entire villages, women and children included. Where was his love when his friend walked onto a land mine? His questioning made him wander from his faith; he even delved into drugs somewhat.

Following his eventual return to Grey Falls, the church wasn't the same – only a few hangers-on who met in homes here and there for prayer and bible study. The locals were taken back by Malcolm's rejection of church life, and he would debate with them about the realities of war, trying to convince them of his new world view, but he only ostracized himself.

Out of character, Malcolm went to a singles dance one Friday evening, and met up with his high school sweetheart, Lydia Forsythe. With her eye on politics, a great education, and a fun person to be around, she was quite a catch in Malcolm's estimation. And, Lydia rather liked this new bad-boy ex-church, ex-Vietnam soldier. So, after dating for six months, Malcolm popped the question. Lydia was only too happy to live with this handsome man and raise a kid or two.

Now with a wife and a baby on the way, Malcolm began thinking about a career path. He started as a salesman at Sam's Lumber Yard and Building Supply. Sam hired him on the spot, and his years there gave him the background and experience in the construction trades, which he learned about inside and out. He would visit the sites he was providing supplies for just to learn all he could. Despite his surly side, he did well, moving up through management, eventually becoming president of sales.

Of late, he has been thinking of striking out on his own. The lumber yard can't keep up, and there are a few items he could specialize in without becoming a direct competitor to the lumber yard that has been so good to him. He walked into the local credit union with a thick binder of plans, forecasts, spreadsheets, and commitment from suppliers – they were impressed with his due diligence.

The gas in his leaf blower runs out, so he gives it a few shakes to milk out all the fumes he can, but it sputters to a dead halt. Good thing – he hears the phone ring through the open kitchen window. He runs inside.

"Hey Toby! How are you? What's up?

Malcolm and Toby go back a ways, though they're not really close buddies. Different social strata, different backgrounds, but – Malcolm occasionally attends the same church as Toby, and they share stories of being soldiers in a war that made no sense. A friend in need is a friend indeed, and Malcolm has helped out Toby in the past.

"Hey Mac…" Toby has a speech impediment and can't pronounce his name… "Listen Mac, sorry to bother you on a Saturday, but the church board thinks I should talk to you about something."

"Sure Toby, what is it?"

Toby continues. "You remember that big store that came into town last spring? Well, I quit my job at that printing place… you know, Johnson's… to go work for them, but they went and laid me off. I'm stuck. We don't got any more money to pay rent. Mac, I'm not askin' for a handout, but maybe you know someone in your company who needs some odd jobs done around the house and yard. You know how handy I am. Plus, hunting season is a couple weeks away, and I needs gas so I can get meat for the winter."

Malcolm smiles to himself. It's a familiar smile, one that comes every time he bails Toby out of another bind. He doesn't mind… Toby is the kind of guy that everyone loves, and knows that he'd be the first to help out in any squeeze. And he has.

"Listen Toby, what are you doing right now?"

"Well, I'm talkin' to you on the phone."

Malcolm shakes his head. "If you got enough gas to get over here, I have half an acre of leaves that need raking and bagging. Let's start with that."

"Mac – you're amazing." Toby squeals with excitement – "Mac" can hear him pass on the news to his wife. "I got enough gas – I'll see ya in twenty minutes!"

Malcolm meanders back to the tool shed and refills his leaf blower, his mind rekindling thoughts and questions from decades ago. He recollects asking one of his profs in bible college: "Sir, why is there so much death and murder in the bible, all in the name of God?"

His professor strokes his moustache, and responds authoritatively: "God is the ultimate answer to everything. Who are we, as mere mortals, to question the eternal wisdom of the creator of the universe? God does as he sees fit, and it is not up to us to doubt his reasons for anything". The professor then finishes the lecture with a barrage of bible quotes from the old and new testaments, which Malcolm notes for future reference.

To this day, he ponders the justification of murder for the greater good. Is God-sanctioned killing right? Serving in the army didn't help – his experience overseas did nothing but cloud his judgment in this area. *Thou shalt not kill.* Yet, the bible is filled with mass extinction, supposedly ordered by the architect of the universe. *Maybe I'll go over those bible verses…*

Malcolm is startled by the sound of the leaf blower starting up – here is Toby, all dressed up in dungarees and work gloves, finishing the job Malcolm was too distracted to continue with.

"I'll have this done in a jiffy," yells Toby over the roar of the little gas engine – "You go make us a pot of coffee!" Toby knows Malcolm doesn't drink coffee, so he'll end up with the whole pot to himself – a ritual they'll go through time and again.

Thus begins a new era in Toby's life. For some unknown reason, Malcolm is able to find dozens of people needing Toby's particular talents. Yard work, light carpentry, vehicle repair… Malcolm's influence and connections in the community are enough to keep Toby quite busy for the next while. Needless to say, Toby worships the ground "Mac" walks on.

Malcolm looks out his kitchen window. "Typical redneck!" he says to himself. Up on Malcolm's lawn is Toby's three quarter ton pick-up, the national symbol of freedom: two CB antennas each sporting an American flag, mud flaps reading "Back Off," and a rifle rack filled with his favorite hunting rifles. The trailer with a camouflaged quad rounds it all out.

Wouldn't want to be his enemy, he thinks, looking for the ground coffee.

Chapter 6

Medical school is grueling, and if you're not from a rich family, seven years of education racks up quite a huge bill. Dr. William Kao doesn't like things hanging over his head, so he's motivated to pay it off as quickly as possible – he decides to specialize in plastic surgery. It's good money. On the other side, there's this pro-bono work that his wife "strongly suggests" he get involved in. An intelligent man, Bill is also very polite and cordial, a perfect fit for Grey Falls. He and his business partner found out about Grey Falls from a relative. *You should set up there. It has a growing economy, and no womens' clinics.*

A few years ago, Bill and his classmate Steven were sharing a coffee in a hospital's cafeteria. They go back a long time – from the old neighborhood in Chicago's west end, to high school, and on into medicine – they had each other's backs through the years, and could always count on one another.

They were talking future plans as a gorgeous nursing student sauntered from one corner of the room to another – seems she recognized a friend and decided to join her for lunch. Neither of them spoke for a few seconds, as their eyes followed this red-haired beauty as she crossed their sight lines. Their heads hardly moving, yet eyes straining, Steven finally broke the silence.

"Who in Christ's name is she??? I've never seen her before… you?"

Bill shook his head and responded -

"Uh – no – but I did hear the nursing college was bringing in a new class of third-year students for their psych rotation. Whoa – quite the class, wouldn't you say?"

"Let her analyze *this*" Bill said with a nudge-nudge, wink-wink posture.

This teaching hospital has a constant influx of students hoping to some day be doctors, nurses, respiratory technologists, and lab technicians. Massive in both size and patient population, the hospital itself would qualify as a small town on any day of the week. Learning and interning here brought about its own rewards, such as preferred status in certain fellowships, a chance to study under the country's best surgeons, and most important – the highest nurse-to-doctor marriage statistic in the country. Not surprisingly, many alumni have nicknamed it "Ultrasound Central."

A quick rock/scissors/paper left Steve at the table. He watched as Bill gathered his courage, did a thumbs-up, and walked over to the redhead's area.

"Hi, I'm Bill, and that's my friend over there – Steve. We're wondering if you girls have been informed by the university's registrar department about the new intern appreciation initiation application masturbation and observation protocol?"

The girls roll their eyes and smirk.

"Ahem – well, I can't say we've heard about *that* per se, but we *were* warned about horny medical students on campus who should be reported immediately to security."

They all chuckle, exchange looks and eventually phone numbers, after a bit of serious "converswasion" as Bill was known to call it. *I'm not busy tomorrow night* says, Colleen. Steven's future wife was a little harder to convince, but as they say, the rest is history.

Bill's decision to specialize in surgery split him and Steve up from their usual afternoon coffees, but they stayed in constant touch as good friends do.

What are you and Colleen doing this weekend? – Steve emails Bill.

"Why don't the four of us get in some skiing before they close up for the season?"

"You're on. I'll book the cabin."

The women's health and wellness clinic Bill and Steven co-founded years later was an instant hit – breast implants, tummy tucks, and face lifts melted their student loans away like ice cream on a hot sidewalk. No one talked much about the therapeutic abortions also conducted there; they relied on Colleen to coordinate everything, and they simply did what they were told. The threatening letters, anonymous phone calls, and suspicious packages in the mail kept everyone in the clinic on their toes. The press they attracted was more than they expected, though today, Steven gave it a good spin on local television amongst all the protesters.

"As co-founder of Grey Falls Women's Health Clinic, what is your response to those who argue that your client education falls short in comparison to the local right-to-life chapter?"

The question catches him off guard. *What am I doing here?* he says to himself, as he scans the parking lot of the new clinic. The protesters seem more organized than usual, with their placards and banners. A full on-location television crew is there from the station nearby, and the strong presence of a police vehicle reminds everyone to remain civil.

He agreed to be the public face for their new clinic, even though his partner's wife would have been a better choice – but, she had other involvements in the community and could stand a little anonymity. Steven simply was not prepared for the onslaught of attention brought to them by their clinic's practices, nor the question he's supposed to answer with this camera in his face… Yet, he handles it like a pro.

"To start, let me please assure everyone here that our clientele are treated with the utmost respect – not the way these protesters are suggesting."

Camera two pans the crowd; the switcher in the microwave truck splits the screen in half top to bottom, showing Steven and his interviewer on the left, the hundreds of protesters on the right. A few viewers recognize Toby's truck off in the distance.

"Our staff are the best in their field, and we are here to fill a very important need that has been missing in Grey Falls for years.

I'm not here to debate the morality of medical science – we can do that another time. But I can say that we are indeed here at the request of many people from this city. That's all I have to say for now – please excuse me."

Colleen is watching this live at home.
"Whew – glad *he* was there, and not me."

Recently married to make things "official", Colleen Patrick kept her last name because of all the associations, fraternities, and clubs she joined during the time she put her husband through his last couple of years of medical school. One of her roles in the community is at Grey Falls High School, filling in as a guidance counselor for a peer who is away on sabbatical. She is a favorite to many of the students, including Leslie Hodges. Growing up in a tough inner-city environment and having to raise her own younger siblings, Colleen relates well to teens, so Les opened up to her right away. They sometimes stroll around the high school grounds at lunch time, Colleen listening and helping Les navigate around many typical teen issues. They both know they have a friend in each other despite the age difference.

Leslie asks, "How can I get Sean to take life more seriously? His problem is his good looks, talent, and brains... he hardly has to try at anything, and you should see the marks he gets!" She avoids mentioning the marijuana.
"Well, Les, it's tough to watch someone like him take life so easily – maybe he's the kind of guy that doesn't have to try as hard as the rest of us, but he will come across some kind of hardship or testing – then he'll discover how strong he really is. None of us know till we're put through the wringer how we'll react.
"Think of why this bothers you... search your heart and ask yourself if you're jealous of him. If not, then just be happy for

him. It sounds like he's happy for you, with your good marks and musical talent."

Les ponders her words. "You know, maybe you're right. I mean – I do have to study harder than him to get the same marks, and that is annoying, so yeah – maybe I shouldn't let it bother me. Thanks Nurse Patrick – I knew you'd understand."

"No problem," the nurse responds, rubbing Leslie's shoulder. "I have to meet my husband for a team consultation in a few minutes; I really should head towards the parking lot."

"Sounds interesting! I didn't know you worked with your husband. What do you do together?"

Colleen pensively responds… "We get involved with young teens in trouble, you know – who find themselves expecting. We offer them choices. It's a new service in Grey Falls. Used to be that only the big cities could help them, but now this town has grown so much, we're just as well-equipped."

Leslie feels uncomfortable, but doesn't know why. She understands what Nurse Patrick is talking about, but doesn't want to give it thought.

As they part ways, Leslie waves – "See you next week!"
"Thanks Leslie, take care, and remember I'm always available for a chat."

Chapter 7

If Grey Falls has a good high school, they have an even better support industry for the local developers trying to keep up with housing demands. Malcolm saw a business opportunity, and with the help of a bank loan and a couple of grants, he opened up a new manufacturing plant that provides custom doors, windows, and roof trusses to local builders. Months later, Hodges Enterprises also opened a cement plant three miles south of town. *Talk about cornering the market* though Malcolm as he closed the deal.

His manufacturing plant is in the east end of Grey Falls, the industrial sector. It is the perfect size, even considering future expansion. The front offices were remodeled by his own staff in one weekend, and the basement cleared out of junk left behind by the past occupants. All the workers' spouses showed up with coffee, doughnuts, pizza, and the odd massage for the few office workers who hadn't lifted a hammer in the past few years… Everyone was in on it, with even the mayor attending the official ribbon-cutting ceremony. Lydia was never shy about making a public appearance.

Malcolm it at the podium: "Ladies and gentlemen, this is a major milestone for Hodges Enterprises. We thank everyone for being here, especially Mr. Gromwell from Grey Falls Trust, and Lydia Forsythe, our mayor. Both have been instrumental in making this happen, and I am truly grateful."

Lydia did have some zoning bylaws overlooked for her ex-husband's new venture. After all – it's for the good of the city. *OK, get on with it you gasbag.*

"Our hardworking staff have gone beyond the call of duty in preparing for this grand day. Hodges Enterprises acknowledges and recognizes them all." He raises his hands to clap; the crowd follows. He patters on about the great city they all live in, the importance of economic growth, and the close sense of community in Grey Falls.

"Now Your Honor, if you will…" he says handing her a pair of large ornate scissors. Lydia steps forward and takes her place beside Malcolm, holding the scissors over the ribbon. They hold the pose. There's a TV cameraman recording the event for the evening news while the professional photographer steps forward, bends to one knee and asks "Smile!"

With all of the formalities out of the way, and the crowd dissipating, Lydia says to Malcolm –

"Hey, it's not often we see each other. I stuck around to give you a heads up about a new company coming to the area. You may want to create some new employee retention bonuses or something… I hear mining companies pay exceptionally well. I'd hate to see all this hard work go to the dogs."

Malcolm knew exactly what she meant. Companies have been poaching employees from each other for the past year now, creating a skilled worker shortage.

"Mining? Shit, what does Grey Falls have in its soil worth digging for?"

"Uranium. 12 miles south. A test dig has apparently caused some stir in the industry. Someone I know saw the geological reports and thought that perhaps I should know about it. There's nothing I can do or say – it's on property owned by a doctor who lives here in town, but he doesn't want a mining operation in his back yard."

"Hm. Thanks Lydia. This is good intel, right? I can bring this up at the next board meeting?"

"Yup. Just be quiet about where you got it from."

With that, he squeezes her arm and makes for his office. *More bloody money out the window. More stress. Dammit!*

CRACK!!! The aluminum bat connects squarely with the baseball, sending it out to right field, bouncing off the chain link fence. The team out in field is comprised of the executives of Malcolm's company; the team at bat – all the floor workers. Last game of the season – the air is crisp, and everyone smells frost. They figured a family picnic and ball game would boost company morale, particularly the surprise bonus checks coming that Friday.

None of the outfielders know baseball very well – Malcolm grabs the ball first and throws it to the general area of second base, but Gerry the accountant is busy waving to someone in the crowd… the ball flies past him, and everyone roars with laughter as he realizes his gaffe and tries to recover – too late, the batter is at second thanks to him. A couple more slips from the outfielders, and the bases are filling up.

Gord "Slugger" Osborne steps up to the plate. The pitcher looks nervous and catches a glimpse of his brother Toby chatting with one of the exec's wives at the hot dog stand.

"What a suck-up," he whispers to himself, while winding up to send his best curve ball over home plate.

"Why, Mrs. Hodges, I'm not used to seeing you at a baseball game. How are you?"

Marjorie responds – "Great! But – why are *you* here?"

"That's my brother, the pitcher. He's kinda embarrassed of me, but I like to watch baseball, even if it's not the pros. I tagged along with him this morning. Hey – I asked first – I thought *you* didn't like ball?"

Marjorie blushes a little. "No Toby, I'm not a big baseball fan, but I thought I would show some support and cheer for my husband. Though I have to say, I'm rather enjoying this new book." She pulls out a rather thick hard cover novel, with lots of yellow stickies marking her favorite passages. She winks at Toby. It takes a second for him to get it, but then he exclaims…

"So let me get this – you find your book more interesting than Mr. Hodges' ball game," cracking a huge, knowing smile. They have a chuckle together. "Is it a good book?"

Marjorie launches into the story – "It's called 'Crimes of Passion, Moments of Love.' It may be a little spicy, but I like that," she says in a whisper – "The story is very intriguing, and even my sister's husband liked it. He said it's more than a sappy love story; there's macho stuff in it for the guys too." Other than all the temporary yellow-stickie bookmarks, there's an ornate quilted one that Toby comments on – she opens it and reads a quick paragraph out loud. He nods with approval. "Almost like words to live by!"

They both ignore the crowd's noise, and the game's obvious turn-around. The lineup to the hotdog stand dwindles…

She continues – "We're discussing it in our book club. You should come by some time we're meeting – every Tuesday evening at the high school library. Oh here we are…" Marj places her order.

"I'll have nacho chips with cheese sauce and a hot dog please. Toby? My treat."

"Well thank you, ma'am! One hot dog and a coke please."

"The book sounds interesting, Mrs. Hodges, my little Jacquie keeps telling me I should socialize more and make friends. And I do like to read. This one sounds good."

"Well, Toby, nice to chat with you again. I guess I'll see you in church if I don't see you raking leaves again at our place. Take care."

"Thanks for the invite, Mrs. Hodges. And the food."

He mumbles to himself something about having a bad memory, that he should have written the title down.

"Slugger" had hit a home run, emptying the bases and winning the game for the shop boys. Everyone starts packing up, with some headed over to the Loose Goose for a couple of cold ones. Marjorie hands Jake his nacho chips and says, "Share with your father – here he comes." She takes one bite out of her hot dog and offers the rest to Malcolm.

"Gee, if I knew you guys were going to suck so bad, I would have stayed home," she says with a smirk.

"Yeah, well, whatever you were reading seemed more important anyways."

Jake chimes in – "I can throw better than you! I've got a right arm my coach loves!"

"Well, I tried to get you in, but it was only employees. Maybe next time, son."

Jake continues… "Can we go home? I have to pee, and the outdoor toilets here are gross".

"Well," says Marj – "I guess there *is* hope for this young man! I bet you didn't even wash your hands after *you* went…" looking over her reading glasses at Malcolm. "Some example!"

"Let's head back home. I can't wait to hear the gloating at work tomorrow," Malcolm says sarcastically.

At the Loose Goose, Toby is sharing a table with his brother Gord and some his brother's co-workers. There are many rounds of beer, glasses clinking with "Here's to kicking corporate ass!" They all roar with laughter and order another round of dry ribs, potato skins, and veggie platters. Earlier Malcolm gave Gord his company credit card saying, "No more than $1,000. Let the boys know the office is paying for it – kind of an early Christmas present. Have fun". Toby wishes he could work for Malcolm too, but his applications don't ever seem to go anywhere. Still, he's included in the revelry.

"You know Gord, Mr. Hodges' wife – what's her name? Marj – that's it. She invited me to her book club Tuesday nights."

Toby's brother listens, pauses, and measures his response.

"Bro, she's an executive's wife. They do that kind of thing, just to appear cordial. You know what cordial means, right?"

The next five minutes sees Gord explaining the intricacies of social decorum to his brother, the second time this week. Toby slowly shakes his head, and says:

"I think I understand. Thanks Gordo. But I think I just might show up at the library next Tuesday," he says with a determined look.

"You forget what we do every Tuesday evening…"

A knowing look comes over Toby's face. He remembers rule number one: never utter their group's name in public.

"I should have remembered *that*" he says embarrassed.

"You're new, that's OK. And hey listen – you go to the same church as they do. I'm dropping hints about the group to Malcolm. He might be interested – maybe you can drop hints to him as well. Just remember rule number one…"

"…don't mention the name of the group."

Chapter 8

Despite all the smoke and mirrors, Maria must perform well enough to keep Midwest Mining's president on board. She has studied the company's HR records very closely. But any time a member of her staff slips a bit, she takes him clubbing, or sends him a case of scotch. Five months into her mission, and the company's stocks keep dropping. She hates to see someone else benefit from her hard work, but such is corporate life. Her reward is on its way.

"Ms. Ramirez, call on line 2." Maria has her own corner of the 20th floor.

"Talk to me."

"It's an IT guy crabbing about his nine years on staff. You know, kids and all."

Maria knew this would happen.

"Has Lynn not interviewed him yet?" Lynn is her hatchet man, but he can't keep them all away from this "faceless bitch" responsible for their termination.

Sigh. "Put him through."

"Yes... hello? Ms. Ramirez here..."

"Well finally! I thought *her highness* didn't speak to us plebes down below the 10th floor."

God. I hate this.

"Ms. Ramirez, I'm Glen Aldrich – I've worked for this company for almost ten years, and you're letting me go without any severance... I've talked to my lawyer and he says I have a legitimate complaint that I can take to the labor board. I have kids with braces, car and mortgage payments... you think I can just find a job tomorrow?"

No severance? What is Lynn doing?

"Mr. Aldrich, let me pull up your file."

Seconds later…

"I can assure you, no one will leave Midwest without the minimum requirement as stated by law. My personal promise is twice that. Do you understand that Mr. Aldrich?"

"Uh – yes. I have your word?"

"There's obviously a misunderstanding here. Sir, you will not leave here empty-handed. I personally assure that. But you know what…"

Mr. Aldrich listens intently.

"Glen, wasn't that you who spearheaded the Y2K task force back when you first started? Yes – here it is. No budget, no staff. You sequestered two peers to patch all the company's PCs and laptops."

"We missed two. Had to re-image them."

"I like that kind of initiative. Greg, you're on the short list for re-hire. I'm sure the senior manager's job will be open in a month or two. Hang in there…"

"Thank you, ma'am."

"Good afternoon, sir."

Maria ends the call, then phones her hatchet man.

"Lynn, what the hell are you doing? I just got a call from a techie who said he wasn't getting any severance." She lets him explain.

"You said to be brutal, I'm being brutal."

"You asshole. When's the last time you've been fired without a minimum of holiday pay or some kind of package?" She lets the silence linger… he gets her drift.

"Here's what you're going to do. You will phone our friend Mr. Aldrich, apologize, send his wife flowers, send him twice his holiday pay, then crawl on your hands and knees and beg to weed his garden. Do you *get* me??? We're pragmatists, not Nazis."

She slams the phone on its cradle. *I'm not cut out for this.*

Friday afternoon. Maria has timed this meeting perfectly, and is ready to pounce. Months of scheming and preparation are about to pay off. With Underbridge's help, and her cunning strategizing, the pair's efforts are about to culminate. *Here goes nothing…*

The boardroom is somber, filled with barely a quorum of voting shareholders. Everyone is eyeing each other as they wait for Maria to start the meeting. Joshua Gerenberg is not present; he's off schmoozing on the golf course, something arranged by Maria.

"What good has she done so far?" someone asks another. "It's been weeks."

"*Months* you mean. It does take time." answers Glenda – "She'll be announcing a new strategy this morning – you wait and see."

Just then in walks Maria.

"Good morning, ladies and gentlemen." She opens her briefcase and passes out a one-page financial overview of the last few years, with colored graphs and pie charts. She stands to speak after everyone has a chance to study the numbers.

"Ladies and gentlemen, I draw your attention to the top graph. It represents an important 10,000 foot view of the company's performance over the past three years. The red line is our share price, the blue line our EBITBA – you know – earnings before interest, taxes, depreciation, and amortization. I have been studying these numbers since I got here. Please note that around May last year, we change from a plateau, to a slow decline of our *ebitiba* closely followed by our share value. It's a no-brainer if you think about it, but I was curious as to what may have initiated this decline. Anyone care to offer an explanation?" She knows the answer.

They look at each other – someone at the back speaks up.

"Diversification. I was against it from the start."

"Right you are sir. This is two months after Midwest's leadership changes and a new mandate is presented. I am frankly surprised this hasn't been pointed out before. Any junior analyst would have…" she's cut off by Zachary Hersch.

"Ms. Ramirez, the numbers are obvious to you because you're an outsider and have objectivity."

He clears his throat, then stands and nods to his peers, as if to thank them for listening.

"These numbers mean the same to us, but for different reasons. All the time Joshua's father was alive, we did things his way or the highway. We were in fact growing a few percentage points a year. Then he took ill and changed a few things around, trying to leave a legacy for his family. He bungled it. We all knew this day would come. After his passing a year ago, some of us have been anxious to do something, but our hands are tied. Ms. Ramirez, you're the change we've been looking for. Some of our numbers have been improving, even in the short time you have been here – we are likely to start seeing an upswing. I read reports too." He looks around the room. "Now, I didn't intend on highjacking this meeting; we would like you to continue."

"Thank you, Mr. Hersch. That helps me understand things much better, and leads me to my next very obvious question. When Midwest began to diversify its operations, was that in fact the new mandate brought forward by Mr. Gerenberg Junior?"

The reaction is interesting. At the mention of his name, half the room shake their heads as if to say, "Oh you mean *that* piece of work."

Someone answers – "Yes, that is correct. Ever since he's been at the helm, we've been in a consistent nose dive."

"I thought so. The numbers don't lie. So – here is what I am proposing. Um – just to remind everyone, I am not here to make anyone feel comfortable. I am simply acting on the mandate I was hired to execute."

Everyone senses something is coming...

"If we were to politely but firmly request that Gerenberg Junior step down, and allow his second in command to take his place, I guarantee Midwest's value will begin to rally the next day. You then pursue what you do best: mining. Forget about refining and distribution. I have spoken with Mr. Rudman, your vice president, and he is on board. I understand him to be the force that has kept Mr. Gerenberg from totally destroying Midwest – he's your obvious choice. Madam Chair, may I leave the rest to you?"

She threw them the bone they've been wanting to chew on for a long time.

Glenda shifts in her seat. "Members of the board, I would like to see a show of hands as a response to the following question: should we vote on new leadership?"

Every hand is raised.

"May the secretary please note the unanimous response."

"I therefore put forward a motion that Joshua Gerenberg be removed from his position as president of Midwest Mining Corporation. All in favor, raise your hand."

Unanimous once more.

"Motion carried. May the secretary please note the unanimous agreement once again."

"So done," responds the secretary.

Glenda steps up: "I put forward the motion that Gregory Rudman be elected to the position of president of Midwest Mining. All in favor?"

Unanimous.

Maria's heart is pounding. Her first coup…

"Motion carried." declares the chairperson. There's loud applause. Someone shouts, "Hallelujah! Finally!" Someone else – "Christmas bonus, here we come!"

Glenda continues.

"Well ladies and gentlemen, we have ourselves a new president. I'm sure we're all looking forward to Midwest turning a new leaf. I have one question to throw out to everyone." The din settles. *What's up now,* they think.

"In all the excitement, we have left a station in the executive team empty. Does anyone have someone in mind to fill in Mr. Rudman's shoes as VP?"

Most are slightly bewildered. They haven't had much time to think about it. Someone from the left side of the room starts to talk. Maria can't make out who he is – there's sunlight coming from the window behind him.

"Madam Chair, I'm wondering if there's anyone in this room willing to throw their hat in the ring."

"Do you have anyone in mind?"

"Yes I do. It's someone who has been influencing our bottom line of late. It's someone who has the proven abilities of leadership, focus, and a can-do attitude." People are staring around the room. Two or three know whom he's talking about.

"Ms. Ramirez, my name is Donald Benoit. You only know me by name because frankly, I couldn't be bothered with these meetings. But after following what has transpired today, I am asking you to consider joining the ranks of Midwest Mining as our new vice president."

She gasps, placing her hand over her chest. *I didn't know it was going to be this easy!*

"You don't have to answer today. But we could use someone like you working with Rudman – you'd make a great pair actually."

Maria measures her response.

"Mr. Benoit, Madam Chair – everyone – I'm overwhelmed by your vote of confidence. You've only known me short time, so I am humbled. I'm not sure I can respond today if that is OK – I have my own company to run, contracts coming up…"

"We understand Ms. Ramirez. Would a week be adequate time to come to a decision?"

She feigns surprise quite well… "Well – yes, that would be fine. I will have a firm answer then."

The chairperson responds: "Thanks Maria, you've been a god-send. I would be delighted to see you on board."

All this time at Midwest, Maria has kept Josh from three important shareholder meetings. *The company has lost its vision and direction once and for all,* say the experts at the Financial Times. Leaks to the press about an absentee president result in one last terrible slide in Midwest's stock price: $3.78.

Buy, you greedy prick – buy all you can! That's the essence of her fax to Underbridge. She shreds the original immediately after it has been transmitted, then receives a call on her private line minutes later.

"Alone?"

"Yes."

"OK. Stage two. Tell Rudman there's a new gold mine in Venezuela that was just discovered. It's virgin. First rights. I'll fax you the geologist's report. Tell them he's some free-lancer looking to cash in."

What a player, she thinks. *I'm glad I'm on his side.*

Glenda Boyer calls an emergency board meeting for Monday, 10AM sharp. She was up past midnight getting staff to re-write, proof, and photocopy the geologist's report. She writes a quick executive's summary to be tucked into the front for the ones less acquainted with such technical matters. *Good news* she tells everyone. *Perhaps a turnaround.* A leak to the press, and Midwest's stocks will skyrocket.

Monday morning. Maria's driver isn't accustomed to such an early rise. The whisky shots and beer chasers didn't help much. But that was 8PM last night. *C'mon with us, there's this great club on 60th Street – you'll never forget it!* Morning-after regrets are drowned in a double-espresso.

"Rough night?"

"Aw – you know. My new girlfriend is half my age. I can't keep up with her."

Maria doesn't say anything for a few seconds.

"As long as you answer your phone and can drive – that's all I care."

"Yes, Ma'am."

"A word of advice. In ten years, the age difference will mean nothing. I know."

The driver is intrigued. *I think I like her.*

Fifteen minutes later, Maria is leaving the car.

"Stay here. I shouldn't be longer than an hour or two."

The noise in the boardroom is deafening until Maria walks in. Her eagle-like stare scans the room to ensure only the right people are there... including the source of the last two leaks to the press.

The company's president takes the floor and announces Mid-west's salvation: a new find in Venezuela.

"Yes, it's brand new, and our very own geologist found it." A lie.

"Preliminary tests are extremely positive. Do you know what this means? A vein of gold three miles long no one has ever seen before in South America... Folks, we'll be in the black by year-end!"

They can't believe their ears. Most have scanned the report in front of them and first thought the projections were typos. Apparently not.

"Ms. Ramirez, it hasn't been a week, but are you ready to come on board yet? The stock options are great."

Maria slaps her hand on the large boardroom table. *"Damn right I am!"* she exclaims in a loud voice. The room breaks out in applause. She raises her finger – "But I *do* need a break if you don't mind!"

"You name the terms," pipes in the chairperson.

Back in her limo, Maria reports to Underbridge on her car phone. He tells her –

"You did it. Check your bank balance tomorrow morning for an early Christmas present."

Maria is very relieved. *This has been a tough go,* she concludes. As she slumps into the back seat, she craves a gin and tonic. She's not had a drop of booze since her new role as a 'business consultant.'

"Well Argyle, it's been a slice. Looks like I won't need you after today, but don't worry, you've got a nice bonus on its way. I'll cancel the phone rental and car lease tomorrow. You've been great. Good luck with your new squeeze. Now let's go have a drink together."

Conveniently, the info about Midwest's new find is leaked to the press before they have a chance to announce it formally. Their shares indeed begin to climb… The stage is set. Peter reads the paper a few days later, coffee in hand. *Well shit – looks like I'll be one rich son-of-a bitch by this time next week.*

———————————

Such is the life of Peter Underbridge, the conquering capitalist. His peers refer to him as *Attila the Hun.* His methods are somewhat questionable, but legal. The companies he buys pay their shareholders well, and Midwest Mining will be no exception. He leaves this corporation to their own devices without interfering much – with Maria on board and Rudman at the helm, who knows how helpful they could be in the future.

His methods do not escape the attention of a small group of influential individuals in the corporate world. *He's made of the right stuff. We could use him.*

On a miserably cold and rainy autumn night, Underbridge has his first encounter with Senator Gleason in a mansion that rivals his own. The library is traditional Bostonian, with dark-paneled walls, bookshelves everywhere, a large pool table in the middle, and a bar with every single malt dating back thirty years. With only the two of them in the room, the politician tells Underbridge about a small group of people interested in his talents.

"We're small, but effective. We simply got tired of these liberal left-wing tree hugging judges in the supreme court, overturning appeals. Big business is under fire, Underbridge – I know you fight lawsuits all the time. So, we now move things around in each scenario without lobbying, without buying votes, without getting bogged down in trying to change legislation. We all scratch each other's backs. I do my part in the senate, but there's more to life than politics. You're a shrewd man Underbridge – we think you joining could be win-win. We're meeting tonight."

Underbridge swirls his whisky in the oversized snifter and stares at the senator for a few seconds. In a reflective voice he responds…

"I look forward to it."

The meeting room is filled with pungent cigar smoke, but Underbridge doesn't show his discomfort. A butler had been through earlier asking for drink orders and places glasses of brandy every-where on various ornate side tables, as well as the main oval table in the center. The 'cigar' room as it is referred to, many decisions and deals have been made here by the country's power players. Tonight is special – the induction of a new member. The leader clears his throat and begins…

"Gentlemen, we all know why we're here. But before we get into business, I have the pleasure of introducing Mr. Peter Underbridge. You've all read his dossier. We've been watching this rascal do business, and we like him. Do we not?"

Someone responds – "Hear, hear."

"He does business as we do. And he knows how to play the field for the betterment of the shareholders he is responsible to. And

– he likes to get his hands dirty. Again, as we do. I propose we get on with the toast."

The *Toast*.

"Mr. O'Conner, please do the honors."

Mr. O'Conner steps up to a bookshelf and removes a small, very old leather bound book. Each of these men have one in their home. He looks in the index, then flips to somewhere in the middle. He clears his throat and raises his glass with his other hand.

"Hear ye, all worthy gentlemen."

The crowd responds in unison…

"Hear ye!"

"Step forth from common pursuit and conquer."

"Hear ye!" – the crowd responds louder.

"Take hold of strength and courage as they are your birth-right."

"Hear ye!"

"Let boldness go before you."

"Hear ye!"

Mr. O'Conner places the book down, and almost shouts…

"Let all that are present pledge their honor and their life to *Specialis Ordo!*"

"Hear, hear!"

They all clink glasses and down the brandy.

"Welcome Peter." they all say to him. The senator hooks his thumbs in his vest pockets and says to him:

"Now, you'll see how we really get things done in this country."

Chapter 9

It's Monday morning. Two inches of snow on the ground don't bother this veteran of Colorado winters. Always ready each November with snow tires on his four-by-four truck, Mr. Clark pulls out of his driveway, chuckling at the city before him in panic. Cars on bald tires are skidding everywhere, trying to get to the local grocery store to buy up a week's supply of bread. *Jesus, it's only two inches.* He laughs every time a dusting of the white stuff appears on the streets of Grey Falls. Still, every year this phenomenon called "snow" strikes panic in the heart of this otherwise sane town.

Mr. Clark pours himself a strong, fresh cup of coffee from the cafeteria's huge aluminum drip dispenser. *Must get these guys into the 21st century – a latte would really do me right now.* His usual sojourn to school this day was broken by a side trip to the bus station.

He shows the claim ticket to the person behind the counter, who says, "One moment please."

After signing for the medium-sized brown box, he excitedly walks out to his truck and places it on the passenger seat. The familiar yellow logo in the upper left corner confirms the contents of the shipment. His class's long-awaited DNA kits are here.

Mr. Clark carries the box down the hallway to his class past the principal's office – he gives a quick wave to Mr. T, who is on the phone. He waves back. As he enters his class, he finds the students beginning to seat themselves. Many are late that morning, so he gives his obligatory "Here's how you drive in snow" lecture which everyone has heard before. "When I was a boy, I used to see six foot snow banks everywhere!" They roll their eyes.

"Class, our DNA test kits have arrived. Chris, would you be so kind as to open this up and hand them out." He hands him a box cutter.

Christopher eagerly opens up the box and passes them around, reading each of the names out loud that are printed on the individual envelopes. Everyone is excited at the prospect of finding out their biological heritage.

"This is better than Roots," someone exclaims, referring to a novel they're studying in English. It took the world by storm when it came out decades ago, causing a tidal-wave of interest in genealogy.

Sean leans over to Leslie and whispers: "Mom – you know – Lydia – seems uncomfortable with this."

"Maybe you look too much like the postman," jokes Leslie. Sean sends her a disapproving frown.

Mr. Clark reads the direction on his kit, then says,

"OK everyone, please quiet down. When you open up the kit, follow the directions precisely. If the Q-tip gets contaminated with anything but your DNA, they can't use the sample. So – go ahead and get a good swab from the inside of your cheek, and immediately place it back in the container. Chris will gather them up when you're done."

Five minutes later, the kits are collected and repackaged for delivery.

"I'll send these out tonight class – now it's just a matter of time before we get our reports."

Chapter 10

The studio is quiet, the lights come up, while the producer counts down...

"Three – two –" ... The set of Breakfast Television sparkles to life.

"Good morning, ladies and gentlemen, I'm your host Jamie Philips with all your news, sports, and weather for this beautiful autumn morning in Grey Falls. George is on location this morning at the mayor's office, and we'll get to him in just a moment. First, the news."

The talking heads do their jobs impeccably at this newly funded television studio, making it a quick favorite amongst the morning news watchers in town. Young, funny, and always on the scene of any significant event with their camera crews; this morning they're about to cover an interview with Lydia Forsythe.

Off-camera, Lydia's assistant whispers... "You got everything?"

She is annoyed with him. He means well, but she doesn't need coddling by this ambitious, but inexperienced boy-Friday who always seems to have a cell phone stuck to his head. Her last assistant left the position for "other interests," but everyone knows how hard it is to work directly for the mayor.

Last night, the war room at city hall was the scene of near panic, and Lydia Forsythe was in the middle of the fray, as always. She hates getting news second hand. Seems someone high up in the mayor's office has some ties to a new uranium mine that is about to begin operations just outside of Grey Falls. The company that had announced their intent to extract uranium by tunneling quietly re-announced last week their intent to use open-pit instead, without any environmental impact studies.

The tree-huggers caught wind of this and immediately hired a lawyer to expose their goings-on to the public, and to dig up as much dirt on them as possible. This lawyer found John Goshen's name on some paper work. Knowing he was the CFO of Grey Falls' municipal government, it wasn't long before the news was leaked to the press. John Goshen's name was not mentioned; they wanted to drop the bomb the next day. The phone lines lit up at city hall. "We have to do some damage control, maybe a press release or something," says Lydia.

"Mayor, we're ready to go in 15 seconds." The technician in the microwave truck outside city hall gives the interviewer the green light. Signal strength back to the studio is 86%.

"Another story now on the environment and political front – While researching the public documents of Midwest Mining Corporation, a lawyer named Jack Bane stumbled across the name of city hall's Chief Financial Officer, John Goshen. Mr. Bane was hired by the Coalition for a Greener Planet, a collection of environmental groups who are protesting the mining of uranium south of Grey Falls. Although the CFO was not available for comment, mayor Lydia Forsythe is standing by at city hall. Over to you, George."

"Thank you, Jamie. George Kenworth here at City Hall, with our mayor, Lydia Forsythe. Good morning Your Honor."

Lydia twitches in her seat. "Yes, good morning George, good to see you again."

"Thank you mayor, you as well. Ms. Forsythe, I'd like to get right to the point – we know you're busy. Are you aware of the dealings John Goshen has with Midwest Mining? Would it not be a conflict of interest for Mr. Goshen to have financial ties to any company that the city has dealings with?"

"I was not aware of Mr. Goshen's relationship with Midwest Mining, but – technically, the city has not had financial dealings with that company. Because the land they plan on mining is close enough to our city, we had a say about possible environmental issues, so they complied and sent us their impact study. That's as far as it went."

She dodged a bullet – hopefully. Maybe the city has no financial dealings with the mining company, but she suspects this goes deeper – she takes a sip of water… A number of offices in city hall have televisions, and they're watching their boss like a hawk. A few employees speak out what most are thinking… "She's really nervous – more than usual."

"Ms. Mayor, are you then saying Mr. Goshen has no direct financial dealing with Midwest Mining?"

She moves uncomfortably in her seat. "I have no record, and am not aware of any information that exists to prove – or disprove – that my CFO has any ties to Midwest Mining. What if he does? This company has nothing to do with our city, so my CFO can do whatever he wants."

"Really?" questions the interviewer… "I have information that says your chief financial officer has ties – through family – to the employment agency used by the mining company to hire locals from Grey Falls. What is your comment?"

The interview went well up to this point…

Lydia is visibly frustrated by this witch hunt. "You media people should not assume all politicians are guilty until proven innocent. We're looking into it, and our findings will go public at the appropriate time."

George clears his throat and finishes with, "Thank you mayor for your time today. Back to you Jamie."

Wow, that was short and sweet. Anyone watching the interview at home or at work saw it for the first time: the mayor of Grey Falls lost her composure in public.

———————————

John Goshen knew he had it coming, so he hides himself in the archives building, claiming to be researching some old budgetary items mentioned in long-past city hall meetings. Lydia tracks him down like an owl after a mouse… she closes the door behind herself.

"What *THE FUCK* have you been doing behind our backs?" She is livid, hands on hips.

"Look, Your Honor, I know how it looks, but it isn't that bad."

"Dispense with the bullshit formalities, John; we're old friends. Spill."

John sighs, sits in a chair, and looks up at his boss.

"OK. Well, a few years before I was in public office, my sister and a business partner started up an employment agency for office workers. It blossomed into what it is today – they now hire temps for any industry you can think of. I didn't think anyone would care really…" his voice drops off…

He clears his throat.

"So yes – of course my surname is in print in their offices, but I'm not connected with them directly."

"Dammit John, you know I don't like surprises. Why didn't you fess up last night at our meeting?"

"I didn't think they would have found out – I was thinking maybe they discovered the deputy mayor's ties to that new housing development no one talks about around here."

"You left me hanging John. Perhaps it was just a tempest in a teapot, but I was totally unprepared. I'm going to be issuing an announcement to the news shortly. I'd like it if you were there."

"Sure Lydia. Count on it."

The so-called "scandal" is quashed, and city hall regains its squeaky clean reputation. The next day, Lydia's assistant cringes as he sends out an inter-office memo via encrypted email:

From: Office of the Mayor
To: Undisclosed recipients
Subject: Conflict of Interest
Priority: High
Message: I would like to thank everyone for their hard work and dedication to their careers here at City Hall. I am aware of the extra work everyone puts in, so I thank you – it does not go unnoticed.

As you most are aware, my television appearance yesterday was by far not my best performance. I was sideswiped by information I should have been aware of, but was not. For that reason, I must ask that if any employee of this government is involved or has ties to anything that may be construed as a conflict of interest, I want to know about it. Thank you.

Sincerely,
Lydia Forsythe

Everyone receiving the memo squirms in their seats. They know she means business. To top it off, Lydia requests the human resources department to clean up the wording and include the gist of her email in the City Employee's Handbook.

Chapter 11

The north-facing corner office on the 43rd floor has a great panoramic view of Central Park, but this particular company president takes no notice. With his back to the large windows, his admin assistant reminds him occasionally that he should stop and smell the roses a little more – perhaps relocate his desk for a better vantage point of Manhattan. *I don't need distractions,* he retorts every time. *And no, you can't have my office.*

Running a conglomerate is rather like spinning a dozen or so plates all at the same time, except people's lives and reputations are at stake, *namely mine* thinks Underbridge. He knows a thing or two about rolling up his sleeves and getting his hands dirty – you can't always delegate, and you can't trust everyone. Such is not the case though with Midwest Mining Corporation, his recent acquisition. Their operations are spread around the States, Canada, Mexico, and Venezuela. He keeps upper management and the executive team intact – they have a proven track record. He quite likes the current president, recognizing in him the qualities it takes to get things done.

The legal sized folder open before him is a summary of the company's financials for the last five years. He likes to review all the various companies he owns at least once a quarter. *Hm. My boys said they were doing good – I can see that...* 19 percent growth since acquisition. He pats himself on the back. Mr. Underbridge and the president of Midwest Mining Corporation have history together via mutual friends, acquaintances, and a particular fraternity few people know the name of. Their membership was confirmed in boardroom meetings, with handshakes, and nuances of speech everyone else was clueless about. The old boy's club is tight. Things are asked for and answered without question. Things happen no one knows about. Things are shuffled around for the higher purpose of the Group, all under the radar, all silently.

Reviewing the reports further, Underbridge can't help but notice the anomaly in one report regarding a new project in Utah. There have been multiple communications between MMC and a certain landowner who doesn't want to play ball; his property's mining right are tied up, putting a strangle hold on anything MMC can do until things change. He ponders his options… *Hmmm. It's time for an intervention. I hate doing this…*

Mr. Underbridge pushes his intercom button.

"Mary, will you get Greg Rudman on the horn for me? Buzz me when you have him on line. Thanks."

"Right away, sir," Mary's voice crackles.

The president of Midwest Mining Corporation is en-route to an airport. He is a stocky man in his late fifties, with a tie that has stains from lunch, and a comb-over hairdo that currently needs attention. A man connected to the old boy's network in the senate, his company does well thanks to his uncanny ability to squelch protests, hire the best lobbyists, and keep the best lawyers on staff who know people in the Environmental Protection Agency. He's in touch with every aspect of his company. *The machine rolls ever forward.*

The limo ride to the airport is plagued with call after call on his cell, but Rudman loves it. The company stocks have been rising steadily, so he'll field a call from anyone owning more than ten percent.

"Yes, yes – I told you – don't worry about our little change in plans. I know people who fix this kind of thing as a hobby. Your investment is safe with us Mrs. Johnson, you have my word. Listen – Mrs. Johnson, I have another call I have to take. Nice to hear from you… yeah, please call anytime." He punches a button.

"Maria! Yes, I'm 10 minutes away. Got the topo maps? Good. You talk to the land owner? Excellent. See you there."

His cell hums again. *Dammit, this is crazy…*

"Mr. Rudman?"

"Speaking." He recognizes the voice, but can't place her.

"This is Mary Chen of Underbridge Holdings. Mr. Underbridge would like to speak with you if you have a few moments."

The light goes on. "Absolutely, put him through."

Elevator music. Seconds later…

"Greg – Peter here. How are things?"

"Hey Pete! Good. Things are busy; I'm on my way to the Utah for a couple days – that new mine."

"Sounds like you're getting your hands dirty as usual, good for you."

"Well thanks Peter. So – what's on your mind?"

"Is there anyone with you?"

"Negative."

Mr. Underbridge eyes the phone console for any other open lines and turns his back to his desk, speaking in lower tones. As he does so, Rudman scribbles something on the palm of his hand with a ballpoint pen. *First connection with Underbridge in a while. Hm. This changes my plans for Utah…How the hell did Underbridge know about the cranky landowner?*

"I was going to speak to him – you know, maybe some face time would grease the gears a bit. I don't know how he did it, but the greedy bugger owns a good majority of the mineral rights."

"I know all about it" comments Underbridge… "He hasn't budged since he bought. This takes care of it, and the cover is genius."

"Consider it done. Thanks for your help."

"No, thank *you*."

Mr. Underbridge spins his chair back around, speaking normally again – "No problem. There's an engineering and construction company I own that's building a reactor in India, but I'm told uranium may be hard to source. It's a good thing there are people like you Rudman. When you get back give me a call and let me know how it goes. I've set things in motion. And – listen – I'm having a party at my yacht on the 17th – I'll have Mary send you an invitation. Black tie and all that BS. You in?"

"You kidding? I saw the article in *Forbes*... that's some fishing boat you got there. How many decks above water? Four? Two helipads? How many staff again – something like eight?"

"Fourteen."

Christ!

"Count me in. I'll bring my tackle box."

Underbridge likes Rudman's sense of humor.

With that, they hang up. Rudman lets few people refer to him simply by his last name, except perhaps for this multibillionaire who just so happens to be his boss.

In less than thirty minutes, a Learjet with only two passengers leaves LaGuardia airport in the dust. The flight attendant offers tea and coffee, but Mr. Rudman asks for a whisky. At a large table, he and Maria pore over a topographical map of central Utah, their fingers pointing to an area not too far from the number 15. Rudman lifts his head and peers over his reading glasses –

"Oh Maria – by the way – no face time with the owner. We have other plans now."

"Is he not still pissed?"

"Yes, and that's the point. You'll understand later. And let's get the table relocated to Grey Falls. Our first meeting there is coming up shortly, and our main guy says there are lots of good candidates for our special 'group'. It helps being in the buckle of the bible belt."

"Sure thing. I'll make a call."

They look back down at the map...

"What's close to here? Are there gas stations or diners for people to go for lunch?"

"Absolutely. It's a Ma and Pa operation, and they won't know what hit them. They'll retire rich I'm thinking. Being bible country, there's not much in the way of bars though."

"That's OK," chuckles Rudman – "I'll fly in everything we need."

Chapter 12

RIIIINNNGGGG! Five minutes to first class. Sean and Leslie are going to be late for Social Sciences if they don't move it. "See you tonight" they both chime as Marj drops them off in front of Grey Falls High. "Thanks for the ride!"

They usually take the family's second vehicle to school if Marj doesn't need it to run errands; today is one of those days.

Sean and Leslie go to their separate lockers to organize their books for the morning, then meet again at Social Sciences. After settling down in their seats, Mr. Clark speaks.

"Class, I hope you did your research for this morning. I asked you to read up on two medical ethics issues: stem cell research and pre-birth sex selection. They're related, but I'd like to see how much you really understand the issues, so – instead of giving you a written test, we're going to have a debate. Two teams, chosen by me. It's worth five percent of your final grade." He silences the protests.

Mr. Clark knows what he's doing. All these students are in the "gifted" stream, hopefully on their way to great things. He's a great educator, and is always looking for ways to improve their intellect and prepare them for post-secondary education.

"Ooh, I love debates," says Mark.

Mr. Clark divides the class in two; as they rearrange their seating, the rules are read… *no put-downs, or any dirty play, no raising your voice – just the facts.*

"Team A, you have to argue the pros. Team B, the cons. We'll mix it up a bit later. OK, who wants to start?"

After a bit of a pause, Kathy starts. Kathy is an eager learner, quite certain she'll be studying political science or anthropology next year in university.

"As I see it, we all live in a society that has benefitted sometimes from past indiscretions of our forefathers. Morality isn't black and white, and we have to sometimes sacrifice a few for the greater good. Using stem cells from human embryos is one of those cases. I just think there's a difference between the rights of one person, and the rights of us all put together. Look how well-off our society is."

Mr. Clark nods in approval. *She's been thinking about this.*

Mark from team B responds. "I kinda agree with you, but I have to argue the cons to get marks here..." Everyone chuckles. "You mention the rights of both sides. Are you saying unborn babies actually do have rights?"

"I didn't really mean to say that, and we know many people do perceive an unborn baby as a human being, who has the same right to live as anyone else. But my point is that these people need to see that the rights of all of us put together are bigger than the rights of just one individual, born or not."

"Very good dialogue people," interjects Mr. Clark. "What's your response Mark?"

"Well, I'm not sure if we're talking about the pros and cons, or whether it's morally right or wrong. If it's both, then morality itself is on the table for discussion, which opens all this up to a million topics."

"Astute point Mark, I should have clarified that at the beginning. I did say 'Pros and Cons', let's go with that. You're right, morality isn't up for debate. Anyone else?"

Both Sean and Leslie are on team A. Sean pipes up.

"Well, maybe experimenting on human embryos can go bad. In the future, I mean. Think of what could happen if scientists could do anything they wanted. With no value placed on each individual, or at least less value than the collective whole as Kathy says, then who is to decide if I live or die? I think individual rights are important

– think of all the fighting for minority rights that we've won in the past 75 or so years."

Mark comments, "Yeah, like black people, women, and the disabled. I worry about leaving the decision of where value lies with scientists. They're paid off by the pharmaceuticals anyways."

Kathy tries to speak, but is interrupted by Mr. Clark. "Give someone else a chance."

Team A all glance at each other. "I'll go," says shy Melanie.

"I don't think scientists should say when *you* die, Sean, but there's a difference between cruelty and advancing our society. Say, there are five thousand people on an ocean liner. It's starting to sink, and the only way to stop it is for one person to sacrifice his life by swimming underwater and fixing the hole. Doing so causes that person to drown, but they save the rest of the ship. What's better?"

Les chimes in finally. "Mr. Clark, I have a point that shouldn't be missed – but it's for the other team to argue."

"OK Leslie, go ahead."

She addresses Mel, "You say that one life is saved for many, but what if it's that they don't all drown, but they just have better health?"

"Whoa! Good one Ms. Hodges! No points deducted…" says Mr. Clark with a smile. He's impressed with the banter.

Melanie from team B picks up on the thought. "Yeah, it seems the only life and death issue here is for the human embryo. All the material I could find on this says it's for medical research for things like Alzheimer's, spinal cord repair, things like that. We're not saving lives from extinction; only making the quality of life better."

"Well done class. Let's move on to sex selection."

The class loves debating. There are no harsh words or lost tempers; Mr. Clark is very proud of their well thought-out comments and responses. They continue on to pre-birth sex selection, but Team A finds it hard to focus. It is unspoken that most of the class thinks the practice of terminating a fetus simply because of its gender is a bit over the top, so Mr. Clark drops the "Team A – Team B" rule and opens it up to free discussion.

"Look what's happening in China," an Asian girl brings up. "They abort over seven million a year, and they're mostly girls. Talk about discrimination against women! Whole sectors of society will start to go missing if this continues! What if they find a gene for gays? Are they next?"

Mr. Clark joins the discussion, guiding it to its end. "Well folks, think of all these moral dilemmas we're discussing. Scientists, with all their supposed objectivity, search to make things better for mankind and give us tools to improve life as a species. *Are* they bought off by the companies funding research? Not all – We as a society take their discoveries and do things with them they did not intend, such as the atom bomb. Do we blame science for the millions dead? I think we have to evolve as a society quicker than we have in the past. All these new technologies popping up everywhere are putting a strain on our value systems… goodness knows, we don't need more stress!"

Everyone appreciates his insightful overview, and thank him for "making" them research today's topics.

The students start to gather their books, when Sean fakes a radio voice with right hand cupped over his ear, and booms out loud – "Next week in Dr. Clark's Social Sciences class: Pork versus tofu. Are your bacon bits real? Over to you, Mark."

Leslie bonks him on the head with her scribbler. *You knob.*

Mr. Clark has one more thing to say. "Oh guys, listen – our DNA test reports are in, I just have to go pick them up at the post office. Whatever we're spending time on tomorrow will be put aside as we sort it all out and discuss how I want your reports formatted. Other school staff are interested as well, so I'm asking you to put extra effort into this. See you tomorrow."

Football practice is a little tougher due to the cold weather, but the only person complaining is Sean's math teacher and coach… he's not moving around quite so much as the students. *The season is just about over, thank goodness. I'm freezing out here.*

Mr. Robertson, like many other teachers doing double duty at Grey Falls High School, will cut slack for any student showing talent and promise. Sean's absence today sealed it though – no more Mr. Nice Guy. Either it's the band, or football. He hasn't seen Sean at practice in weeks

He blows his whistle. "OK guys, we're done here. Wrap it up," he orders. After making sure everyone is out of the showers and changing room, he locks up the gym and heads over to his other favorite hangout. He doesn't need to be at the airport till after nine when his wife lands, and he has already cleaned the house top to bottom.

He always wished he could teach science and sociology instead of math, but that position was already covered. His interest in these sciences always took second place to the scholarships available for someone built like him; a natural athlete with a neck as thick as his skull, he defied all stereotypes about football players. Mr. Clark, a single man who spends much time at the high school after the students leave, enjoys the coach's company.

The principal thinks he has a story or two – but listening to these two ex-marines' experiences could fill a book. Or two. They knew some of the same people from decades ago in the military… Grenada, then Desert Storm – they were both decorated and would brag while the other listened with respect. A tight friendship can quickly evolve between anyone sharing such a background, and these two gentlemen are the best of friends.

Mr. Robertson walks into Mr. Clark's home room.
"What's up Rick, you look busy."
"Hey Adam, yeah I am. How was practice?"
"Good, though it's too cold for me, just standing there."
"These DNA reports finally came in. Help me out here."

95

They unpack the large, flat pizza-box of envelopes. With each student's name on them, they sort them alphabetically by last name on a large desk.

"They're not sealed – let's look."

"That OK?"

"If you're half the voyeur I think you are, you'll be just as curious as I am."

Mr. Clark first went through his own report and whistled at the findings.

"I told my wife I had Norwegian in me! Look at this nose," Mr. Clark says as he turns his head 90 degrees to the left.

"Yeah, maybe. Although I'm not an expert in the field of rhino-geometrics." Adam says with sarcasm.

"F – G – H… Hodges. Oh say, I have an interesting idea. Families are supposed to share a lot of the same DNA, right? Sean and Les are cousins. It'd be interesting to compare their DNA."

Neither of them can resist. In each envelope is a transparent acetate with a bar-code looking graphic of their DNA, so they remove them and overlay one on the other. Mr. Clark holds them up to the ceiling light.

"Hm. I mustn't be doing this right. Let's get the overhead projector out."

Adam walks to the front of the class and pulls down the screen while Mr. Clark plugs in the projector. After a few minutes of comparing the two acetates, trying to align them as best they could, Adam pipes in…

"You know Rick, we're not experts here, but I do know genetics somewhat. This isn't kosher. My sister is a doctor at the hospital, let me give her a call." He yanks out his cell and is quickly chatting with his sibling.

"Sorry for bugging you at supper Helen, but I have a question."

He lays it out and ends with "Thanks sis, I owe you one."

Adam slaps his cell shut – "There's no doubt. At least 12 percent of these bars should match up. The results are from the same

96

lab, using the same equipment so there's no guesswork here…
She said something about register marks for lining them up just for
this purpose."

One last attempt fails.

"They could get a paternity test done, but we're essentially
doing that right now. Wow – interesting. We should maybe talk
to them."

"Hm… You know, this goes back a long way," remembers Mr.
Clark, arms folded, tapping his cheek – "I remember rumblings of
something way back when. I wonder if this is part of it. Too bad
both their parents didn't participate in this, then we'd have the big
picture." He sighs.

"Look, you've got them in the morning for math at second
period, right? Why don't we see what they say – they may already
know something we don't."

Sean and Les certainly didn't see it coming. Just as they are
packing their books up to leave, Mr. Robertson asks them to stay
behind to chat. In walks Mr. Clark, but that's normal – everyone
knows how close they are as friends.

Mr. Clark starts – "Hey, you guys doing OK?"

"Um – sure… " They look at each other.

Sean looks at Mr. Robertson – "Did I do something wrong?
I know I've missed some football practices…"

He smiles – "No no – nothing like that. But we've got something weird to share with you. As you know, your DNA reports are
back. Well, Mr. Clark and I decided to do a cursory review of them.
We couldn't resist – we looked at both of yours together."

Mr. Clark recounts the details of their discovery. He
carefully asks:

"Is it maybe *possible* one of you is adopted? I mean, that really
is the only explanation."

The look of surprise on both their faces leads the two teachers to conclude Sean and Leslie are as shocked as they are.

Sean responds: "I've never heard anything, I mean – I'm fairly certain my parents are my parents…"

Les: "I only knew my mom and dad till I was fourteen. I suppose it's *possible.*"

"Look you guys – it's time for next class. Let's meet at lunch in my classroom so we can go over it all together and talk about this more."

"OK – we'll see you then."

Les looks at Sean as they exit the classroom.

"What do you make of this? Do you know for sure you're Lydia's?"

"I don't know what to think to be honest." They part ways, each picking up the pace so they're not late for their next period.

Lunch bell rings, and they're in Mr. Clark's class in a flash. The two teachers have the overhead projector and screen already set up. Mr. Robertson shows them the acetates.

"OK – here we go. See look – these are registration marks to line up multiple sheets. There – perfect. Now – cousins are supposed to share – at the very minimum – 12.5 percent of the same genetic material." He moves the top acetate around a bit. "See – *nothing!* Not a single one of these bars line up."

Sean and Les stare at each other in shock. *Holy shit, who could it be?*

Mr. Robertson contributes:

"Just to illustrate the point, I looked it up last night on a medical website and found this." He replaces Sean's and Les's DNA sheets with one he photocopied from his research.

"This is what siblings look like. See the red circles? Someone has marked this up obviously, but it's so very clear how they share 50 percent of their DNA. So again, although 12 percent is a smaller number, we should see *something* line up." He places their acetates back on the overhead projector to emphasize his point.

"Leslie, your background is far more northern European than Sean's. If I were you, I'd be looking into that. Do you have any idea of your parents' heritage?"

"No, none. I mean, growing up people would say I didn't look much like either of them – you know, my round face and dirty blond hair. Hm. You know, my only tie to them is Lydia, Sean's real mother. Sean – let's see if she knows anything." Sean opens up his cell phone and punches in a quick text message, finds Lydia's number, and hits 'Send.'

Chapter 13

Driving home early from work thanks to a migraine, Lydia receives a text message on her cell. "Mom – Les & I need to talk to you."

Sigh – "I hope it's not what I think it is." She doesn't need this just before the holidays. Her performance on the job of late is causing her public support to wane a little; she's feeling the pangs of loneliness, but won't date anyone. No time. Her last partner couldn't handle her schedule and her self-centeredness; she kept too much to herself he said… She taps the steering wheel a few times in thought. After a pause, she decides to face her fear. She hits a button on her dashboard, and a mechanical voice responds, *Name or Number Please.*

"Sean Hodges."

Thank You. Her IDEA (In-Dash Electronic Assistant) dials Sean back.

"Hello."

"It's your mom. What's up?"

"Not on the phone mom, we need to meet."

"I'm leaving tonight for the lodge. I'll be gone till after New Year's."

"Then we're coming over right now." Click.

"Sean? SEAN?" The line is dead.

Once in her condo, she drops the mail on the floor, kicks off her shoes and mixes a strong Martini. Three gulps and it's gone. Her hands shake mildy as she pours another strong one and drops ice on the floor.

"Shit!"

She's uncomfortable with the thought of what's coming. She digs through her writing desk for some legal-looking papers and places them in an envelope, leaving it on top of a pile of notebooks and bills. *Perhaps they could have found out? Sigh.* If so, it may mean a change in the Hodges' household, depending on how they take it. Her thoughts wander back a couple years...

"You sure you want to do this?" Malcolm asks. "I mean, I'll go along with it if I know that you won't change your mind in two or five years, or whenever. That would be unfair to Les especially."

"You don't need to worry about that; I've got the message that I'm not mother material, and they both would be better off in a stable home with a stay-at-home mom. Besides, we can all visit whenever we want, right? I can watch Les grow up as her aunt. It's not easy letting go of Sean though. I'll be spending a lot of time with him – I know you won't mind." She pauses...

"Oh Malcolm, where did we go wrong?"

The doorbell shocks Lydia to the present. She holds the intercom button... "Come on up, guys."

After a few moments, a knock at the door... she lets them in. They hug and exchange pleasantries. Nervous to bring anything up, Lydia asks about the band, football, school in general.

"That's it mom, we need to talk about something that happened at school. Remember that DNA test our class had done? I have a real tough question to ask you about the results."

Lydia knows what's coming.

"Mom, the results show I'm not related to Les. You get a transparency with all these bars of your DNA, and Les and I should have at least 12 percent of them line up... but they don't. We're cousins, right? What's going on?"

Les has the transparencies with her, so she holds them up to a window.

Pointing her finger, she shows Lydia: "See – they're like a barcode, and everyone's is different. But relatives have some that line up because they share some of the same DNA. Siblings share at least 50 percent – cousins 12.5 percent. But look here – nothing. What's up with that?"

"I told you not to believe all the results; DNA isn't an exact science!"

"Yes it *is!* Please don't insult our intelligence," replies Leslie.

Sean remembers… "I *knew* there was something funny when I mentioned it in the car a while ago."

Lydia sighs and says – "OK guys, no more cat and mouse. Promise. Come sit down. I need to tell you what really happened."

In a conversation that she never really wanted Les to hear so soon, Lydia explains. "A couple of years ago, I was contacted by a Florida lawyer. Les, your parents had a will, but it was not up to date – so, you weren't named as an heir. Your grandmother thought that to be terrible, and because she felt bad about not keeping you, she tried to get you an inheritance. When she found your birth certificate, she realized you were in fact adopted. Your 'parents' couldn't have children, so they visited a country in the Eastern Bloc and brought home a newborn. You."

"So, that's why you're not related. My mom had her lawyer sent me the papers." She walks over to her antique writing desk and comes back with a manila envelope.

"Here you are, Les. This is who you really are."

Les is dumfounded. *Adopted? Eastern Bloc? What the hell…*

"Why did you keep this from me? I don't get the secrecy…"

"Well Les, I didn't want to make you any more a stranger than you already where. As long as Malcolm thought you were blood, I thought why rock the boat? And I thought it was bad enough for *you*… I just never thought it would be productive to make you feel any more estranged. God knows you've had it bad enough. We all love you deeply; why make anything worse?"

Lydia puts a positive spin on it.

"Look, the papers have your real parents' names, address, everything. If you felt like it, you could maybe try to contact them. One of them speaks English I think."

A long silence. Lydia stands up and walks around the living room.

"Can you forgive me?" she asks as she directs Les to open the envelope.

"Look at this… it's a trust fund held in your name." She lets it sink in… "My mother, your adoptive grandmother, wanted you to have it when you turn of age. That's real soon." Lydia smirks. Les responds, then eyes the paperwork.

"Wow – really? 50 grand? Shit man!" She sighs deeply, drops her arms, looking almost relieved. "Look Lydia, my mind feels like mush right now, but thanks for what you did. I get why you kept it to yourself. But – were you planning on telling me anytime soon?"

"Just before your 18th birthday."

"Oh I see. Wow, what a heavy…"

"So Les, who else knows you and Sean aren't cousins?"

"Mr. Clark and Mr. Robertson. We made them *promise* to keep this silent till we figured all this out. They were really good about it – they said our secret is safe."

Sean's face takes on a look of annoyance.

"Mom – *I'm* kinda upset with you. Why did we have to find out this way? You could have told us long before now; hell, we're old enough."

"That you are. It's been at the back of my mind for a long time wondering if I should have broken the news before now, but I've been too damned busy to gather the courage. I'm sorry it had to come out this way – really I am."

Les ponders her future and says in a low tone, "Hmmm – I want to meet my real parents I think…"

Sean sighs deeply, and walks over to his mom's bar. "I'm having a drink. Anyone else?" Lydia allows Sean and Leslie to drink when around her, and will hardly object to Sean's suggestion.

"You know how I like my Martinis."

"Guinness please, and I'm stepping out for a quick smoke. This is heavy."

Lydia pipes in – "You haven't quit yet?"

"Workin' on it – first one this week."

Sean gets drinks ready, and hands his mother a Martini with two olives. They chat about the consequences of this new information for a few minutes when Les comes back in from the balcony. They talk more about her parentage, and of course the money. "A great college fund perhaps," says Les. "A kick-ass sound system!" pipes in Sean.

Leslie raises her glass – "Here's to 50 grand!"

———————

Back home, Les and Sean stop in the garage to talk before entering the house.

Sean sighs and leans back against the van, folding his arms – "So, wow – you're not my cousin. Weird, eh?"

Pregnant silence.

"Could be a lot worse," says Sean. "It's all out in the open now, at least for us."

Les responds "Yeah, but we're *not related*. Makes me feel strange. Doesn't it to you?"

The ringing phone pierces their conversation. Sean sighs deeply and picks up the cordless off the wall.

"Mark, how are ya. No, just got in. Practice? Tonight? Listen dude, Les and I have to take a break tonight. Leave your bass at home and take that girlfriend of yours out for a hamburger. She's always complaining you ignore her…"

He hangs up.

Leslie apologizes – "Oops, I forgot about tonight – I was supposed to tell you they were coming over for practice."

"No sweat cuz, I've had enough for one day. Oh – I can't call you that any more," Sean says, trying to add some levity.

"You better – no one knows but us, your mom, and two of our teachers. I hope we can trust them."

"Yeah, sorry. Some charade, eh? But I think it should become common knowledge at some point. What would be the harm in that?"

"Hm. Not sure, but now that your mom's conscience is clear, now it's *our* burden. She owes us big time. I'm not hungry for supper. Let's talk about this later – tell mom I'm in my room."

Although their family history is somewhat abnormal, Les and Sean both refer to Marj and Malcolm as mom and dad most of the time. Marj especially likes it when they're all together around the dinner table.

They both enter the house and are greeted by the aroma of Christmas fruitcake baking away in the oven. Sean's stomach growls.

Dinner time at the Hodges' is often cut short by someone having to leave for hockey practice, band practice, theater… This evening, no one has to go anywhere, so Marj is anticipating a nice quiet sit-down meal with her entire family. The hot Irish stew, dumplings, and apple crisp are piping hot as they join hands to say grace. Malcolm raises his voice slightly, looking towards the hallway to Leslie's room…

"Les sweetheart, we're waiting for you!"

"Oh sorry, Dad," says Sean – "Les isn't feeling well; she asked me to tell you she wasn't hungry."

"Oh…" Marj says sadly – "That's too bad. I hope she isn't coming down with anything. I'll put a plate of food aside for her."

Jake, the household vacuum cleaner, says…

"I'll eat her helping! I love beef stew!"

"You're a piggy winkle!" Marj says as she pinches his belly.

He does indeed like to eat, and it's starting to show around his midriff.

The family recites grace and digs in. The conversation is unusually toned down.

"What's new at school Sean? Did you get those DNA results?"

Sean replies, clearing his throat.

"Yes, and they were really interesting. We're not done our reports yet, and we'll be doing a big reveal at school assembly in a week or so. They're making a big thing of it, so they asked we keep the results under wraps. But parents are invited. Each of us will be giving a quick, high level overview of our ancestry, then publishing the details on our school web site, graphics and all."

"I can't wait to see it!" exclaims Malcolm.

Maybe you won't want to.

The school assembly starts with the national anthem, guided by the senior band in the orchestra pit. There are announcements about volleyball, football, and the upcoming band exchange with a high school in Mexico, asking for families to billet students. Mr. T approaches the podium and thanks Ms. Cooper.

"Students, teachers, parents – I'm excited to announce the completion of grade 12-A's DNA research project. Just so you understand, anyone can do this individually, and we plan on posting the details on the school's website. Mr. Clark's Social Sciences class took it upon themselves to participate in this study as a group. Mr. Clark, over to you."

Mr. Clark approaches the podium, notes in hand.

"Good morning everyone. As our principal noted, our class embarked on a DNA study. *The National Geographic Society* has something they call the Genographic Project. By sending them a sample of live skin tissue, they can track your ancestors' migration patterns around the world based on DNA evidence. The findings have been most interesting, and each student is now going to present a quick overview of their findings."

Mr. Clark looks over his reading glasses at the audience and asks –

"Ms. Amy Galleta, please introduce your findings."

Amy steps forward, takes the remote from Mr. Clark, and talks about her Italian heritage and their long distant roots in Africa. A map of the world projected onto the white screen behind her cleverly morphs from 60,000 years to 10,000 years B.C. in incremental steps, depicting her tribal ancestor's movements across the globe.

Sean takes his turn, then Les is next. She describes the same details as the others, except for the very different migration patterns around 10,000 BC, located much further north-east on the Eurasian continent. Marj is in the audience sitting with a church friend. She notices how different hers is compared to Sean's – *Huh – that must be where Lydia's brother in-law is from.*

Mr. Clark keeps each student's presentation within its time limit, and begins to draw the assembly to a close after the entire class has gone over their results. The students, teachers, and parents respond with a few questions during the Q&A period, and are finally dismissed by Mr. Templeton.

"Thank you everyone for your interest in this project; I'm sure there are many more questions, so please visit the school's website and click on the FAQ section of our DNA project results. Further inquiries can be directed to Mr. Clark.

"Students may resume their class schedules, and we appreciate all the parents showing your interest today – thanks for being here. Good morning to you."

"Man, we need a break from all this," whispers Leslie to Sean. He nods in agreement.

Chapter 14

Spring sees many tourists swarming to Grey Falls in their vans and motor homes, gobbling up the local history and culture. The hotels are booked solid, as are the popular walking tours coordinated by the historical society. The water park with its wave pool is ever popular with children from 8 to 80. This season is also a good time of year for the three real estate offices in Grey Falls; they do their best to keep the photos of properties for sale in their storefront windows up-to-date, but it's an uphill battle. Visiting tourists can be seen poring over them first thing in the morning. They do notice property values are much higher than last year.

"It's so busy downtown," complains Leslie to Marj. "We'll never find a dress in one day."

"Maybe not," responds Marj, "But keep your hopes up – we're getting out there before most of your classmates."

This is Marj's way of doing things. Christmas gifts are bought in August. Birthday presents two or three months beforehand – and today hopefully – Leslie's prom dress. She thinks back to the wonderful time she and her mother chose *her* gown. Her mind wanders back decades…

"Are you sure this is appropriate?" asks Marj. Her mother answers…

"Of course sweetheart, you don't think they'd sell it in this store if it wasn't, now do you?"

It was a bit racy for the time, but Marj pulled it off with class.

Marj starts the van; Leslie opens the passenger door and reaches in to click the remote garage door opener.

"Just a sec mom, I forgot my cell phone." Les rushes back into the house.

Marj can't help but reminisce about her graduation so many years ago. Her admiration and interest for that young upstart preacher was never reciprocated until years later, in less than ideal circumstances. *Nevertheless – we're here now. I got my man.*

Driving towards the four corners, Marj asks Leslie…

"So, are you taking Mark up on his offer?"

Leslie is somewhat fond of their bass player, but not in a romantic way. She has high standards, and isn't too impressed by the slim pickings in her high school. She needs a date for the prom, so …

"Yeah, Mark's going to pick me up in his dad's limo if he can fix it in time. Some guy couldn't pay his repair bill, so his dad put a lien on this huge Cadillac. The guy went bankrupt, so it was granted to him in an estate settlement. Could be cool!"

The downtown core, though crowded, ends up to be a breeze to get through. And the three dress shops they visit are mostly empty at this time of day. After a few fittings, Leslie settles on a beautiful white designer gown Marj thought might suit her.

"I usually wear real dark stuff," Les says to the young salesgirl, "but I want to blow their minds on prom night. I want to highlight my hair too."

Marj eyes the plunging neckline and winks at her daughter…

"Ooh – sexy! I think our next stop is Shirley's Underthings. She's got push-up bras that'll knock any guy's socks off."

"Mom!! What's with you?" Everyone laughs. The staff are accustomed to such antics. After eyeing the price tag, Leslie looks at Marj with a big question mark across her face…

"Huh?"

"You weren't supposed to see that," responds Marj. "Malcolm gets a lot of bonuses, and hands me extra cash for things like this. Congratulations for graduating sweetheart."

They both well up with tears. "Thanks mom – you're great."
The salesgirl hands them each a tissue and comments to Marj –

"You're great. Most of the girls who come here with their moms are so embarrassed to be seen with them."

Les replies – "Well, I guess some of that depends on how easy or how hard your life is, and how you react to it. It's all about choices, right?"

Senior prom night was as special as everyone planned it to be, with the limos, evening gowns, tuxedos, and dance. The parents chipped in and ordered a catered banquet – a lovely sit-down meal, the waiters themselves dressed to the nines.

Sean and his date Amy arrive, each sipping on a flute of fake champagne just outside the gym. He eyes a tastefully decorated beige limo decked out with streamers and red flowers arriving just behind them, noting the artistic touch. *I've seen this car before.* He stares to see who steps out.

As if in a Hollywood movie, cameras flash as the rear door is opened by the driver, aligned perfectly over the red carpet. First he sees a shoe – then an ankle – then a leg… Out steps Leslie, adorned in the most incredible gown, makeup, and coifed hairdo he has ever seen. Some don't even recognize her. Guys gawk. Girls stop for a second to register… *who is this?* She's out of her element, normally dressed in black jeans, a hoodie, and Doc Martins.

"Holy shit, is that *you*???" People catch on it's Leslie by his reaction. There's whistles and clapping. Mark then climbs out and offers his arm. Leslie smirks as she saunters past Sean, purse in hand, doing her best catwalk imitation.

Whoa – lucky Mark! Sean thinks to himself.

Following the meal, Mr. Templeton and the senior teachers have their turn at the podium, poking fun at the students, and recounting some of the ups and downs of the last few years. Of course, they don't forget to offer the kindest advice one could imagine.

Finally, the principal of Grey Falls High School announces in the loudest voice he can muster…

"Ladies and gentlemen, let the music begin!!!"

The curtains fly open – spotlights hit the stage, and the twenty piece orchestra breaks into a modern hip-hop interpretation of Glenn Miller's "In the Mood." The students bolt to the dance floor, including Leslie with Mark, and Sean with Amy. Malcolm and Marj watch them on the dance floor.

"Boy, they sure are a tight bunch," Malcolm says to Marj, leaning into her ear.

"I sure wish them the best," Marj responds. Malcolm stands and takes his wife's hand.

"May I have the honor?" Marj blushes at Malcolm's unusual gesture.

There's a mix of students, teachers, and parents on the dance floor. The swirling lights and live music make for a fun experience, and after the next tune starts, people start swapping partners. Sean takes Marj's hand, Malcolm grabs Amy by the waist, and Leslie two-steps with a classmate. At one point, Sean cuts in to dance with Les…

"So kiddo, that's one helluva get-up. Seems you set out to blow everyone's mind."

"Uh huh…"

"It worked."

Leslie pulls him in a little tighter as the tempo slows down to the song's ending.

"Thank you, kind sir, and you clean up pretty good too – that cummerbund adds a touch of class. Rental?"

"What else! Not like I'll be wearing *this* too many times in my life."

"What about our first Emmy?"

"Now I have to say – I never did think about *that*." They both smile. Sean notices how easy it is to be close to Leslie just when Mark cuts in…

"I do believe you have stolen my date. Out of the way you thief!"

Sean kids with them – "She's got bad breath anyways. You can have her."

Leslie slaps his arm.

The four of them are inseparable, and through the evening they talk about the future of Indigo Insight.

Huddled at someone's empty table in the corner of the gym, Sean is the first to chime in…

"You never know what's on the horizon, but most of us have plans for the next couple of years. Change is good; I think we all could use a break from Grey Falls. I know Capital will eventually want to talk to us, so let's keep that option open too. Hey, everyone tells us we're young, so let's not rush anything. Besides, we're here for a good time, *and* – someone told me there's a stash of wine hidden in the cafeteria!"

"I'm on a mission!" exclaims Amy, raising her glass. "Sirs and wenches, I'll be back with a report of where and how we pillage said cache of fine drink!"

Off Amy goes with the grit of a conquistador, Mark in tow.

Les pokes Sean in the arm…

"Hey you – you ready to go outside and share a joint with your *cousin?"* she asks, mocking the word *cousin*.

———————————

The graduation ceremonies are a week later. It is a momentous event for the Hodges family: Leslie won a partial scholarship to an art college in Minnesota, something Sean encouraged her to pursue. *Thanks for the push,* Les says to him as they cross paths in the school gym, waiting to walk onto the auditorium stage in their blue robes.

Sean's future is interesting as well – he had many offers from various educational institutions, but his interest was piqued by a scholarship that included co-op experience in England sponsored by *IncoPharm,* a drug company looking for the brightest and best. They have all the scientists they need – their next phase of expansion is to groom exceptionally smart and bright salespeople to expand their market penetration. Sean fit the bill to a tee.

Mark landed a promotion at the grocery store on Main Street as head of produce.

"Stick with it," he was told, "and you'll soon be managing customer relations and maybe even payroll."

Amy's marks weren't quite high enough for her college of choice, so she opted for a position with the municipal government's Parks and Recreation department. It is outdoor work, something she loves. She'll take night classes to boost her SATs before re-applying to get a law degree.

The ceremony lasts over two hours, with the valedictorian's address, a speech from Mr. Templeton, and awards – lots of awards. Amy gets one for proficiency in music. Les for top marks in history. Sean for highest average in his class. He does a thumbs-up to the crowded auditorium right after receiving his diploma. *Done. Finally!*

Part Two
Chapter 15

Eighteen months later

Jake's love interest just rang the doorbell, but if you asked Emily Swarovski, she'd know nothing of it. Today's field trip to the airport is coordinated by some homeschooling parents who want their kids to socialize with "normal" children, despite their objections to most things worldly.

"Jake, open the door. Be polite."

Emily, dressed in hand-me-downs, has learned to be embarrassed by her parents, and now by her clothes. Friends from the same church, she shares her opinion of the world with Jake, who listens attentively. He doesn't really care about the latest styles...

"You know stuff on television is not real!" she whispers to him during Sunday school.

"Says who?"

"My mom and dad! And guess what else – doctors are bad. If we had more faith, we wouldn't get sick."

Grey Falls Baptist Church draws a diverse crowd of people, ranging from the casual attendee looking for a preacher to marry them, to hard core evangelical fundamentalists who take the bible quite literally. Emily's parents fit into the latter category, with the righteous conviction that the world is evil, waiting to test their faith at every turn. Homeschooling suits their beliefs and lifestyle.

It all actually fascinates Jake, though he isn't sure Emily believes everything she is told. When they play hooky together during Sunday school, Emily will "borrow" cookies and pop from the church cafeteria, and they'll hide under a stairwell. She spins yarns about how she'll build churches in Africa and China when she grows up, then live as an old granny up in heaven.

Jake's affection for her is likely what is behind him voluntarily refraining from dessert of late. *Puppy love,* thinks Marj. *My, how he is growing up fast for a nine-year-old.*

"So, off we go," says Marj as the small school bus makes its way to the airport. She arranges the seating so that Jake and Emily are together, intentionally playing cupid. *They're so cute together.* It's a bumpy ride to the airport, and once there she fishes out a little digital camera from her purse to take some shots of their experience, and perhaps sneak one or two of Jake and Emily together.

In a hangar at the airport, a small crowd gathers around Mr. Longworth, the president of the Grey Falls Homeschooling Association. An austere middle-aged man, his children are off to Princeton and Harvard – quite an accolade for this teacher who has no teacher's degree.

"Parents, children, Mrs. Longworth was able to arrange today's outing. We're all excited about flying in a company jet. Thank you, Mrs. Longworth" he says slightly bowing to his wife. Everyone applauds.

"The jet is coming in from New York to pick up some business people, but they have agreed to delay their trip by an hour to allow us this time. So, for those of you who are homeschooled, please have your questions ready. I believe that is the plane now…"

Everyone watches the sleek aircraft touch down, then taxi over to the hangar. The closer the jet gets, the more excited the children become. Marj notices the "MMC" logo on the tail. After a moment, the door drops open, and the first to disembark is the flight attendant. The parents look at each other…

Oh my – that's one tight miniskirt. Marj smirks as she watches the cloistered 12 year old boys gawk like they've never seen that much skin before. They likely haven't…

The pilot and co-pilot are next out. He eyes the crowd, whispers something to the attendant who disappears back into the jet, then approaches Mr. Longworth. They shake hands and have a couple of words.

"Children, parents, my name is Captain McLaren, this is my co-pilot Mr. Beal, and our flight attendant Trudy is gathering some printed information about the jet for us. While we wait for her, I'll tell you a little about the plane you will be flying in today."

He rhymes off measurements and statistics about the plane's wingspan, flying altitude, range, cruising speed, and any other numbers he can remember. The co-pilot takes over and explains his role in keeping the aircraft on course and safe. The flight attendant is now passing out the information brochures about the plane – she doesn't miss the adolescent boys taken by her appearance, so she lingers just a bit as they begin to ask her questions about her job. Someone shushes them. She makes her way to the front of the crowd.

"Any questions?" asks the pilot.

"When did you learn to fly?"

"Does your airplane use a special kind of gas?"

"How long does it take to fly around the world?"

"How long does the landing strip have to be?"

Field trips like this are common for the homeschooling community of Grey Falls. Companies, restaurants, businesses, and the various manufacturing industries have a lot of time for these families that take their children's education so seriously. The children are inquisitive, ask many intelligent questions, and impress most people with their maturity.

I don't blame them for taking their kids out of school, Marj thinks. Drugs are starting to make their way into the Grey Falls education system, so her and other volunteers attend drug awareness seminars geared to educate and equip community-minded parents.

Marj's cell phone vibrates in her purse. She doesn't notice it till the last ring. "Rats, I guess I'll see if they leave a voicemail."

Today, the children get to sit in the captain's chair, one at a time. Then the airline attendant hands out chewing gum to everyone in preparation for their twenty-minute flight over Grey Falls. Fuel and time are kindly donated by the Midwest Mining Corporation.

What a treat for these kids thinks Marj, who wishes her parents had done the same for her. *Maybe these home-schoolers have it right.*

Mr. McLaren's voice comes over the intercom...

"This is your captain speaking. Please ensure your seatbelts are fastened, and your trays are in their upright and locked position. We've just been cleared for takeoff, so we should be in the air momentarily."

The passengers are pulled back into their seats as Captain McLaren pushes forward the airship's throttles. Within thirty seconds they are airborne. He keeps it low at 1,800 feet so he can point out various landmarks, buildings, and bodies of water the children know about, but have never seen from the air.

Jake says to Emily, who is in the seat ahead of him – "Look, there's where dad works!" He recognizes the large square industrial building with the baseball diamond and basketball hoops in the back parking lot. "Where does *your* dad work?"

"At the church – over there I think." The two of them scour the horizon for the familiar steeple. "There it is!"

Marj is snapping pictures out the window when one of the children's parents leans over to Marj and asks...

"How are Sean and Les doing in school? Sean is in London, right?"

"Yes, and Leslie is in Minnesota studying music. They're both doing well; I just heard from them both Sunday after lunch. We usually have a conference call with them both every month to catch up on news and make sure they're doing OK. But I still miss them dearly, it seems so long since their last visit." Their conversation is interrupted by the captain describing the landscape below.

"Passengers, if you look out the left side, you can see the water park. On your right is city hall. And of course, Grey Falls River just below."

Marj continues. "So, Malcolm and I have been talking about our future. You know, it looks like the kids may be out of the house for good once their schooling is finished. We signed up on a web site for information about hosting international students. Doesn't that sound interesting?"

"Oh my – yes. Think of the things you'll learn from them! Sounds like fun to me."

They chat about retirement, church, and their children. The pilot's tour is thorough, but their twenty minute tour of the sky ends far too quickly.

I should get out more thinks Marj. *This is far too much fun.*

The captain receives applause after a very soft landing, and the flight attendant hands out 5-dollar gift certificates for a restaurant chain to each person as they disembark, winking to the young boys.

The "business people" are waiting in the hangar as the jet is refueled for its trip back to New York. One says to the other –

"There better not be any bubble gum stuck to my seat. I'll send Rudman the bill."

———————————

Marj's voicemail is hard to make out – obviously an overseas call from either Sean, or her brother in Africa, a relief worker she sends money to every month. She has to wait to the end of the message before being offered the choice to dial back. It *is* Sean, but his cell goes directly to voicemail, so she phones his dormitory...

After two rings, someone answers in a strong British accent.

" 'Ello? Who's this?"

"I'm looking for Sean Hodges. He lives on that floor – can you find him for me? He left me a voice mail a little while ago."

"Oh *Sean!* Lucky mum you are, with such a bright lad for a son! Excuse me while I go fetch him."

Marj hears him place the receiver down, and pace down the hall. Minutes pass.

"Mom! How are you?"

Marj always appreciates his warmth towards her, realizing he has divided loyalties in this area.

"I'm good Sean! I'm returning your call – you don't usually phone me on my cell on Saturdays. What's up?"

"Well, I've got a bit of news. How's everyone back home?"

"Great Sean, I just took your step-brother to the airport for a quick flight with the home schoolers. It was lovely! What news do you have for us?"

"Well, Mark phoned me a few hours ago and told me some guy named Devon from Capitol Records wants us to meet up with him in Los Angeles. He heard us play a couple times last year, and our CD finally made its way to him. He thinks we have a shot at getting a record deal. No guarantees, but he claims he knows a good thing when he sees it. Isn't that COOL?"

Marj's heart sinks. Sean and Leslie are well into their post-secondary education. Les with another four months to go; Sean, another two years. *This is a distraction.*

"Mom, you know I kept the band's bank account going – we've got a few grand still there. Why don't we all gather in Grey Falls for Thanksgiving compliments of Indigo Insight?"

The thought of having her family back together over a holiday feast was enticing.

"Well Sean, you know I usually trust your judgment, though I'm not sure you're thinking long-term here. You sure about this?"

"I talked to my school today, and they say I can pick up my studies any time within three years."

When Sean has a bit between his teeth, no one dare stand in his way. He's proven himself to be successful at anything and everything he's put his hand to. His passion for music has been resurrected – he didn't realize how much he missed playing.

"Besides mom, it's not a done deal. We've yet to see if Amy and Mark can realistically take time off from their jobs."

Leslie's third-grade harmony class is tough. A more technical side of music theory, this class challenges her the most, so she digs in and studies hard for tomorrow's test. Exams are coming up soon, and with numerous assignments to finish all at once, she'll get the easy ones out of the way first, then tackle the toughies. She goes over her to-do list:

"Compose an alternate bass line for this fugue in C Sharp."

"Write a 400 word report about a Renaissance composer NOT influenced by his peers."

"Critique this poem by the author's own standards. Why did he compromise so easily after achieving such recognition?"

Leslie can taste the end. *Only four months to go.*

Her closest friend and confidant, Silk-Anne, can't stop chattering about her movie-producer brother who just landed a job in Hollywood north, A.K.A. Vancouver.

"He didn't even finish film school!" she brags. Apparently neither did Spielberg or Lucas. "He pitched the script I wrote, and they liked it. He's gonna do an Indie film with a couple big-name cameos. He won't tell me who, but isn't that too cool?"

Leslie cocks her head…

"Really? Wow, he must be connected. Who does he know up there in Vancouver?"

Silk-Anne opens her mouth when there's a rap at the open door.

"Call for you down the hall Les."

"Hang on to that thought," Les says to her friend "I'll be right back" as she disappears through the doorway.

Silk-Anne is a consummate latter-day hippy. Her long straight auburn hair is adorned with feathers and beads; she has narrow leather straps on both wrists; one finger sports the obligatory mood ring, and crystals of various colors and shapes hang from her neck. She'd have sandals on if it wasn't so cold in the dorm. She is an unlikely friend for someone like Leslie at first blush, but they hit it off very quickly, soon referring to each other as soul mates.

With her friend down the hall on the phone, she sits on the edge of Leslie's bed and glances around the dorm room. Books are piled up on her study desk, open notebooks strewn everywhere, and an Indigo Insight poster on the far wall with the venue and date scrawled in the white box at the bottom. *That's over a year ago. She must miss it.* Her eyes then fall on her bed next to her, where there's a dozen or so printed email messages. She can't help but notice the "From" and "To" in the header – *Her and Sean are sure tight* she thinks to herself. Then she eyes a large envelope with international phone numbers scrawled all over it, and a foreign-looking name in the upper right corner: *Laszlofi.*

Leslie runs back to her dorm room squealing with excitement.

"Guess what – guess what – I'm flying back home for Thanks-giving!!! Isn't that cool? I haven't been home in a dog's age, and Sean is going to be there from London!"

"Wow! All the way from London! You must be excited!"

Her friend knows about Leslie's family, the death of her parents, her move to Grey Falls, the DNA results. They both have dark things they have shared over the past year; they've been a strength to each other at different times when all they wanted to do was give up. Silk-Anne was especially comforting and understanding of Leslie's adjustment to the loss of her parents.

"Leslie, I'm so happy for you! I'm going to miss you over the holidays though!"

"Well, seems to me I remember a certain somebody in our Theory and Composition class who has an eye on you. Maybe *he'll* be around to keep you company."

Silk-Anne blushes. She actually *knows* he'll be around. She drops the subject.

"So listen, are you still into going to Sherman's piano recital tonight? There's a wicked after-party in his room and everyone's going to be there, if you can imagine a recital after-party being *wicked!*"

They both chuckle.

"You've been hitting the books real hard – it's time you took a break."

Les agrees. "Ya, why not. I've been studying every night for days on end – this good news has me all excited, I can't concentrate anyways!"

"So – Les – nosy me… you have relatives overseas? Who do you know there? I've a cousin living in Russia…" Her friend points to the envelope.

Les shows slight embarrassment as she flips over the pile of printed emails. "That's Romanian – I've tracked someone down. Hm – I guess I never really told you the whole story."

"Do tell! Is it juicy?"

"Not really. See, I usually keep it quiet, but I was adopted as a baby in Romania. I don't know why yet, but my parents contacted an international agency that matches up couples in the U.S. and Canada with families in what used to be called the Eastern Bloc. Apparently I'm from Bucharest."

"That's a bit of a heavy. On top of loosing your parents – I mean *adoptive* parents here in the States."

"Ya, when I was barely 14. It was horrible. They leave for an evening out, and I never see them again. The funeral was closed-casket. Screwed me up. I'm still not over it I guess…" Silk-Anne takes her hand.

"Oh, I'm OK. Don't worry about me. Anyways – I get shuttled from my grandmother's to my aunt's in Grey Falls, then a year later *they* split up. Me and Sean end up with the father and his new wife, and a seven year-old boy of hers. Quite the blended family, but it's actually turned out OK."

"Do you feel stranded? I would. Here you are, with this family you're not even related to. That must do something to your head."

"I'm always processing it I suppose, but they're a great family. Supportive, fun. Sean and I get along really well.

"So anyways, it turns out my aunt in Grey Falls was mailed my adoption papers and a trust fund for me. Sort of a double-edged sword. She was going to fill me in when I turned 18, but we found out beforehand as you know. Fifty grand later, I'm in this school, and I've been trying to track down my real parents. They've moved around, but I had a breakthrough just last night – I found a sister who knows a bit of English. I don't think she realizes I'm *her* sister, but she gave me her parents' – hopefully *my* parents' – phone number. I've been trying but there's no answer – I'm so excited, but scared too. I'll be trying again tomorrow morning early."

"Oh Les, what a story! I'm so glad you told me – makes me feel closer to you." They hug. "Let me know how it goes tomorrow, OK?"

"Sure thing Silky. Hey, let's go to the cafeteria. I'm starved."

They have fun that night after the recital, sharing a few bottles of wine, passing a guitar around the room from person to person. Leslie takes the guitar and tries to form a G chord, but forgets where her pinky goes.

"Here, let me show you," says Sherman.

"Hey, amazing playing tonight, Sherm. I wish I was that good on the keys."

"Thanks. Look, here's a G-chord. Here's a C, and a D. With those three, you can pretty well follow along most songs out there."

"Ya, I forgot about those!" Her chest then puffs with pride – "You should hear my *cousin* play, he's really good. He fingerpicks too."

She quietly strums an intro to one of their songs, and hums the vocals. She feels her heart long for Sean's company. *Damn, I miss the fun* she thinks. *Now I'm here 'cause of him, doing really well. I can't wait till Thanksgiving.*

"Sing louder," some tipsy classmate yells at Leslie from across the room. It brings her back to the present.

"No way – I play drums, that's it!" she retorts, handing Sherman's guitar to the person next to her.

Chapter 16

Heathrow Airport is a mass of people anytime of the year, day or night. A bottleneck of people, cars, busses, and airplanes, it is the hub of western European air travel. Just getting there and finding a parking spot can be an ordeal, so Sean and his flying partner decide to take a cab from campus. *Worth the cost,* they both agree.

A little four-year-old girl is trying to keep up with her parents as they weave single-file through packed crowds, finding a way to the ticket counter. This end of the airport is notorious for congestion, and this day is no exception.

The little girl is the apple of her mother's eye, all dressed up like a princess. Her little knapsack is color coordinated with a tiny wheeled suitcase, which she pulls behind her, carrying some snacks for the flight to New York, her favorite books, and a blankie. Simon, her teddy bear, is bearing the brunt of this trek through the rushing crowds. She drops him for the third time, but can't find him…

"Come along dear," says her mother.

"MOMMY!" she cries. "I dropped Simon, but I don't see him!" she exclaims with panic in her voice.

Not knowing what it was, someone in the crowd mistakenly kicked Simon out of the way, out of the little girl's eyesight.

I told her to pack him in her suitcase.

Carol is joining Sean on the same flight to New York, where she is staying the weekend upstate at her parents' cottage.

"What city is it you live in again?" asks Carol.

"Grey Falls."

"Oh right, your flight is a milk run out to Utah. That's too bad."

"Well, at least I have company to New York. I don't like flying over the ocean; makes me feel totally at the mercy of technology."

"Listen to you, techno geek – you love that stuff."

"Technology yes, flying no."

Their cab driver opens the trunk and unloads their suitcases.

"Well, here we go. Just *look* at this crowd!" exclaims Sean.

Inside the building Sean steps to the side to open his knapsack and retrieve his pre-printed boarding pass. He sees a child's stuffed animal on the floor and picks it up.

Showing it to Carol – "Some little kid's parents are going to regret not packing this in a suitcase. I remember losing my teddy bear at the fair when I was really small. I cried for hours."

"Hey, do you think that's them?" Carol points to the little girl about fifty feet away, her parents scanning the floor. "I guess you're her hero today."

They approach the family, waving the stuffed animal in the air.

"This yours?" Sean asks the little girl.

She yelps with joy – "SIMON – I told you to not run away like that! You could get stepped on!"

Her mother dusts it off, and thanks Sean for being so kind.

"Not everyone is so helpful like that, thank you so much."

"Well, have a good flight." says Sean. Bending over to the little girl – "And you're going to hold on to Simon really tight now, aren't you?"

She beams a huge smile and shyly turns her head away.

"She'll be a heartbreaker some day!" The young father nods in agreement, rolls his eyes, and holds up his little finger. "All wrapped up around this!"

At the check-in counter, Sean lets Carol go first. She has two pieces plus one carry-on. Sean steps up, shows his paper work, and while tucking it back into his knapsack, the attendant says..

"That was cute what you did over there. I saw the whole thing. You'll be a good father some day."

Carol sees the flirt going on, grabs his arm, and says out loud "Come along, oh husband of mine; no time for dilly dallying." The attendant's face drops.

Sean is shocked. "What the f…. you think she was… " Then he laughs uproariously as they walk away arm in arm, pretending to be a "couple." Carol is almost twice his age, but they get along well enough to call each other close friends. Students on campus have rumored they have a romantic connection, but there's nothing of the sort. They just get a kick out of playing the cougar-with-her-boy-toy role in public. Makes them laugh. "We should do stand-up together," they would often say.

The flight to New York is uneventful except for the odd bout of turbulence. In first class, the little girl is very well-behaved, occupying herself with the games and snacks her mother packed into her pink travel case and knapsack. Simon is safely perched on her lap, temporarily serving as a prop for her book. Other seats are occupied mostly by executives and their assistants with open laptops, financial magazines, and third-quarter reports.

Travelling coach means little leg room, and no free alcohol. That doesn't stop the people in 14-A and 14-B, who become more obnoxious as time goes on, buying multiple bottles of wine from the flight attendant. The family in front of them try to keep their baby from crying from all the racket… they beg an air flight attendant to cut them off.

"Another reason to hate flying," Sean says to Carol, who is staring a hole into the backs of their heads.

"I hear you. They must have been oxygen-deprived when they were born."

Sean chuckles. "You really speak your mind, don't you?"

"So do you; I'm just a little more caustic. Works well for a woman who is creeping in on 38."

"What made you decide to get into business school? Didn't you already have a career?"

"Sure I did – if you want to call running a hair salon a career. I've always been interested in big business, so I thought I'd start by taking night courses at university. That gave me itchy feet, so I wanted a business degree from a reputable university. Next might be a law degree, perhaps in Boston.

"See, my ex-husband has some money. Not a whole lot, but the alimony is enough for me to live on, plus tuition. Besides, he always said I had the brains. He even sends me extra if I need it. Pisses his fiancée off to no end…"

"No doubt!" replies Sean.

"So Sean, what are your life plans?"

"Well, funny you should ask. They're up in the air right now. As you know, I'm in London on a scholarship. The sponsor is a pharmaceutical company that is interested in my sales abilities. They say I could climb fast, and pretty well create my own little empire if I so desire. Lots of perks like cars, private jets, the whole nine yards. I'm not sure I'm the type though, what do you think?"

"Well Sean, don't go asking me to make up your mind, but if I was living your life, I'd be grabbing at any opportunity that crossed my path. You're still young – what – eighteen? Nineteen? I say do it all. You're talented enough to succeed at most anything. So, why is it up in the air?"

"I'm in a band that did really well, and someone in LA wants us to show up and convince his producer we're top forty material. But we've all hung up our instruments for work and education, though our drummer is in music college.

"A few weeks ago I get this call, and it's like – I forgot how much I miss the whole music scene. Not to brag, but we were good. Booking agencies started approaching us, and a talent scout from a big record company came to a couple of our concerts. We're getting together over Thanksgiving to chat more. Plus, I needed an excuse to clear my head and be home for a few days. I really miss my family."

"Will I not see you next week? You going to skip out on us?" Carol casts her famous raised-eyebrow, hairy eyeball look of disapproval.

"Nah, you'll see me. Although, if it turns out we get an offer, we may put something in motion after Easter some time. Those are just my thoughts – this is what we'll be talking about this weekend."

"I see! You have an intriguing life, Mr. Hodges. If you did pursue a music career, you'd be missed. How on *earth* would I make sense of professor Lacey's lectures? For the life of me, I can't understand that thick British accent of his! He's the worst of the lot."

"Deidre takes good notes like me. Although she thinks your outspoken opinions are out of place most of the time."

Carol chuckles and elbows him, feigning insult – "What, lil' ol' ME? A big mouth? Well I never…"

"Hey – can you imagine the look on her face if Mr. Lacey assigned the two of you as project partners? How *funny* would that be!"

They continue chatting about this and that; their classmates, teachers, London. A lull in the conversation gives Carol a chance to excuse herself and head to the back of the plane. Sean really likes Carol, and would miss her as well. *Now I know why I like her. She's got lots of spunk, just like Leslie.*

Their parting at JFK in New York was quick but very warm. They exchanged hugs, and promises of more great talks when they both get back to classes in a few days.

———————————

American Thanksgiving at the Hodges is something to behold, with everything imaginable coming out of Marj's kitchen… ham, turkey, yams, both sweet and baked potatoes, mixed vegetables, and three choices of pie for desert. She's got it covered, from snacks to the multi-course meal. There are seasonal decorations everywhere, and bowls of candy and nuts spread throughout the house – Marj loves to entertain. *Martha Stewart* look out.

Malcolm is always proud to have a guest or two from the plant for supper. Every year there are a few stragglers whose relatives are too far away for just a weekend trip, so they're invited to the Hodges for a meal they'll never forget. There's the usual Mr. Hansen, an elderly janitor who can't speak English very well. No one knows much about this gentle quiet person, except that he does indeed love the Sunday afternoon football game. Some say he keeps his money in a secret holding place in his little apartment.

When Malcolm has a couple of drinks, he drops his surly manner and will wear his corny old Quaker's hat around the house if encouraged enough, but he can't find it this year.

"I think Jake probably hid it on you," says Marj. *I don't blame him* she giggles to herself. After a brandy or two, they give each other a hug in the kitchen. "Thanks for all your hard work, Marj. You really make this a special day for so many people."

Marj is too shy to take the compliment, and Malcolm knows this about her, so he keeps pouring it on....

"Listen sweetheart, this is all your doing. You're a superstar! You make it comfortable for everyone. I just thought I should tell you that."

"Oh Malcolm, thank you!"

"Just think, our whole family will be here together for the first time in a year!" She looks up at the clock.

"You should get going honey, it's thirty minutes to the airport."

Malcolm acknowledges.

The doorbell rings. It's Mr. Hansen with a paper bag cradled in his arm.

"Well hello, Gerald! I'm so glad you could make it again this year." exclaims Marj, extending her hand to shake his.

"For you!" He hands Marj and Malcolm the present, a small house plant with beautiful purple and orange blossoms.

"I grow it this year. Maybe more come next year," he says excitedly.

"How beautiful, Gerald, thank you!"

Mr. Hansen asked permission from Malcolm months ago, if he didn't mind cutting slips and gathering seeds from the array of greenery he tends in the large foyer at the plant. He has a green thumb, and Malcolm was only too pleased to grant him his wish.

"Come in, come in," he motions to his fellow worker. "The pre-game show just started."

His eyes light up. "There's your favorite chair – please be seated!"

Malcolm doesn't easily relinquish his easy chair to many people. Mr. Hansen was one of a few exceptions.

"I'm just on my way to the Lincoln airport to pick up my children. John should be by any time soon."

With that, he's on his way out the door, throwing his coat on as he fumbles for his keys.

At the airport, it isn't long before Malcolm and Sean see each other through the arrivals crowd, and race towards an embrace.

"Sean! How are you?"

"I'm great! It's good to see you. It's been way too long. How's mom?"

"Oh, you should see the feast she's prepared for you guys. All your favorites."

"I can't wait. I'm starved."

They make their way to baggage carousel number 5. Malcolm can't figure out why he looks so different. *Oh – it's the hair.*

"For God's sake, what did you do to your head?" Malcolm asks.

"Dad – you forget I've been in Europe for a year. It's called 'highlighting.' Guys do it all the time."

Carol had left her mark. As a hair stylist, she loved helping small-town boys get up to speed. And apparently their parents as well... *I suppose it's better than a nose ring,* thinks Malcolm.

Just then, a public announcement informs Malcolm and Sean that flight F9107 from Minneapolis via Denver will be late thanks to poor weather. A quick scan of the arrivals board confirms what they just heard.

Malcolm looks at his watch and exclaims "You know, I did hear Denver was getting hit with a storm – I hope she's not *too* late, Marj will be getting Thanksgiving dinner together in a couple of hours."

"Well, why don't we go grab a soda while we wait. Maybe I'll have a beer."

Malcolm thinks his eldest is growing up *far* too fast.

"Sounds good Sean – pardon me, I'll phone Marj and let her know." He pulls out his cell phone.

Just then Sean's two suitcases tumble down onto the luggage carousel. *They made it.*

Sean sighs to himself. He normally travels lighter, but he's been away for so long that he's gathered gifts and souvenirs for everyone. It'll be an early Christmas at the Hodges this year.

"Oh – let me go find a cart for those," says Malcolm.

The airport is busy with holiday travelers, but it's not long before they're in a short lineup waiting to be seated at the restaurant. In a couple of minutes the waitress is showing them their seats.

The small talk meanders around each other's news of the past few months, stories of losses and wins, when Sean begins to wonder if Malcolm has learned about Leslie's parentage. It has yet to come up in conversation, so he concludes things are still the same as when he left...

"You look like you want to talk about something Sean – what's up?"

"Oh, nothing. I'm just tired from the long flight. It was a milk run, with a stop-over in New York."

"I didn't realize that. Well, you're bedroom hasn't changed – you can hit the sack any time you want after supper. What's the time difference anyways?"

"Seven hours I think – it's almost midnight in London right now."

The area usually receives about five feet of snow a year, and this November everyone swears they got it all in the past week. The Airport Authority is doing its best to keep the runways clear for in-coming flights first, then departures. Leslie's plane has been on the tarmac for over an hour when the pilot announces that they're next up. Everyone applauds! They're in great spirits – the co-pilot had been keeping everyone in the holiday spirit with jokes and songs for the past twenty minutes, so there wasn't a grouchy soul on board.

Going against the rules, Les pulls out her cell phone and sends a text message to Sean giving him the news. *Cya in 1 hour. Taking off shortly.*

Sean is half way through his beer when his phone vibrates. His face lights up as he reads Leslie's message.

"Woo hoo! She'll be here in an hour!"

"That's a relief – I had nightmares of us eating our Thanksgiving meal at midnight. Can you imaging the fit Marj would have!"

The hugs and kisses are liberally shared when Leslie walks through the doorway.

"What an ordeal!" She says, eyeing Sean's new look. "Look at you, all Euro and everything. You look good." She plays with his hair a bit.

"Thanks, so do you – cool duds!" She's been wearing more colors of late.

"Aw, you know – the Goth thing was getting tiresome. I know a lot of kids in fashion at my school, so the advice is good, but never ending."

They chat as baggage is retrieved; they make their way over an overpass to where Malcolm parked the family van on the second level.

"I'm glad you're all finally here. My stomach is starting to rumble," says Malcolm, "Actually, let's grab a candy bar at the machines."

While Malcolm scans the machine for his favorite snack, Les leans over and whispers into Sean's ear – "I found my sister and parents in Romania. We've been writing – they have no Internet."

Sean's eyes grow huge. "No way!" he whispers back. They hug. "Tell me more later." Les winks at Sean.

———————

"I'd like to make a toast."

Malcolm raises a glass, and everyone follows suit.

"To the Hodges household, and especially our children. I'm thankful we can all be here for Thanksgiving. And special thanks to my beautiful wife Marjorie who put on this wonderful spread."

"Hear hear!" spouts Leslie. They all touch glasses, take a sip, and Mr. Hansen speaks out in his thick accent.

"Tank you again mister and missus Hodges, for the lovely food and lovely wine!"

"Hear hear!" shouts Malcolm even louder than Leslie. His speech is getting a little slurred. "Pass that bottle, son!"

They all have their fill of Marj's feast, and start heading into the living room. Malcolm belches for all to hear. Leslie rolls her eyes and comments:

"You're cut off Daddy-o. No more booze for you."

"I'll have you know little girl," he slurs – "it was my hard-earned money that paid for that beautiful Chardonnay." He tries to tickle her in the ribs, but she's too quick for him.

"Get away from me you slob!" She grabs a bun from the table and throws it at him. He returns with a croissant. "Take that!"

This happens almost every year. Malcolm gets tipsy, then begins to actually have childish fun with his family. Two years ago, after a ladle of gravy found its way onto the dining room drapes, Marj made everyone swear never again. Everyone promised. No one listened.

"Food fight!" yells Jake, eyeing the dining room, daring not to enter. He knows what's next. Marj flies into the room waving a big wooden spoon in the air, chasing after the two combatants.

Almost normal, thinks Sean, staying out of the fray. *It's not Norman Rockwell, but I'll take it the way it is.*

The doorbell rings, and Sean jumps up to get it – he knows who it is. Opening the door, he invites Mark and Amy in.

"Hey!!! Great to see you!" After greeting, they walk into the living room where Malcolm and Marj get up to greet them as well. They chat about the latest things going on; Malcolm asks how each of their parents is doing, and Marj offers them a plate of food.

"Oh goodness, no, but thank you. We each just had dinner at home; when I picked up Amy at her place, they offered too. You're so kind."

"Sean, why don't you guys all go to the kitchen. You can chat there."

He motions to Leslie – "C'mon Les – there's lots to talk about."

It takes about twenty minutes to get through the news and gossip. Indigo Insight are together again, and they all can't wait to hear more details about LA.

Sean starts in – "So, tell us the good news, Mark."

"Well, Sean, you remember the CD we sent to all the different A&R people a while back. One of them called all the contact numbers in the promo material, and I was the first live person he got to talk to other than an answering machine. His name is Devon, and he says he heard us at that first big concert we did in the gym. Then a month or so ago, someone *else* dropped our CD on his desk. He took the hint and played it to somebody he just refers to as "big daddy," some big exec in the business.

"He wants us to go up against another band; they can't decide who to go with until they see how we do in a studio. I told him we had some experience, but he said we haven't had *LA* experience. So – it's up to us when we go. The sooner the better."

"Whoa, this is heavy," comments Amy. "I've got a full time job, and so do you Mark. We can't just walk away from it all."

Sean's excitement betrays him. Smiling as he talks, he offers input.

"I've been thinking about this – I'm wondering if we could all take a few days off and coordinate a trip to LA. Listen guys, if we don't try, we won't know. Imagine getting a record deal with Capital Records – you guys could blow off your dead-end jobs, Leslie gets to *not* graduate from art college just like every other successful artsy, and I already have an understanding with my university in London – I can resume my studies at a later time – *if* I so desire."

"Don't go making up my mind for me," pipes up Leslie. "I'd like to at least get my diploma for all the hard work I put in."

"I get that," replies Sean "but think of how much better a musician you are *already*. We could conceivably set ourselves up quite nicely with a couple of music videos, a couple top hits – the royalties would keep us going the rest of our lives. We're talking big bucks here. You have any idea what Coopers Hawk make in a year? And they're not even main stream. $100,000 a year just in overseas royalties. Tour Europe and Japan, and we could double or triple what we'd make just here."

Mark, Amy, and Leslie are stunned. They don't know what to say. Opportunity is knocking; they just need to walk through the door. Sean gets out of his chair and removes the large calendar from the bulletin board over the phone, then flips it to the new year.

"It's too late for this year I'm thinking. Maybe we should look at spring break. Les, you'll be done, and I have a week off."

"Hold on boss man," Leslie interjects – "You brought this up as a realistic thing, so I say jump on it now. Sean, you're already here. So am I. We need to practice – it's been a year since we played together. Plus, we have Christmas holidays coming up. Amy, you essentially work for Sean's mom, so he can pull strings if you can't get the time off. And Mark – you look *so* ugly in that green apron. Ya *gotta* get another job dude! This is your chance."

"Hey, I'm produce manager!" he says laughingly – "Many people want what I have, especially the low pay and long hours!" Then he squints his eyes at Sean…

"I'm trusting you man, I want to do this, so let's not blow it. My mom depends on help from me financially."

Amy grabs the calendar.

"OK – here we are now. I need to give at least a week's notice. What about you Mark?"

"I don't want to burn bridges, but I *could* leave tomorrow. I joke about it, but there are two people who work for me that want my position. I'll work with whatever you guys want to do."

Les continues – "Excellent. I can get all my shit mailed to me from college; Sean – you can too. We stay here, start practicing, and wait for these jokers to join us after they quit. In the meantime you and I start writing again. By the time January rolls around, we'll be in peak form."

Amy looks at Leslie with a surprised look – she likes her new take-charge personality. Sean likes what he sees too. Leslie isn't usually so aggressive, but apparently college has served her well.

"Wow, this is spinning my head. I need a beer."

"Me too," everyone replies.

Conversation turns to details, the logistics of the trip, and finances. Sean assures them of the funds they still have, so the LA trip is taken care of. Someone suggests a fundraising concert, but the rest disagree – *it's just a distraction.*

"So – who's going to tell mom and dad?" Les asks Sean. Reality sinks in. He chuckles. "Flip you for it!"

"Nah, let's both go tell them now."

Marj and Malcolm know something's up. Marj hasn't whispered a thing about this to her husband. The chatter in the kitchen has been quite animated, so when the four of them walk into the living room with that "we-have-an-announcement-to-make" look on their faces, Malcolm grabs the remote and mutes the volume.

"What is it kids?"

Sean can't wait… He clasps his hands together in excitement.

"Mom, Dad, as you know, a talent scout called Mark and asked us to come to LA to audition. They think we're a natural fit, so we're *this* close to landing a record contract."

Malcolm looks at his wife – "You knew this?"

"Shhh. Let them talk dear," she whispers.

"So, we've cooked up a plan to go. The thing is, well… um…"

Les takes over. "Thing is, we're staying here. I mean – now. Sean's going to take up his studies later if he needs to. He won't because – we're like – going to the biggest band *ever*" she says in her best valley girl accent, twisting her hair. Mark chuckles.

More seriously – "Amy and Mark have their job situations figured out, so we're going to start practicing this week. We leave for LA late January and maybe come back with a big fat check. How's that for life planning?"

Malcolm and Marj are surprised, but not all that much.

"You guys really sure about this? I mean, what if this guy in LA turns you down when you call tomorrow?"

"Mark has it on letterhead. Dad, they're serious. They're just waiting for our response. Mark told him to hold off till after Thanksgiving, and he said that was fine."

"Well, as you know, your bedrooms are always here." He stands up, looking a little awkward. He reaches out to Sean for a hug… "Welcome home you guys!"

They all clap in excitement. Mr. Hanson's English isn't the best, but he understands it better than he can speak it.

"You make good record, and put Grey Falls on the map!" he says in support. Leslie thanks him and says, "I'll send you a free CD – promise!"

Amy and Mark exchange hugs; Marj calls out over the din… "Malcolm, get that bottle of champagne out – my kids are going to be home for Christmas!"

As Sean is pouring some into everyone's glass, he steals a quick few words with Leslie. "When am I going to hear about *your* family?"

"Not now – over at Lydia's. She should hear too."

"Cool."

Everyone could feel the excitement in the air as Indigo Insight talk about their future, making plans as if they were already millionaires, all the while helping Marj clean the kitchen. They plan their first practice for Sunday night.

———————————

"Aw *man* – we're in G, not C," complains Sean. Leslie keeps the beat going, but much softer. "Mark, crank it up a bit, and go to a low A half a bar after I hammer on the F sharp." Mark quickly scrawls something on his lyric sheet. His vintage Rickenbacker bass will rattle the windows.

"Sorry man, it's been a while." Everyone forgot how hard practice was. As good as Sean is, he does grate on everyone's nerves just before a big gig. Leslie mediates…

"OK – from the first chorus. Shut up Sean, we're doing OK."

The noise from the garage is somewhat muted by the loud television, but Malcolm eventually gives in and enters the garage.

"Hey guys, tomorrow's a new week, and you can practice all day long while we're all away. Do you mind if I head off to bed now?" That's Malcolm-speak for 'please shut it down, I can't sleep with that racket.' Mark checks his watch –

"Oh sorry, Mr. Hodges, I don't think we realized how late it was."

"That's fine guys. Good night."

Everyone responds.

Chapter 17

Two weeks before Christmas in Grey Falls marks the annual parade. Just about every business with an account at the local credit union has the funds to participate, thanks to Mervin Gromwell's attitude, that "investing in your community is investing in your family's future." Not that Malcolm's company needs any extra financing; Grey Falls Manufacturing and Building Supply Center sponsors a float that gains much applause, with its huge one-story high cartoon characters, and some of his employees dressed in *Disney* costumes waving to the kiddies. The large banner across both sides of the float proudly displays his company's name and logo.

Almost the entire town is out for the parade, that is, unless you're the next hot band meeting with an A&R rep from a major record label. They slaved away at practice, hardly noticing the time fly by. Just after a week they were getting their edge back, and they could *tell*. The creative juices were flowing, and Sean and Leslie had two more originals in the "can" as they say it in the industry. The odd reprimand from their parents to pry themselves away from their practice schedule was met with resistance; they were bound and determined to wow everyone in LA.

Occasionally Sean and Les would visit Lydia at her condo. She didn't mind if they drank, of if Leslie had her odd cigarette on the balcony, as long as they kept things civil. Not that they ever over did it, but it was still nice to indulge without a lecture and a wagging finger. During their first visit after arriving, Les filled them in on her family back in Romania. Lydia and Sean couldn't wait to hear it all.

"Well, my mom's English is kind of OK, and her accent is really strong. I have an English-to-Romanian dictionary to help me out. They were all totally blown away when I phoned, as you can imagine. So – my mom's name is Sabina, my dad's is Petru, and my sister is Dana. It was hard to understand, but the reason I was put up for adoption was because my dad lost his job at the factory, and they couldn't afford groceries. Rent was overdue, and they already had Dana. They found out about the adoption agency, who basically pitched to them the idea of having their newborn children raised in America by well-to-do couples. They promised constant contact, which was a lie. They never heard anything till I phoned."

"What a rip-off," Says Sean. Lydia agrees. Les continues.

"There was still a lot of political unrest after Romania was no longer under communism, so they opted for what was best for me. Here I am. I told them I'd visit when I got the time off. They're doing better, but they still are poor. I've sent them some money to help them out."

"Well, shit, then this record deal is just in time. But even if it falls through, I'll donate some. How about you mom?"

Lydia answers – "You got it! Just let me know when you want to go, and I'll guarantee you one grand. And it's not a loan either."

Leslie's eyes well up. Sean squeezes her shoulder.

"I can't believe this, you guys… thanks so much."

Their visits with Lydia evolve into shopping trips, a spa weekend… though not intentionally, they both were benefitting from Lydia's guilty conscience. At their utter surprise on a weekday evening, Lydia announces –

"Hey you two – I have to go to Canada. There's this conference for municipal movers and shakers that the city wants me to attend. If you can believe it, no one else from the office is going. Wanna come? Everything's covered."

Without a single protest, they immediately made plans and booked a flight to Calgary, and a car rental to Banff, a resort town in the Canadian Rockies. *I've always wanted to learn snowboarding,* thought Sean. Downhill skiing was fun, but a friend from England was semi-pro and always chatted Sean up about giving it a try. Leslie found a website with pictures of the restaurants and the nightclub at the Banff Springs Hotel and emailed the link to some of her friends. *Guess where I'm going for a week,* she bragged.

Mark and Amy were ready for a break as well. Weeks of hard-core practicing were beginning to take its toll. It was a tough regimen: 10 to 10:30: individual warm ups comprised of finger exercises and chromatic scales for the two guitarists and keyboard player, full-body stretching for the drummer. Les would adjust her drum kit's position on the mat, while everyone tunes to Amy's 88-key Korg M3. After two songs, they're sounding warmed up. Then the band will play more covers, then eventually work their way into some of the originals they're preparing for LA. Sean then gets their input on the creative arranging, making notes as they talk. Then a quick lunch break. At 3:00 in the afternoon when they're looking for a break, his musical genius pours out. They keep a digital recorder going constantly, should there be a chord change they can't quite remember on second try. It was a good formula all in all, and it was serving them well. *But man, we need some time off from this boot camp.*

Not long before touchdown, Leslie removes her headphones and comments to Sean –

"Look at those mountains. They're awesome. And all that snow! Can't wait to try snowboarding down *those!*" Sean leans into Leslie to get a better look. Les had called dibs on the window seat not long after they left their house four hours before.

Sunset is back-lighting the Canadian Rockies with an orange glow, and illuminating the few clouds they are passing through with the same color. It was almost surreal as the plane makes its approach and banks right, opening up even more landscape below them.

Calgary International Airport is busy with holiday goers, business people, and elderly volunteers in white cowboy hats waiting to help anyone looking lost. The flat-panel LCD monitors above the various baggage carousels display the flight numbers of the most recent arrivals. *Delta flight 4640. Let's see if they got all our baggage.*

At the baggage carousel, Lydia, Sean, and Leslie are chatting away, keeping an eye out for their luggage. Lydia eyes the car rental desk and says –

"You know what my luggage looks like. I'll go ahead over there to get the rental paperwork out of the way."

Lydia doesn't like flying like she used to. She still loves being in a small aircraft, but these airports grate on her nerves. The less time in them, the better. Her suitcases all have a bright pink and orange tassel hanging off the carrying handles, so they're easy to spot. Anything to make this experience go as smoothly as possible.

"There you are, Ms. Forsythe. Your car is just out those doors, in stall G24. Is there anything more we can do for you?"

Sean and Leslie have all their luggage in the cart; they're just waiting for Lydia.

"No, that should do it I think. Insurance, GPS, keys… How long is the drive to Banff? I'm wondering if we should stop for some dinner first."

"Well over an hour, Ms. Forsythe. If you're hungry now, perhaps you might want to have a bite to eat before heading out of town. I can recommend a number of good places to eat if you wish."

More of a concierge than a clerk, the young man flirts with Lydia while showing a few restaurant options on a map. Deciding against anything at the airport itself, they opt for a higher-end hotel restaurant at the corner of Barlow Trail and 32nd Avenue. Lydia likes to live it up, especially when on the road.

"My brother manages the place," he winks. "Best beef in town. I'll phone ahead for you if you wish."

"Wow, these Canadians *are* friendly," Sean whispers to Leslie.

Lydia is pleased with their plans. "Done deal. I love cow parts. Let's go troops!"

"Enjoy your stay in Alberta."

Making their way through the large double doors, Sean says to his mom –

"Still got it, eh mom. That guy was gushing all over you!"

"No way," said Les – "He was as gay as they come."

"Who cares, gay – straight – I'll take the attention from anyone these days."

Sean and Leslie look at each other and laugh, Sean exclaiming loudly –

"Uh oh!!! Trouble! Guess who'll be chaperoning *who* this week!"

"Listen you two, I have changed a few diapers in my time, a few of them yours. Don't you go all holier-than-thou on me now! I come from a long line of serious party animals, so I'll expect you to hold up your end!"

Sean, always the clown, puts on a well-honed upper crust British accent, raises his nose, and says to Leslie –

"Dawling, can you believe what comes out of the mouth of this so-called politician. Dear me, I do say the world's morality is crumbling."

Les plays along.

"Dearest, we shall never survive her gregariousness. What *shall* we do?"

Lydia's accent is pretty good too.

"Mummy. Daddy. While I turn around and bend over, I do invite you to bite the big one." Roars of laughter fill the enclosed parking lot.

The party has begun. They're all in high gear for a great time in this winter wonderland. Lydia has a full day before having to show up for seminars and workshops, so while driving to the restaurant she suggests that they all take a dip in the pool after they check into their rooms. Maybe go dancing. Everyone agrees.

"I don't have to get up tomorrow morning, so we can let Banff know we're there!"

Now at the hotel restaurant, Lydia comments on how impeccably the meal is prepared. The head cook does his job making sure the presentation is up to his standards before a thing leaves his kitchen. Every customer has two or three various attendees filling water glasses, brushing crumbs from the table, and delivering their meals. The sommelier is friendly and informative, going over his wine list making suggestions for each of them.

"I've never tasted beef this good," comments Lydia after the first few bites, drawing on her glass of French Merlot. Sean is loosening the thin cucumber that is wrapped around his salad tower.

"Everything looks too good to eat," he replies. The food prepped table-side is a new experience for both Sean and Leslie, as they watch the server skillfully prepare the restaurant's famous Caesar salad.

Approaching the end of their meal, Lydia brings up a subject that hasn't been talked about in a long time. The wine is loosening her tongue a bit...

"Listen guys, I know things haven't been easy for either of you. All of us older ones, supposedly your 'parents,' haven't done a perfect job. I mean, god, I think of what your family has been through and I cringe at the role I played in it all. But I just look at the two of you, and I can't help but be amazed at how well you turned out. Really.

"This week is for you guys. Whatever you want to do, it's on me. I have a fat expense account, so don't worry about anything financial, OK? You can have my credit card to carry with you, but guard it with your life. I have another one, so keep this one for the week." She digs in her purse, finds her wallet and hands Sean her personal Visa.

She continues.

"Malcolm phoned me before we left and thanked me for taking you guys on this trip. We get along OK as you know, but that was out of character for him. He really loves you guys, and is as proud as can be. Your trip to LA is causing a bit of a stir in the community, and I think I can speak for a whole lot of people that we're behind you 110 percent." *Leslie gets to see my mom's soft side,* thinks Sean. Away from home, away from the office, Lydia is letting her motherly, protective instincts surface.

Something began to happen that no one planned; out of total spontaneity… the mood, the fun, the beautiful atmosphere, Lydia's soft words – they all reach for each other's hands. Sean in Lydia's, Lydia's in Leslie's, and – Leslie's in Sean's. They look around the table and notice it at the same time. They let it linger, but Sean and Les are the first to let go, slightly embarrassed. Then Leslie takes Lydia's hand with both of hers.

"Lydia, I'm not angry for what happened. Who knows what I would do in the same circumstances – it must have been hard to conceal such a secret all these years. I get why you kept it to yourself all this time. You know, it's been well over a year since all this came to a head, and I've had a lot of time to get over whatever crap I held in my head. I just don't want you to feel like you owe me anything. Sean and I talked about this, and we've enjoyed you spoiling us, so – please don't stop."

The levity gets them all chuckling; a waiter stops for dessert orders. Lydia asks him to come back in a couple of minutes.

"Please don't do it for the wrong reasons."

"Leslie, those are the kindest words. You're a sweetheart… " Leslie smiles and wipes a tear. *Thank you.*

"Yeah, it's all good. I did want to bring something up though."

"Please do, Leslie."

"The only thing about all this is that it puts a strain on home life a bit. Malcolm isn't really my uncle. Maybe we should think about letting him in on it too. But – I know that puts a bit of pressure on you. Have you thought about this at all?"

Neither Sean nor Leslie mention they each had confidants back at school who know the entire story.

"Yes Leslie, I have." She responds assertively.

"But let me think about it more the next while. It's not like he has to know tomorrow."

"Very true. But whenever you do tell him, would you like me there with you?"

"Perhaps. Let's talk more about it after you guys get back from your LA trip."

She then asks Leslie a sensitive question –

"Les – where's your head in all this? I mean, knowing you're not related to Sean?"

Leslie gathers her thoughts and sighs.

"It's been quite a trip. We're close – we spend a lot of time together because of the band. I don't see him as a cousin of course… never really did at the beginning 'cause we never met before. More like a really close friend. I don't know, we're so busy with everything, I don't think about it much." Her cheeks betray her words.

She does in fact think about it.

"Well, you're both strong kids, and you know I'm always there for you. It hasn't been easy, and as you said Les, it's not quite over. I've got to deal with Malcolm. That won't be easy… but I think it'll be OK. It was all my deception, so you guys are safe."

Changing the subject, she looks around the restaurant… "Where is that man with the dessert cart?"

––––––––––––

A large delivery truck makes its way through town into the industrial sector of Grey Falls, heading for the Hodges plant. Turning into the parking lot, the driver skillfully backs up the five ton into his usual spot as the hydraulic ramp lowers onto the delivery bay floor. The shift foreman notices the arrival, and meets with the driver to sign off on a few small boxes bound for their electrical department, and also a large wooden crate. "Big one today," comments the driver.

"Yep – hope you didn't roll it down a hill on the way over."

"Almost missed one – sign here too, please. Some new form for large crates."

He waves off the *Purolator* driver with a "Thanks again. See ya tomorrow." They meet daily in this environment and often chat about their families, children, the weather. He reads the packing slip: "From: Underbridge Holdings." *Ah, thought so.*

He tracks down one of their larger forklift trucks and jumps into the driver's seat, just when a worker approaches…

"It's my job, I'll move it. You supposed to be boss!" he says in a thick accent.

"Sambo, hey – I'll take it down. Special orders. Go have a smoke."

Puzzled, the short Italian shrugs his shoulders and follows orders.

The freight elevator is just big enough for the forklift and its cargo. Once in the basement, he jumps out of his seat to open the elevator doors, at the same time turning the service mode of the elevator to "lock" position to ensure no one follows him. *Sure is musty down here.* Negotiating the maze-like path is difficult in the low lighting, but he knows the route.

He lowers the crate to the floor, drops the forks and backs away from the crate. Driving around it, he begins the task of removing a large section of boxes that are also on skids, exposing a section of a large cinder block wall. The blocks are much newer than the originals, making it easy to landmark. After jumping out of the forklift, he turns the key to kill the motor. Silence. A good look around

151

ensures he is alone. At the cinder block wall, he counts the rows from the top and locates a special spot on the wall. Pushing on it, it gives way with a clunk. Then miraculously, a huge section of this false wall begins to move away from him, into a room very few people know about. After a few seconds, it then shifts to the right, slowly creating an opening wide and tall enough to clear the crate and fork lift.

Once inside, the wall moves back into place. He finds the light switch and heads back over to the forklift to locate his crowbar. After prying off the top and sides, a cursory inspection of the large object reveals no damage. The oils used to preserve this ancient table lend a musky, almost animal smell to it. He admires the intricate carvings in the pedestal, and notes the various letters and words that encircle the outer rim. *I've no clue what that alphabet is* he thinks to himself. Pulling out a cell phone, he punches in a memorized number and texts a message –

The table has arrived safe & sound. Awaiting further instructions.

Chapter 18

The desk staff are busy with a long lineup of travelers checking in and out. At the far end of the foyer, Leslie notices a group of journalists and photographers trying to get the perfect shot of a couple descending a large granite staircase. *He looks familiar somehow...* A quick scan around the room and she sees a large sign announcing that the hotel is hosting a benefit this weekend, and the celebrity roster is impressive. Actors, politicians, movers and shakers from Hollywood.

"Maybe we'll see them on the ski hill," Leslie says to Sean.

"Please don't embarrass me by asking for autographs..."

Lydia makes her way to a clerk. "Two rooms under Forsythe."

The clerk punches her name into his computer terminal –

"Lydia? Yes, here we are Ms. Forsythe." The clerk goes through all the details about parking, valet service, where the rooms are located, elevators, restaurants... finally handing her two card keys for each of their rooms. Lydia turns around.

"Here you are Sean – Les and I are bunking together. Don't go trashing the place."

"Mom, I may be in a rock band," feigning disgust – "but I do know how to behave. *Sheesh!*"

As they head to the elevators, Leslie asks, "So everyone, we going for a swim like we said?"

"You betcha."

After checking into their rooms, the trio all don their bathing suits, put on the comfortable white hotel robes, and head for the outdoor heated pool.

"Swanky!" comments Sean as they survey the pool area. They place their robes in one spot, and begin descending into the water.

Lydia can't help but notice Leslie's young, well-endowed shapely body. Sean can't help but steal a look or two.

"And you say you have no boyfriends?!?" she exclaims in a lowered voice, pointing to her cleavage. "Holy smokes, I'm surprised you aren't swamped with phone calls!"

Sean contributes – "She wears baggy clothes, lucky for her." *And me…*

Les sends him a dirty look, then plunges into the warm water. Sean does laps as the girls wade and chat. The warm water and cold air makes for an interesting experience, especially with snow piled up here and there. There's even a small snowman someone made in a corner, out of sight, but not escaping Sean's eye. He chuckles to himself. *This is surreal.* The frolicking lasts all but 20 minutes when an attendant comes to the side of the pool to remind them of the time. *Oops – we forgot the pool closes at ten.*

"Is there a bar open?" questions Lydia.

"There sure is folks, including a dance floor. Lower level – just follow the noise."

They all dry off quickly and head to their rooms, which are all on the same floor.

"OK kiddos, a quick shower and let's all meet in the hall in – say – 15 minutes?"

Sean inquires – "Why shower? We just…" then it dawns on him. Their hair.

"Oh! I forgot how vain you are, Your Honor!"

"Bite me." Is her response with a smirk.

The restaurant-turned-nightclub is posh. Old world craftsmanship mixed with a modern flair, the environment begs you to spend money. The late dinner crowd is leaving, and the DJ is lining up tonight's songs. No laptops or CDs here – it's all vinyl. And *very* hip. The funky background music is boosted just a bit; the lights are lowered ever so slowly. A new shift of waitresses in black miniskirts and push-up bras swarm the room, asking for orders. Crowds are coming in from other Banff establishments via foot, car, taxi, and private bus. This conference, that seminar, and of course the benefit – apparently this is the place to cut loose.

"We better get seated quick, look at all those people swarming in."

"Over there in the corner – that booth…."

They hustle to their spot when a cocktail waitress smiles at Sean from a distance and holds up her finger – *Be there in a sec.* Sean's jaw drops. She's a knockout.

Les catches the interaction and says to Sean – "You flirting with a waitress? Or just wishing to have something you could never get?"

"Well, how's that for a vote of confidence!" comments Lydia. "If I was a fly on the wall, I'd say you were jealous."

Leslie's reaction is a little dramatic: "Jealous? Of what?"

Sean defuses the conversation with – "Hey, I don't get out much. Anything looks good to the musical recluse who doesn't date. Hey – what's on the drink menu?"

They all scan the menu and someone suggests appetizers along with drinks. *Sounds fine to me,* someone says. Settled. A dry martini, a hard lemonade, a Pilsner, and veggie platter number two. The waitress arrives and Sean orders for them all, which impresses her.

"Good memory. You should work here."

"Would we be on the same shift?" With a slight smirk on her face, Les kicks Sean under the table.

Ouch.

Lydia notices three businessmen walking through the door, all middle-aged and very handsome. As they remove their outerwear, stuffing scarves into arm sleeves and gloves into pockets, their waitress guides them to a table a short distance from them. One of them makes eye contact with Lydia and smiles. She reciprocates. The dance is on… over the next few minutes, Lydia doesn't involve herself with Sean and Les's conversation – she's rather distracted…

"Mom… *Mom* – " Lydia is startled.

"Sorry, what where you saying?"

"Les and I want to take snowboard lessons – I found a brochure in the lobby that has all the info. It's a full day with a small group of people on the other side of the highway. Maybe we'll do that tomorrow. That OK?"

"I told you guys, this trip is for you. You have my credit card – knock yourselves out. I'll be tied up at the conference center all week, but we can hook up for dinners and have fun at night."

"Great, I'll sign us up first thing in the morning. Doesn't start till 10 I think… This'll be fun."

"You know what would be fun – is if that hunk over there asked me for a dance."

Sean and Les look at each other… "Man, we're hardly here half an hour and you're already scoping the crowd."

"He scoped *me*. He hasn't stopped staring at me since they arrived five minutes ago. I'm thinking he'll make his way over here when the DJ starts."

At the table of the three gentlemen, one says to another –

"Heads she's yours, tails she's mine." The third one just rolls his eyes, commenting on how sophomoric his buddies are. The coin flies in the air, lands in his hand, he flips it over…

"All yours, lucky guy. I'm not sure she'd appreciate me hitting on her daughter, what do you think? Kinda young for me anyways."

"I'll take'm both. I'm in the mood to celebrate – oil just went up 10 bucks a barrel, so I'll be paying off my ranch house faster than I thought."

"*Another* house? What about your place here – you don't go there much, do you?"

"I keep it staffed, plus my sister and her family use it when they come up to Canada to ski. It's a nice place to call home away from home I suppose. Besides, I don't like hotels when I'm up here for meetings. The food's not the same as home cooked."

Everyone nods in agreement. These high-stakes players have been at the game for decades, and in their younger years didn't mind the jet-set lifestyle. With age, they prefer the comforts of home, a familiar bed, and no check-out times.

"You guys are welcome to it anytime you're up here – I'll have my assistant make up keys for you if you want. Just check with her if it's available."

"Thanks Herb, that's a kind gesture. I'll have to get you that case of 15 year-old *Springbank* whisky I was talking about… though I suspect there's a bottle or two missing. It's a limited run product, but I was able to locate a case through my restaurant friend in Soho. Maybe they'll have some here we could taste…" He looks around for a waitress. Just then the lights dim more, and the DJ starts up his playlist.

The subwoofers call upon the tribal in Lydia, and she yanks on Leslie's hand –

"C'mon Les, let's cut up this rug." They are joined by a mass of people onto the dance floor, and the DJ cranks it even more. Sean's at the booth alone, but not for long – a group of single girls file up to the dance floor, and one of them grabs him by the arm. A group of locals, these girls form a core of friends that are mostly transients from one country or another, working as kitchen staff, cooks, waitresses, any job one can find in this famous resort town. They can spot a newbie from across the room. Sean will be their boy toy on the dance floor for a couple of hours, but that's as far as it'll go. 6AM comes fast, and they just need to blow off a little steam.

One of the businessmen nudges the other –

"Time to cash in on your win. Go up and dance with her."

Herb doesn't need much convincing after his double whisky sour. He removes his jacket and tie, rolls up his sleeves, and slinks into the crowd.

Lucky bastard. Why does he always win the coin toss?

Lydia picks up on her quarry and moves in for the kill.

"I'm Herb – may I have this dance?"

"Most certainly. I'm Lydia, that's my son Sean over there with the white shirt, and this is Leslie. Um – Sean's friend. But they're not a couple so-to-speak"

157

A few more pleasantries and they keep dancing. It's hard to make out words so close to the vintage Tannoy speakers just overhead; the songs meld into one another with no breaks. After 20 or so minutes of constant music, Lydia invites him over to their table. He gladly obliges and peers at his two business partners and winks. The booth is far enough into the corner to make decent conversation.

"Good seating choice. I couldn't hear myself think over there!" He waves down a waitress and orders a round of shooters and another whisky sour. "What is everyone else drinking? Your glasses are almost empty." Les is dancing with the locals over where Sean is, and she begins to make her way to the booth as well. The waitress remembers all their drinks, and Herb nods –

"Excellent! Another round then, on my tab."

"Thank you Herb – I'll get the next one."

Les joins them and listens while Lydia asks Herb about his job, where he's from, who his friends are… they exchange generalities about each other's lives for a couple of minutes, when the drinks arrive.

"Here's to Canadian winters, and the price of oil."

"I'll drink to that!" Lydia responds. Sean approaches the booth with a curious look on his face; it's the first he's seen of the new guest at their table.

"Sean, this is Herb, Herb, my son Sean."

"My pleasure." Sean likes him: firm handshake, nice smile, no phoniness. Sean has a fairly well-honed bullshit meter, as does Leslie. They're both thinking *what a catch this guy would be for Lydia.*

The evening goes on with more drinks, dancing, and conversation. Just after midnight, the rich guy's friends retire to their respective rooms, and Lydia makes a mild suggestion they find a quieter bar, perhaps the pub down the hall. Herb mentions his house is not far away; everyone is welcome over for a drink. *No one else, just the four of us.* His invitation is met with … "We'll pay the cab fare."

"Oh quiet," he interrupts, "I'm calling my driver."

Fifteen minutes later, the four of them are whisked off to a scene that can only be described as incredulous. His "house" is more than a mansion. *Kings live like this,* they thought.

"How do you like it?" asks Herb. No one speaks for a few seconds.

"Herb, this is gorgeous. This is *yours?"*

The limo makes it around to the front entrance and stops; the driver asks the owner – "Sir, is that all for tonight?

"Yes John, thanks. But I'll need you in the morning."

Lydia's mouth is agape – *Wow – something tells me we're here for more than just a drink.*

The foyer is dimly lit by a few night lights left on by the day staff, but the motion sensors quickly illuminate the entire first floor as they walk in. A large double staircase leads to the second floor, and three massive arched doorways invite them to the living area, the dining area, and another set of stairs down to a games room, home theater, and bar. Their amazement is not lost on the rich guy…

"Hey, look around. It's huge thanks to Alberta oil, so take your time and let me know what you find. There are places here that I've yet to see… I need to make a call before we have drinks."

With that, Herb disappears into door number three. Lydia, Sean, and Leslie spread out to discover this immense mansion the rich guy calls his "pigeon coop." Sean slowly follows the owner down the stairs. Leslie meanders into the dining room and sits at the head of a table she's never seen the likes of, except perhaps in the movies. *This can sit thirty people,* she half whispers. A short trip into the kitchen, and she's soon looking around in the massive stainless steel fridge for something to munch on.

Lydia heads to the second floor and peeks into all the bedrooms, each with their own ensuite, jacuzzi, and massive clothes closet. *I could handle this quite easily,* she says out loud, feeling the bedspreads, towels, and shower curtains. The details don't escape her;

Lydia begins to feel like the little girl in a fantasy castle she used to dream about as a child. Sean bursts through the door, surprising his mom...

"Oh! Sorry, I didn't know you were here."

"That's OK – come look at this view."

In what must be the master bedroom, Sean and his mother gape at the panoramic view of a beautiful pastoral landscape perfectly framed by pine and spruce trees, lightly dusted by a recent snowfall.

"Is that a lake?" Sean asks.

"Not sure – but the moon makes it look like you could dive right in," comments Lydia.

They are startled by a voice coming from everywhere – "Calling all guests – calling all guests. You are invited to the lower level for cocktails and snacks, and the longer it takes you to get here, the less there will be."

Sean and Lydia quickly realize that Herb has summoned his new friends via his intercom, so they rush downstairs. He and Leslie are there laughing together. *You flirt,* thinks Sean to himself.

"So, here we all are. As you know, my name is Herb. Forget last names for now... I know you're Lydia... let's reacquaint ourselves in this quieter atmosphere."

"Sean." They shake hands. "Thanks for the invitation – this is an awesome home."

"I'm Leslie. Pleased to meet you." She bends at the knees slightly. Herb kisses her hand.

"Where's my manners – please follow after me... Someone see if they can find a light switch..." Leslie obliges.

He obviously hasn't lived here long.

"Thank you, young lady. Here we are."

He makes his way to a bar at the other side of the room where there's a tray of four freshly prepared Martinis, and some crackers and cheese.

"My chef is on call, but it's too late to bother her… this is all I could find in the bar fridge. Don't know if these are everyone's favorites, but down the hatch!"

They all slam back the drink, and Lydia, smacking her lips, says…

"Any more where that came from?"

Sean and Les look at each other and copy the scene at the airport –

"Uh oh – looks like we're chaperones again tonight!"

They all laugh and down another two versions of the same drink, this time with a bit more gin, and no olives. Stirred, not shaken. *Screw all that ice.*

Sean's a bit tipsy now. – "Hey, I like'm shaken, not shtired," doing his best 007 imitation.

"Well big boy, get behind this bar and show your stuff," replies Herb jokingly.

Sean slaps his hands and exclaims, "Finally – someone who recognizes talent when he sees it. Thank you, fine sir." – They both bow to each other. Sean speaks in his British accent…

"Madam Forsythe – what is your pleasure this evening?"

Leslie loves this side of Sean – the joker, always quick to make anyone laugh.

"How about a strawberry daiquiri, you smart ass."

"Coming up, your highness."

Lydia's impressed, and nods to Herb – "Smart kid, isn't he? I had no clue he could tend bar so well."

"And you, kind sir?"

Herb answers – "Young man, I would like a rusty nail if you don't mind."

"M'lady?" looking at Leslie.

"A Guinness for your wench, fine sir", bending at the knees once more.

"Coming up everyone" he says, wagging his head.

Sean serves them up with flair and gusto, having the time of his life. Never has he seen such opulence, but never has he seen Lydia and Leslie so loosened up. *We should make this a habit,* he thinks.

The rich guy leaves the room for a second to put on some music. The mansion's elaborate sound system doesn't escape Sean's ear. *For an old guy, his taste is pretty good.* When he's back in the room, he asks if anyone is interested in a dip in his outdoor heated pool.

"There's a hot tub too for the wimps," he says daringly. "Clothes optional."

More booze, some good music... On a dare, they all jump into the huge hot tub barely dressed, having to first race across some snow. They all laugh for hours on end. The alcohol and weed helped a bit...

"Hey mom, when's the last time we had so much fun?"

Lydia replies –

"Son, it's been way too long!"

Leslie, mildy entertained by the rich sugar daddy, says, "Hey Herbie, who do you like, her or me?" The question doesn't need answering.

Lydia holds a lit cigar to Herb's face.

"Who do *you* think, young lady?"

She tries to tease him to have a little fun, but he's had his eye on the prize all night. As predictable as *that* was, no one would have guessed what else was coming.

Sean and Leslie had never seen each other with so little clothes on, and they both were intrigued. Somewhere in their subconscious minds, some barriers had dissolved. They make very subtle, but meaningful hints of sexual interest in each other throughout this night, more so than in the past. The tension had started a few weeks ago for the both of them, and tonight's atmosphere helped it along.

Leslie volunteered to get more drinks for everyone, so she grabs a towel and heads for the house. Herb mentions the heated sidewalk back to the side entrance – "I know the kitchen is only 20 feet away, but it's much nicer on the feet than that snow."

Les turns her head back. "Hey Sean – gimme a hand. You mix better than I do."

"Now you two behave yourselves" Sean says as he leaves the hot tub. Towels are in a high pile within arm's length.

In a dimly lit kitchen, Sean mixes each drink and places them on a serving tray. Leslie is poking around the kitchen being nosy. Sean catches a few glimpses of Leslie's form outlined by the light of an open refrigerator door. His almost twenty-year-old body responds like any red-blooded male…

Les asks – "Hey, you hungry? There's left-over pizza here."

Sean responds, "No thanks, we should get back to the hot tub – I'm cold. And, you know how mom gets without her booze." With that comment, he willingly carries the serving tray.

"Oh thanks – I was going to get that," Les says, then gives him a peck on the cheek.

Back at the hot tub, everyone continues to tell stories for a while when Herb suggests they all retire.

"It's almost three in the morning folks. I think I know where your mom is staying tonight," he stammers, "you two are on your own. I have nine bedrooms, so you figure it out. The maid shows up around eight, so leave your doors closed."

Lydia and Herb grab towels and make their way inside. Sean and Les chat a bit, then Les gets out and begins stacking glasses and ashtrays on the serving tray. Sean can't stop staring. He gets out and wraps a towel around his waist. Their hands touch a few times; they keep getting closer… Sean backs off and says –

"Hey, let's get this shit into the house, then I'll have you a game of pool." He feels more comfortable now… Les takes the hint and replies – "Sure, see you downstairs."

Sean figures the games room in the basement is far enough away from the master bedroom that some music won't interrupt anyone… He dims the lights just a touch and sets up the table. Of all the things Sean is good at, pool really isn't one of them, but he knows the basics. As he is about to head to the wet bar, Les comes downstairs with two martinis, still dressed in her push-up bra and panties.

"How's *that* for a sexy waitress," she says. "Service like this is hard to come by in our little town."

Indeed.

They touch glasses – *Cheers,* they both say. Sean sips his, Leslie gulps hers till it's done.

"Whoa! Go easy there… what's up with that?"

"No time like the present to have fun. So dude, you gonna explain the rules again? It's been well over a year since I played eight-ball at the hall back home."

Sean does his best to stay focused and be serious; this is his typical self when in his 'teaching' mode. They decide on a mix of rules that wouldn't make it into a competition, but they agree it's OK for 3AM on a Saturday night.

"You break," Sean tells Leslie.

"Now *that* I know how to do…"

Les's alcohol intake has not affected her eye-hand coordination, at least from Sean's point of view. Her slightly off-angle break sends one solid into a corner pocket.

"Solids it is… watch this."

Sean watches. Not her cue stick, but her. She looks so intent on making the shot, it's as if she's alone in the room, not caring what she looks like. Her breasts are flattened out on the table, emphasizing her cleavage. A split second before she takes the shot, she catches Sean's eye. *That's all I needed to know,* she says to herself. *Sigh – OK, what now?*

She nails the shot, but then misses the next. Sean steps up for his turn, and calculates his strategy.

"Dude, you look way too serious. I'm getting a beer. You?"

"I'm OK for now. You know, you didn't leave me with much."

"I'll make it up to you."

Leslie walks slowly to the bar, gets a beer out of the fridge and pours it into a Pilsner glass. She draws a long gulp and eyes Sean over the rim.

He misses. Leslie picks up her pool cue, saying, "Do I have to show you *everything?*"

"You're forgetting who taught who."

She tries to aim, but the angle's not right.

"Hey, you'll miss it that way. Look – sit on the edge of the table – the cue goes around your back – like this."

Sean softly places the pool cue behind her, and guides her arms into position.

"Keep your left arm steady... arch your back to clear the stick."

She does, puffing her chest out more by taking a deep breath. His eyes can't avoid what she has been flaunting for the past few hours. Their eyes lock, and Leslie lifts her chin to Sean's face. He can't back down now. They kiss softly at first. Leslie drops the pool cue and reaches behind Sean's head to pull him in tighter... he wraps his arms around her waist.

———————

It was a clear and beautiful Canadian sunrise if you were awake to see it. The housekeeper has already been through the kitchen picking up half-empty glasses from last night's revelry. "What a mess!" she says in her Slovakian accent, pouring it all down the sink. "No wonder they need so much aspirin in the morning."

Her usual rounds of the house are tempered with a light knock on the various half-open bedroom doors – you never know where sugar daddy has brought home his next ex-wife.

Sean stirs. Leslie's arm slaps his leg as she turns over... they both wake up and look at each other. You could literally cut the air with a knife.

Leslie bolts upright... "Oh Jesus... it wasn't a dream" she mutters, hands over her mouth. Sean stirs and looks up at Les. He knew before his head hit the pillow that this was meant to be. It felt *right*. To him, this is life's way of making decisions for him.

Les demands his attention...

"Have you *any* fucking idea what this looks like to anyone but us? We're supposedly related, for God's sake. We may have an album deal, and they think we're related too – that was the pitch – we're cousins!"

"Aw Christ"... He picks up a roach from the ashtray, but Leslie slaps it out of his hand.

"Smarten up dude, we have to act like we hate each other again." After about eight seconds of silence, they look at each other and break out into the most hilarious gut-wrenching laughter. They can't stop themselves; the more they try, the harder they laugh. The housemaid overhears them, saying to herself, "Oh *houseguests*... more sheets to wash."

Sean leans towards Les. They kiss, then begin to make love again. The bedroom is drenched in the bright sunlight reflected off a nearby mountain. They both smell the aroma of fresh brewed coffee.

"Hungry?" he asks.

"Hungry for you," Leslie growls.

Sigh. Finally, after all this time, Les feels strangely whole and very much at peace, like she's finally come home. After climax, their eyes are locked. They each know what the other is asking...

Yes, of course...

Chapter 19

The day at *Sunshine Village* is a great opportunity to blow off a lot of pent-up emotional energy. With no one around, they can be themselves, holding hands, staring into each other's eyes. Rather like a honeymoon.

The day of snowboard instructions pays off; they're both able to hold their own on the beginner's slopes, so they book another day's worth of equipment rentals and hire a trainer just for the two of them.

"I'll see you guys tomorrow. All your equipment will be right here when you get here in the morning."

"Thank you – Now I think we're going to go soak in some hot water."

On their way back down the road to the town of Banff, Leslie looks out over a stone railing. "Let's stop and look. You can park right there." Sean pulls over and they climb out. *Oh, I'm stiff…* The view is breathtaking, with the sun beginning to set, bathing the clouds in orange and red.

"It's so beautiful here. I'm not used to all these mountains."

Sean seems a little quiet. "What's up Sean?"

"My mind is totally blown. I can't believe what has happened with us, and here we are in one of the most beautiful spots in the world. It's like I'm having trouble taking it all in – my eyes keep tearing up; I've got this lump in my throat half the time…"

"I noticed," is all she needs to say…

"Thanks Les." He takes her hand… "It's no wonder this happened, I mean, we know each other so well. We like a lot of the same things, and there's Indigo Insight. But I don't know if it's something we should talk about to everyone, or be quiet about it. I'd literally like to shout it from this mountain, but I'm not sure it would be the right thing to do."

"You know Sean, if I'm honest with myself, I've had feelings for you for a long time. At least since graduation, maybe even before. I always put those feelings aside though, you know – because we're cousins supposedly. But after the DNA thing, something changed. Being away at art school seemed to help a lot. I even told someone about it, a really close friend who said that my feelings were natural, that I shouldn't ignore them. Anyways, here we are."

"Huh! Funny you mention graduation. I'll never forget how you looked stepping out of that limo. You have one fine rack. Nice butt too." Smiling, she slaps him on the arm, and they quickly lock hands again. Sean continues, "I suppose we'll have to keep all this under wraps until we can break it to everyone gently, though – I'm not sure there's any subtle way to do that. Can you imagine announcing *'Ladies and gentlemen, Les and I aren't related. We're actually sleeping together now. Put that in your pipe and smoke it!'* Christ, what are we going to do?"

Leslie detects the frustration in his voice. "Sean, let's just play it safe for now and not mention this to anyone. Keep up the story we're related, for now anyways. Things have a way of working out. We obviously belong together, but we shouldn't change our behavior or people will pick up on us."

"Ya, that sounds like the best thing to do right now. But – I think we should talk to mom about it. Let's not make the same mistake she made – we're all in this same boat together, and we at least owe her our honesty. And to be a little selfish, we could just be ourselves around her."

"I like that. Yes, let's talk to her tonight at dinner. Good thinking, babe."

"Done deal. But no PDAs until then."

Leslie's quizzical look makes Sean explain – "Public Displays of Affection. An acronym. Get it?"

"Got it."

"Oh – hey, do the floor boards creak between your bedroom and mine back home?"

Again Leslie looks puzzled – *Why the hell would you care if the...* it hits her, and they both laugh.

The conversation grounds their love not just romantically, but intellectually as well. They have acknowledged their feelings for each other, and although the future looks unclear, they at least have a short term strategy that won't hurt themselves or anyone around them. They both feel very safe in each other's love, and yet they also feel the unfairness of having to hide it from everyone. Their hands clench tightly all the way back to the hotel, not in desperation, but with an eager and fresh energy they both find wildly invigorating.

"I feel all toasty inside," Les purrs, as she leans her head on Sean's shoulder.

"Me too. Let's have an awesome week together, what say you?"

"You're on big boy! Woo hoo." she yells. They high-five each other.

Sean leads with a suggestion: "I do believe we have a couple of hours to kill between now and dinner."

———————————

"So children, how was your day on the slopes?"

She is interrupted by the waiter, dressed in a finely appointed black suit, delivering buns and butter to the table. He inquires about drinks. The restaurant, one of many in this resort town, is top notch. Sean even spied an actor across the room he once saw in a movie theater as a child.

"Strawberry daiquiri for myself. Children?"

They pick up on Lydia's upper crust behavior.

"Thank you, mother – I will have a vodka martini, Grey Goose if you have it."

"Certainly sir. Miss?"

Leslie eyes the drink menu. "Same as mum."

"Very good. I shall be back in no time." The waiter turns on his heel, swiftly vanishing.

"The hills were great mom. I'm feeling muscles I never thought I had though," replies Sean, twisting his torso side to side. "We'll be back tomorrow if that's OK. It's a blast. You should have seen Leslie. A regular skater girl."

"I'm glad you're having fun. It's about time you two spent some quality time together somewhere away from home. How long has it been? A year away in England?"

"You know mom, we *do* spend a lot of time practicing, with LA coming up."

"I appreciate that, I said quality *alone* time."

If she only knew.

They chat more about their day when the drinks arrive, then place their orders for appetizers and main course. The waiter has also brought the dessert menu at Lydia's request, so she shares it with Leslie.

"Leave room for sweets, Sean, these are decadent."

"I'll be sure to do that. So mom, what did you do all day? You start your conference tomorrow, right."

"Right you are. Well, Herb had to leave for a flight, so he cooked us breakfast then took off. He sent his driver back to me – he told me to use him for the day." Her eyes scan the dessert menu. "Have you any idea how much there is around here to see? He was my very own tour guide. Let's see – well, we went up a gondola just on the edge of town to the top of a mountain – Sulfur Mountain it's called. Tourist trap kind of thing, but very pretty. As you know the day was clear, so we could see for miles up there. Then he took me to a museum on the main drag, after which he took me to this cave where one could smell sulfur from the water. Very pretty but smelly – you know, rotten eggs. Then we took this drive along highway 1-A that runs parallel to the Trans-Canada. Apparently built just as a scenic tour through the area. Absolutely beautiful. Lands you in Lake Louise if I'm not mistaken. All very breathtaking and grandiose.

"And hey – you guys cleared out real early. How did you get back here?"

"Taxi. We hadn't a clue where we were, but after a short description, the dispatcher knew exactly the place to send the cab. This Herb dude is well-known from what I could tell. And he doesn't even live here year-round."

"No, he lives in Texas where he runs an oil company. He hates hotels, so he keeps places like this around the world."

That is Lydia's cue. Smirking, she reaches for her purse and pulls a key ring and dangles it, saying…

"Eat your hearts out people, I've the keys to his mansion. How's *that* for being a weekend hussy!"

"Oh Christ, you gotta be *kidding* me,." exclaims Leslie – "What, are you *marrying* this guy? He'd be a great catch!"

"No way. Neither of us wants commitment. Just the odd rendezvous now and then. He's a nice enough guy, but I don't need his money, and he doesn't need an obsessive compulsive bitch leaning on him."

There are a few seconds of silence when Lydia continues laughingly:

"OK, you could have disagreed with me there!"

Sean, not missing a beat, says…

"Oh sorry – so you *do* need his money."

Lydia picks up a bun and tosses it at her son. The bartender sees it from the corner and shakes his head. The table beside them glance with disapproval.

"You're cut off. Two drinks and you start a food fight in a five-star restaurant." He's actually a little embarrassed.

"Sorry – I'm having too much fun. I'll settle down, promise," she says through her giggling. The waiter approaches and fills up their water goblets.

"Your appetizers are on their way."

They appear seconds later. Escargot, stuffed mushrooms, and a small cheese platter.

"Sean, Les – so-o-o what's going on with you guys?"

Lydia keeps her eyes down so they can glance at each other. *Shit, she knows.*

"Mom, I'm not sure what your question means, but there's something we want to talk about with you. A 'development' of sorts."

Lydia is no spring chicken. When Sean used the word "we", she knew…

"Go on." She lets them squirm.

Both Sean and Leslie take turns setting up the scene for last night – the DNA revelation, feelings they began acknowledging for each other… they're cut off by Lydia mid sentence.

"So, you *finally* hooked up." She keeps her head down, playing with her appetizers. "About bloody time. Listen you two," Lydia says as she leans forward, both hands now on the table – "I can be an impatient bitch, but I have all the time in the world for you guys. I saw this coming years ago. Do I look stupid? God, why do you think I wanted both of you on this trip? No better place for this to happen than somewhere away from home in a romantic setting.

"You're meant for each other. Look how natural you are together. I've had this in the back of my mind since I found out about your adoption, Les, but didn't think it would happen like this. Hey, I think outside the box, so I just nudged it along a bit."

Sean and Leslie are in shock, faces white.

Lydia sighs in contentment and sits back, dabbing the corners of her mouth with her napkin.… "Let me tell you what *I've* seen. You started 'noticing' each other even before the DNA test. At first, I didn't want to be too hopeful, or pry too much – I knew how shocked you both were when you did find out, so I gave you your space. During all those shopping trips together, the spa weekends – your sibling rivalry disappeared. I knew then it was just a matter of time, unless of course either of you became interested in someone else. Not likely though – you're both so driven and goal oriented. Guys, this is *perfect*. You're absolutely *perfect* for each other."

Sean and Les search for each other's hands under the table.

"There's no uncomfortable learning or testing period – you've known each other for a long time; you work and play together well… What you guys have is something I could only ever hope for, and half the world. I mean it guys. You have my approval and blessing. Now, let's see you kiss, and then raise a glass." Lydia's firm words are somewhat betrayed by the tear in her left eye, and the crack in her voice.

Sean and Les interrupt each other…

"You mean – we're here because… because you *knew???*"

"Leslie, when I saw Sean looking at you the way he does, I just knew I had to do something about it. Maybe I'm a freak, but I know my son, and how the odd girlfriend was just a distraction to him. Anyone too serious was always out the door – he had goals. But a good man needs a good strong woman behind him, and that's what you are. You're no push-over, and you're respectful as well. You simply bounce off each other really well."

"More ways than one," Sean interjects in a low voice. The comic relief was well timed. Leslie uses her napkin to wipe a tear from her eye… Lydia puts her hand on Les's thigh.

"I always thought of you as my daughter, and I'm sorry for being so tied up with my upset with Malcolm way back when. But hey, I was no better, so who am I to get angry. Marj is a peach of a woman, and I couldn't argue with the arrangements everyone agreed on. I'm so proud of you, and it's a dream come true to see you two guys together."

"Can I call you mom too when we're together?" Les asks.

That catches Lydia off-guard.

"Why of course!"

Sean feels the lump in his throat get bigger, looks around, and says to Leslie –

"Sweetie, Lydia asked for something we haven't given her yet."

"Huh?"

He leans towards her, lips pursed.

"Oh, *that!*"

The kiss lingers for a few seconds. When they part, Lydia raises her glass, insisting they do the same.

"Now *there's* something to celebrate!" She puffs her chest with pride.

Perfect timing – two waiters appear with three plates of incredible food, and a bottle of 2008 Niagara Merlot. The kids are distracted with each other, so Lydia takes over…

"That plate over there, this one here…" She sniffs the cork and sips the tasting pour. "Perfect. For all three please."

The meal is sumptuous, and dessert even better. Another bottle of wine continues to lubricate the conversation, when Sean asks…

"Mom, listen, there's only a few people who know all about Les and me. What do you think is the best approach from here? We talked about it today and thought to just keep it under wraps for the time being. I know you said you'd talk to dad, but this is something new."

"That's the politician speaking in you. Yes, that's my advice; too much honesty only messes things up. But – I'm not sure what your medium-term goals should be. Maybe at some point, have a family meeting and divulge everything. That would take care of family, but not the rest of the town."

Lydia thinks, with her finger in the air halting any interruptions.

"I got it. Get the TV studio to do a story on you. They do those half-hour shows Sunday nights on channel 10. They could let out a lot of teasers a few weeks before to get a good audience. Kind of like a 'reveal,' or coming-out."

Lydia has another thought, but dismisses it.

"What?"

"Oh nothing…"

"Mom!"

Sigh – "Well, I shouldn't be suggesting this, but – if this is really going somewhere, relocating and starting fresh is another idea. It solves everything."

"Huh – didn't think of that," responds Leslie.

"Just a silly idea. But you should indeed keep this to yourselves for now."

Why did I bring that up? I'd miss them terribly.

"And say – are either of you using birth control?"

Sean and Les glance at each other with a lost look…

"Well, you both should get to your doctors to talk over all your options. In the meantime, well… *you know.*"

"Yes, mother," they both chime.

After finishing half her plate, Lydia swallows her last gulp of wine – "I have phone calls to make. I'm going to head off to my room, so you two stay here till whenever you want. Order a snack to bring back to your room if you like."

"Thanks, mom." Leslie gets up and hugs Lydia for a good few seconds.

"Yeah mom, you're the best." Lydia kisses him on the forehead.

"Sweet dreams!" she says, heading for the exit.

Sean and Leslie hold hands loosely as they look at each other in astonishment.

"I'm totally overwhelmed. I *did not* see that coming," exclaims Sean. "But I suppose I shouldn't be surprised; she does know me inside and out."

Leslie shakes her head. "Isn't it amazing how she saw this way before us. She's a pretty smart lady if you ask me, but then, I suppose our behavior did have tell-tale signs from what she described."

"Which is why we have to be careful back home. It won't be easy to keep apart – maybe we should structure something on some kind of schedule for alone time until it all comes out."

"Sure – let's talk about it tomorrow. My head hurts."

With that, the two new lovers close up shop and head to their rooms. As if in a daze, each of them is opening their separate hotel room doors, when Sean pauses and whispers down the hall...

"Pssst. Get over here wench! There might be a Guinness in the bar!"

"Thought you'd never ask!!!"

After two days of snowboarding, Sean and Leslie are ready for some down time. In the restaurant, they meet a group of students who are over from Germany for language training. Most of them know English fairly well, so what little knowledge Sean has of the area is passed on to the group. He points to a small map on the back of a brochure.

"Take this road up the mountain to a large parking lot, and ask for Monique at the rental counter. She'll set you up with everything you need. Perhaps we'll see you up there for lunch."

"Oh sure. You not skiing after breakfast?"

"Not today. Perhaps in the afternoon."

Sean and Leslie lounge around the restaurant, drinking coffee and enjoying themselves. They decide to spend the morning just walking around the huge hotel to perhaps absorb some history and give their muscles a break. They are quite taken by the architecture: the stonework, the age... *Look how those stone steps are so worn* Leslie points out. They slowly stroll from shop to shop, buying the odd souvenir for friends and family. Upstairs, there is a large banquet hall with staff running to and fro preparing dozens of tables for an upcoming meal.

"It's so classy and elegant, nothing like what they build today," observes Les. Sean lets go of her hand to look at his watch.

"You starting to get hungry? What do you say we meet that German group up on the mountain for lunch? By the time we get there, it'll be 11:30."

They have lunch around a large fireplace with their German acquaintances, who are very friendly and want to know all about Sean and Leslie. They chat about college, family, and their upcoming trip to LA. Then Leslie has each of them tell their name, where they're from, and something about their lives.

"You sound like our English teacher back in Germany." Everyone laughs.

With lunch done, they gear up and head over to a ski lift. At the top of an intermediate run, Sean yells – "Last one down is a rotten egg." It's a very cold day, so after a few runs, everyone heads to the lounge for a hot drink. They eventually part company with the German group... one of the guys exchanges email addresses with Leslie; he is interested in Indigo Insight.

"I think he's more interested in you than our band," observes Sean.

"Look who's jealous," says Les as she pokes Sean in the ribs.

"Ouch! That hurt. Man, I'm sore all over. You?"

Leslie agrees. "I could really use a massage. Hey – I've got an idea!"

Sean figures out what she's thinking... "The *spa!* Let's do it! You know what mom said. She's going to kick my butt. I hope it's not too much."

Back in town, they book appointments for a side-by-side 90 minute full-body Swedish massage. *We just had a family cancel – are you ready now?*

The next day they took the rental car along this highway 1-A Lydia mentioned, and marveled at the vistas, the wildlife, but mostly each other's company.

What's it going to be like in a year or two? Leslie ponders to herself. Sean is still a bit of an enigma in her mind, sometimes calculated and sure, other times not so much… But then she remembers the butterflies in her tummy every time she sees him walk through a doorway, or when he adds a great hook into the lyrics of a song she can't quite complete, or when he closes a concert with his gravelly voice… "Thanks for coming out everybody. We're Indigo Insight," taking Leslie's hand in his while they bow.

The week flies by for all three. Sean and Les get to see many more sights, while Lydia networks throughout the day in her usual savvy way. Each night around the dinner table is a similar experience – not necessarily the same restaurant, but the same routine – dinner, fine wine, and at least some dancing. As the week progresses, Lydia gives in to her tiredness earlier and earlier – *Hey, I'm no spring chicken.* But Sean and Leslie live it up till one or two each night, either in the club, or walking around town and finding a lounge or bar to have drinks, dance, and talk. They sit with other people often, listening to their stories – they're both good listeners, and people pick up on that. Their relationship is strengthened as every hour passes.

This is what it's supposed to be like, they both often think.

———————————

The day of departure, Lydia asks Sean to drive back to the Calgary airport.

"Son, I have some work things to take care of – I'll sit in the back so I can spread out my things."

"Sure – let me set the GPS."

Once on the Trans Canada Highway, the two in front join hands. Noticing it, Lydia smiles. Just then her cell rings.

Sigh – "They just can't do without me for a few days. Yet another panic." – she apologizes as she deals with the third crisis this week.

The hour and a half ride to the airport is mostly quiet except for the odd conversation Lydia engages in over her cell. Sean and Leslie admire the view – it was dark when they drove out five days ago. As they leave Banff National Park, Sean sees the sign for Canmore.

"*Hey* – that's where my classmate in England comes every winter to snowboard. I must have missed it coming in. They had winter Olympics here one time apparently. His dad was in the biathlon. You know – ski, shoot – ski – shoot."

"Huh? That's an Olympic sport?" questions Les.

"Yeah, inspired by the military. Their rifles are really cool – Joe has photos of his dad with his silver medal."

Lydia enjoys listening to the two of them chat as if she's not there. She hears the respect they have for each other in their voices. *Ah, young love.*

———————————

"Well, let's find somewhere to park it for a couple of hours. We're early, and the plane's on time. How about there?"

Sean points to a lounge. With luggage in tow, they make their way to a waitress waiting with menus in her hand.

It's as if they're saying good-bye. Sean and Les know they can't be like this back home, so they drink up every last bit they can, holding hands, arms intertwined. Lydia is quite aware of the dynamic, and purposefully makes herself scarce with her so-called interventions over the phone. Now seated at a table, she senses a quiet lull in their communication. She puts her cell away and squeezes both their hands –

"I don't give a shit what happens. You guys are my family, and I'm your greatest fan. Don't you ever forget that."

Yes, indeed, they are family. The bonding of the past week will carry them through some tough times.

Chapter 20

It's a cold Tuesday evening, and the heating doesn't quite take the chill out of the air. In the basement of an industrial building, a circle of men are seated in metal folding chairs. Guests listen as two or three speak in generalities about how membership to the "Group" has changed their lives, saved their marriages, and improved their outlook on life. Then a half-hour presentation describes the Group's place in European and American history, the ancient vows of secrecy expected from members, and some of the symbology used in their ancient literature. Finally, there is a reading of the Group's charter.

After one more testimonial, they are instructed to stand, fold up their chairs, and turn their backs to a wall about twenty feet from them.

"Everyone close your eyes please." He instructs another member – "Brother, please stand in front of our guests to ensure everyone remains honest."

With that, the guests hear footsteps, a clunk, then something grinding… about thirty seconds later, they are instructed:

"Guests, please turn around and enter this room in single file."

They comply. All are taken aback by the imposing large oval table, obviously very old and not from *this* hemisphere. The room is dark except for the light that a few pedestal candles shed. They are instructed about where to stand, then a few more questions are fielded. Some are left unanswered, such as the meaning of the symbols engraved in the table, and the identities of the men in other chapters. *All will be revealed in its own time* they were told. Once the meeting starts, perfect silence is expected.

Someone approaches the table, picks up an ornate hand bell, and rings it three times. The din stops, and everyone takes their places.

Dead quiet. Everyone could hear the person next to them breathing. The man with the hand bell waits for a few seconds, scans the room, and places it back on the table. More silence... the guests are intimidated by the resolute stillness of the inner circle; they are in perfect formation, hands clasped, heads bowed, eyes closed. *Should I be doing the same?* some think to themselves. *They're even breathing in unison.* After what seems like an eternity, the stillness is broken by someone at one end of the table – he takes a deep breath, and utters a short sentence the guests cannot understand. The rest of the members chant in response with the same low, guttural phonetics that sound very bizarre to anyone hearing them for the first time. They repeat this three times. The same man then speaks in English:

"Dear guests. We thank you for your interest in *Altus Ordo*. You now know some of our history, the reason we exist, and the kind of men that are worthy of such a calling. You may leave here tonight with absolutely no obligation, but may I remind you of the agreement of non-disclosure you signed before entering this room – please know that we take such legal matters very seriously. What you see and hear tonight is of the utmost secrecy and privilege. You are expected to honor your word."

The speaker begins circling the table, waving his arms with passion as he continues. "What you witness tonight is a very small part of how we conduct ourselves behind these wall. For instance," he says spinning on his heel... "we do not wear common apparel, or talk in common language. Certain traditions are kept for membership's eyes and ears only, as the power unleashed by sacred ritual is for the initiated only. We honor the customs and beliefs of our founders, all for very good reason, and it is this: the ungodly world we inhabit would be a far worse place if it were not for the actions, bravery, and steadfastness of our members. If you love your family, country, and God, then we would be pleased to consider you for membership, and honored to have you stand with us in our purpose." He then returns to his station at the head of the table. "Brothers, you know what is next."

With that order, the men in the inner circle open their eyes, then pick up a shallow stone dish, each which has a mixture of sage and other herbs. They ignite the contents with a wooden match, blowing on the embers. They step towards their guests, waving one hand over the dish, dispersing the smoke.

The speaker explains – "This is a cleansing ceremony gentlemen, used by indigenous societies all through mankind's history. Breathe in the pungent smoke. Imagine it replacing anything impure in you mind, heart, and body." He raises his voice as he looks to the ceiling… "Imagine it sanctifying your life's vision and purpose. Imagine it igniting the warrior in you – the poet in you – and the revival of long-past battles lost to mankind's sin, sloth, and greed. Imaging regaining your very own *POWER!*"

The guests feel light-headed. Their hearts are pounding, and most are shifting from one foot to the other, feeling a strange transference of energy directly into core of their flesh.

"I want to hear someone tell me they're sick of the status quo!! I want to hear someone tell me they are tired of how liberal society is letting this country become so ungodly!" He gets a response.

"I am!" someone yells from a corner of the room. "Me too!" A third one pipes in… "Death to evil!" Soon the room is filled with overwhelming responses. The speaker walks around the room, waving his fist in the air… "Then let's DO something about it! Let us become the answer to the moral poverty that surrounds us!" He pauses. "Brother John…" he summons.

The man that rang the hand bell picks it up once more, ringing it three times. The guests know what this means… the room returns to silence as the members place the stone vessels back on the table. The speaker repeats himself in a much lower tone… "Then gentlemen. You know what to do. *Altus Ordo* is a means to an end. The right end. Speak to the man who invited you if you wish to take the next step. Good evening to you all."

The members are back in formation, hands clasped, heads bowed, eyes shut. The final words – the unintelligible words – are spoken again. Just as everyone is asked to close their eyes, they hear a clunking, grinding sound at one end of the room. The cinder block wall begins moving to the left, slowly creating an opening just large enough for the men to walk out single file.

As the final few leave, the speaker remains. Once sure of his privacy, he flicks a light switch on a far wall and begins blowing out candles. A voice from the corner speaks, but he is not startled.

"So Rudman... think you got a few more conscripts? They looked really enthusiastic. You're quite the motivational speaker."

Underbridge steps out from the shadows. His lumberjack shirt, dirty jeans, and five o'clock shadow were great cover... no one had a clue who was in their presence.

"Thanks, I was always good in high school theater you know." He chuckles. "These poor saps actually swallow all this secret society bullshit. We'll have a huge group of zealots before the week is through. They'll be needed soon – things are heating up south of town."

Underbridge is impressed with Rudman's handle on things. "Well Greg, you know I'm not here to look over your shoulder – I enjoyed the entertainment. Good work."

Rudman responds – "Thanks Pete. I'm actually not sure we have the right man for our job yet, but I thinks he's close by. This town is full of these religious rednecks. Listen, if you're in town for the night, why not join me at my hotel for drinks. I've some strategy items to go over with you anyways."

"Done deal. Let's get out of this dingy basement."

Chapter 21

"OK – one more time through the list." Leslie and Sean are piling up gear and suitcases in the garage.

"Drums"

"Check!" (Les did get her digital kit.)

"My guitars."

"Check!"

"Amy's keyboard."

"Check!"

"Bass."

"Check!"

"Patch chords"

"Check!"

This goes on for a few minutes when Mark's step-dad drops him off at the head of the driveway. Sean doesn't miss the opportunity. He races to the side of the car, and before Mark has a chance to slam the car door shut, he sticks his head in and shakes the driver's hand.

"Mr. Cunningham – good to see you again."

He's impressed with his Sean's manners.

"Thanks for letting Mark come to LA. I have high hopes for us there, so your son may come home with a few bucks in his pocket. It's a great opportunity for him, I'm sure you agree?"

Mark's father is not a fan of their band, and gave him a hard time about the trip – he thought going to LA was a waste of time and money.

"Oh sure. I'm glad you're running things son – good luck to you."

"Thank you sir. I'll have him back in one piece." With that, Sean closes the car door and slaps the side of the vehicle a couple of times. Sean really does take after his mom – any opportunity to use diplomacy is seldom overlooked.

A Chrysler minivan pulls up shortly afterwards. Amy's parents help her unload the suitcases, and walk her to the open garage where the other three are organizing everything.

"Good luck sweetheart – break a leg!" They dispense all the love and hugs they can without embarrassing her too much in front of her friends. Les and Sean make small talk with her folks as Amy starts loading the van. Her folks walk to their van as if to leave, but come walking back with their arms behind their backs. *What's this?*

Amy's dad reveals a magnum of champagne; her mother a handful of crystal flutes.

"We know you guys are going to knock 'em dead. Why not celebrate in advance? Maybe your parents would like some."

Les thinks Amy's folks are the greatest. She turns her head and lets out a whistle that deafens everyone for a few seconds... Malcolm and Marj know that sound... In less that two minutes, they're all in the garage sharing a glass of bubbly, raising toasts, and talking over each other. The excitement in the air is electric.

The little band that could – Les, Sean, Mark, and Amy, have a stab at getting a record deal. The A&R agent had a quota to fill for this year – but he couldn't make up his mind between *Indigo Insight,* and some other angry metal band that had an OK sound as well, so they were both going to California to audition before the "Big Daddy."

Mark is a science geek from an abusive family background and never thought he deserved any success. His step-dad is a car mechanic who can't keep a job due to his drinking. "Why should *you* go to LA" he accuses – "*I've* never been there – why should *you???*" Mark's music teacher intervened and convinced him to let him follow his dreams. Besides, he was paying his own way thanks to all the gigs they played – it was no skin off his nose, right?

"Well, OK," he concedes. "But he better not think this house is a hotel when he comes back with no money!"

His mom serves tables at a local greasy spoon and is quite popular amongst the patrons who show up at six in the morning. She's a bright spot in their day, and an even brighter spot in Mark's life. She often brings home leftovers from the restaurant such as pies, chicken, beef. The owner knows her story and breaks the rules for his star waitress.

"You're a godsend Mr. Walsh – thank you!" There are so many leftovers, she often shares them with her neighbor, an elderly man on a small pension.

Amy's parents are very supportive. A cheerleader in junior high, and on the debate team, Amy is everyone's favorite, including both her parents'. A perky, slim blonde with lots of energy, she melts everyone's heart with her smile, especially when playing keyboards… she could channel any great blues or rock musician, emulating their sounds as if she jammed with them personally. In fact, one of her music competition awards was to cut a song with her favorite singer/songwriter artist from the 90s. She hums the tune to this day. Following that, she made second cut on a talent show that was broadcast state-wide – but she was surpassed by a girl with less talent and longer legs. *Damn judges!*

The 747 touches down on hot, dry LAX tarmac. As everyone powers up their cell phones, the group high-fives each other, keeping the emotional momentum going even though they don't have a clue what the next few days will bring. With a carry-on each, they make their way to the luggage area and find push carts for their suitcases and instruments. Sean makes his way over to Les and says –

"I'll go get our van. Meet me with these guys over at that counter."

She nods.

After a fair bit of work stacking all their belongings onto four luggage carts, they follow Leslie. Sean motions them to an exit sign, mouthing the words "Wait there." He settles up at the counter, rushes to the van, and drives to the other side of the entrance where the rest of them are waiting. No one sees him until he walks through the motion-activated double doors.

"Ladies and gentlemen, I will be your tour guide for your visit to the City of Angels."

While they stack their gear and luggage into the half-ton van, Leslie phones home.

"Hey we made it – we're at the airport. What's that? – Yeah, Sean remembered it after we took off." A short pause – "No way! Oh, thanks mom!" She covers the mouthpiece and says to Sean – "mom kinda noticed the guitar sitting out in the laneway. It started to snow when she saw it. You owe her!"

Back on the phone – "Sean thanks you. No, he has two others with him, so he's covered I think. Say hi to dad."

Family obligations fulfilled, Leslie helps with the last piece of luggage and slams the rear door of the cargo van. They all pile into the front two seats while Sean views a map of LA he printed out just before leaving. There's a thick red line from the airport to their hotel, with turn-by-turn instructions at the bottom. He hands it to Amy, sitting in the front passenger seat. She's only too willing to navigate.

Their hotel's parking lot is right in front of their room, adjacent to the road.

"We can keep the gear in the van guys – no more hauling it around. Look – no one's stupid enough to try breaking in to *that*." He's quite right. The bright parking lot lights, the obvious security cameras, and the location – kitty corner from a police precinct – they can sleep without worrying about the contents of the van disappearing.

They all gather in the lobby with their suitcases while Sean checks everyone in.

"Elevators that way, sir."

"Thank you."

Their room on the second floor is a large studio suite with two queens, a small kitchen, and wet bar. Girls in one bed, the boys in the other.

"I have to sleep with *you?*" complains Mark. "I hear you snore!"

"Hey, we'll pretend we're camping out," Sean says when he announced the sleeping arrangements. "It's the best deal I could get."

"OK – who's up for some grub and a beer?" Mark has been looking forward to this since he took the call from Devon a couple of months ago. Everyone responds with enthusiasm. He opens a drawer in the writing desk looking for hotel info.

"There's a pub on the ground floor according to this visitor's guide. Let's go."

Sean and Les each make an excuse to stay behind. Sean needs to locate tomorrow's agenda, and Les has to use the bathroom. *See you guys downstairs in a couple of minutes.* They wait to hear Mark and Amy's elevator door close, then rush into each other's arms.

"God, it's been too long. I'll be glad when it's all out in the open," comments Leslie. They hold each other, then kiss. They linger in their embrace for a few minutes in silence, enjoying the comfort of each other's love and warmth. "You know, I really do have to pee." Leslie giggles.

"So romantic!" replies Sean. "Yeah, let me find that itinerary. It's got the address and directions to the studio… we can go over it with our navigator." Sean likes how Amy will take on a role without question, and live it to the end. She has been to LA once before, so that qualifies her as chief navigator as far as Sean's concerned.

———————

7:30AM. Sean's watch alarm starts to beep. He stirs, then sits up.

"OK everybody," he says rubbing his eyes – "this is your captain speaking. All hands on deck. Be ready for inspection in thirty minutes."

"Shut *up*." Amy throws a pillow in Sean's general direction.

"Insubordination – drop and do 50 soldier."

Les whispers into Amy's ear – "I have an idea. Keep him distracted."

Leslie slips into the bathroom as Amy asks Sean something about the day. He answers in a serious tone. Les giggles to herself in the bathroom as she fills two glasses full of water. She makes her way back into bed, and suggests Sean take the first shower. He agrees, and as he pushes the bathroom door open, two plastic glasses full of cold water come tumbling down on his head. The girls scream hysterically with laughter.

"Good one sistah!" They high-five each other. Sean fills one of the glasses up and makes his way to their bed.

"Oh no you don't!!!" They hide under the blankets, but Leslie's foot is exposed. He winks to Mark who gives him a nod. *Do it!* Sean swiftly raises blankets and douses them both. Mark is enjoying the antics – "Hey, you don't need a shower *now!*"

In less than an hour, the band is having breakfast in the hotel restaurant as they plan their day. *Meet our rep at the studio for ten, warm up, then play for the "Big Daddy" just before lunch*... i.e. the producer who decides which band goes home.

Amy pipes up – "There's a lot of things to see here after we're done at the studio, so I grabbed some tourist brochures in the lobby. Look – we can tour NBC in Burbank, there's a zoo, Universal Studios… whatcha think?"

"I vote for Universal. Anyone else?" Leslie wants to see the movie sets.

"I'll go with that," says Mark.

"Done," says Sean. "Who brought a camera?" Everyone looks around. Amy is scrambling through her purse…

"Damn, I'm sure I… *here it is!* It's only a point-and-shoot, but it's got 12 megapixels."

"Whatever *that* means" comments Leslie.

"Bigger enlargements," she responds.

"Hey, let's get a group shot now. That wall right there is a huge mirror – c'mon." They all walk over to a spot a few feet from the mirrored wall and pose as Amy holds the camera just at shoulder height.

"Back up a couple of steps… Smile!" *Click.*

They finish breakfast and head to the van. Amy yells *Shotgun!* Sean hands her yet another map, with directions from the hotel to the recording studio.

"Man, you're quite the boy scout," observes Amy. Quickly viewing the map, she says – "Right turn up at those lights."

"Yes Ma'am," he says in his best southern accent.

———————————

The recording scene in any LA studio is a sight to behold. In their own sub-culture, the producers, engineers, mixers, equipment technicians, and assistants make for a very dizzying experience for the uninitiated. Producers see this lot… small-town band makes it good, does some recording, and flops in the charts. That's OK; they're his champagne money. The big ones that make it pay for his house and jet. *Let's see what Indigo Insight is about…*

The "studio" is much bigger than they imagined. Not one, not two, not three… there are six massive recording rooms, all with their own technicians, mixers, and wanna-be singer coffee girls… like a movie Cineplex, but without the popcorn and sticky floors. This studio complex demands nothing but the best from its contractors and employees. After all, royalties are everything.

The receptionist directs them to carry their gear through the large foyer, into another waiting room. Devon told them *you only need the basics — instruments, effects processors, that's it. We have drum kits.* Leslie still wanted to bring her Roland electronic drums; besides, everything fits in one duffle bag.

"Dude, where's our rep? Where are we supposed to go?" Mark is awestruck at the gigantic building, known as the "Hit Maker." His nervousness is annoying everyone a bit. Then, in walks Devon.

A few slaps on the back and encouraging words, the band is led to studio #3, "the smallest recording room" according to Devon. It's huge.

"We're running behind a bit, so you got an hour to set up. I have to go meet someone, so are you guys OK for now? Bathrooms that way — cafeteria further down the hall — the receptionist can answer any questions…"

"No, we're good I think. Thanks."

"See ya in an hour."

A sound technician walks in and introduces himself.

"Hey, I'm Don. I'll be at the sound board when you play. Let me help with your stuff."

"Hey Don, thanks."

They situate the drum kit, keyboard, and amplifiers. Don places top-of-the-line microphones in front of the guitar amps, and starts running cables over to a patch panel. He hands an XLR connector each to Amy and Leslie —

"For your DI box." It feeds their keyboard and drum signals to the patch panel, which is then routed to the sound board 20 feet away.

Electronic drums make no sound… the snare, toms, bass, high-hat, cymbals… all have a cable that attaches to a sound module, which then runs to either an amplifier for everyone to hear, or simply a set of headphones for solo practice. Today, the signal is split between the monitor amp for everyone to hear, and the patch panel. Typical stage and recording setup.

It isn't long till Don is at the mixing board, asking for a separate level from each person.

"Drum kit – you're first."

"The drum kit's name is Leslie!" she giggles and looks around at the others.

"Leslie it is." Don replies over the monitors.

"Kick first."

Les pounds the foot pedal.

"Snare."

This goes on for a couple of minutes as the sound tech sets preliminary levels. He's usually pretty close for a final take, but will fine tune later.

"OK guys, think of a song that is an average of the tunes you'll do today. I'll set levels and EQ, then we're done till show time."

"Um – let's do *Blue Blue Feelin'*. It's got a bit of everything in it."

After they reach the chorus and all the harmonies are working together, Don the sound tech takes about 20 seconds to tweak the levels. *The big guy's gonna like these kids.*

He looks up and sees the excitement and enthusiasm in their faces. He also sees their experience; they're young, but sharp and tight. *They'll do OK.*

The song finishes, and the sound tech walks out into the studio and suggests they take a ten minute break and make it back for 10:55.

"There's a fridge with bottled water in the cafeteria if you're interested."

"Sure, let's go guys."

A loud, deep voice with a strong southern accent comes from the monitors:

"Indigo Insight. I like that name. I'm the guy who's deciding which band goes home today. Why don't you introduce yourselves?"

They go around the room. Sean's last.

"I take it you're the front man. I can see leadership in you. So Sean, what are y'all going to play for me this fine morning?"

Sean clears his throat, speaking into his mike. He can be so smooth...

"An original called *I Got Your Message*."

The rest of the band is shocked. They haven't played that tune in a week, so they all stare at each other in disbelief. *Is Sean out of his bloody skull???*

Sean should have been a psychologist. His understanding of human behavior, especially when he wants something from somebody, is very acute. He knew they needed to be challenged; to have something to fight with and fight for. They've been coasting for a while, and he knew "Big Daddy" behind the glass wanted to hear something with a bit of an edge.

Mission accomplished.

The big daddy likes what he hears. *Another couple originals please* he requests over the speakers. He taps his foot along with the tunes, and picks up their CD to look at the credits. *Tracks 3 and 8 written by Sean and Leslie Hodges.*

They finish song number three.

"Sean and Leslie, come on in to the control room please," he says behind the glass, waving his huge hand. They look at each other and smile.

In the semi dark mixing room, they come face to face with their fate. He's a hulk of a man originally from New Orleans who made it up the ranks as a rapper, then began producing his own wildly successful albums, then others'. He developed an ear for other genres of music, and an instinct that helped him discern the difference between the nobodies and the ones about to go places. He introduces himself, shaking hands with Les and Sean. Their own hands disappear into his….

"Doc. Everyone calls me 'the Doc.' So you two, I see by your credits here, you both collaborate, but there's only two originals. I just heard three. If you can give me another seven, Devon here will be glad to talk a deal with you. You OK with that?"

They both hide their emotions… Sean speaks – "Yes sir, this is why we're here. We have enough material for two CDs so far, and more on the way, so we're OK with a multi-record deal if that's where this is going."

"I like you kid – you're OK. Let's get CD number one out of the gates first before we decide on anything more. Your Indie album did good, so it's about time you had a lucky break. I like how you sound, so we're picking up the recording tab. We manage promo and distribution nation-wide. We make you stars if you're up to it. You blow it, and you get a big fat bill, but your chances are better than good – I'm usually right about these things. Keep up the good work and we'll talk soon." They shake hands again. Sean and Les leave the control room and approach their band mates whispering, *We did it!!!*

The Doc leans over to Devon and says: "Send that other band home. I want a deal with these guys by tomorrow night. You can do that, right?"

Devon gathers his composure. He seldom sees The Doc act so quickly on such a short audition.

"They're young. This may kill'em – you've seen it before."

The Doc chuckles in his low baritone voice. "Well now, look who just grew a conscience… you've been feeding me acts like this for five years. Get lost, and have your lawyer send the contract to my lawyer by end of business tomorrow, with all the usual percentages."

Percentages. Hm. More like rape, thinks Devon.

"Play me another original," the Doc instructs. Indigo Insight are happy to oblige.

———————

Outside in the parking lot, Indigo Insight are stunned and overwhelmed, and it isn't long before they're jumping all over each other in ecstasy. Passers-by gawk as they scream with joy.

"Hey guys – this side of the van..." Sean motions. Hiding themselves from the street, he zips open a duffle bag and pulls out a small bottle of tequila and four plastic shot glasses... "I was saving this for later, but let's do it now..." and pops the cork. Some spills on the ground as he fills everyone's glass.

"Oh yeah, pour it on baby," Les says.

"Well guys, we did it. A signed contract is only a day away, and here we are just a mile or so from Hollywood, drinking booze in a parking lot. Does it get any better?"

"Well, that was some prank you played for our first tune. I should bean you in the head!" Amy says with a smirk. "Scared the crap out of me. It was a shrewd move – made us all edgy. I guess that was a good thing..."

"You're some front man!" exclaims Leslie. "We all appreciate how damn hard you work at all this. Nice to see you loosen up. Cheers!"

"Cheers!" One down. A few more to go... Mark belches, then raises a glass. His demeanor is serious.

"This toast is to the Hodges. Without you guys, Amy and I would be in dead-end jobs, hating every minute of it. Who knows how long this adventure will last, but here's to you two geniuses who made it happen. Cheers you guys." Leslie gives him a huge hug as does Sean.

"We love you guys," adds Amy.

The joy and excitement is truly palpable around these four young adults. They keep working on the bottle while chattering about the next few months, the tour schedule they know nothing about as of yet, and of course the money.

"So Amy, I guess your college plans are pretty well hooped for the next while. How do you feel about that?"

"It's cool. I'd rather be doing this for the next year or two, save all I can, then have my pick of schools. There's a couple places I have my eye on."

"Hey, depending on how things go, you may be able to *buy* the school of your choice!" says Leslie. They touch glasses.

"Mark?"

"I'll probably travel some. Buy a new car. Not sure after that… just leave it in the bank till I get an inspiration. How about you guys?"

Sean and Les look at each other, as if to ask *Should we spill the beans?*

Mark and Amy look puzzled as they hesitate. Too late now.

"Well, about the money – Les and I want to record more, and bow out on a high – you know, not wait till sales drop. We're thinking of some kind of promotion and/or production company to get new bands started, like us."

"Like a business partnership, the two of you…"

"Sorta."

"You don't look sure – what's up."

"Here, have more" Sean pours more tequila into Amy's and Mark's shot glasses.

The cargo door on the side is still open, so Sean seats himself.

"Guys – *guys* – you need to know something." He pauses, waiting for their full attention – "Les and I – well, we're not actually related."

Long pause.

Mark speaks first. "*What the…?*"

A million scenarios run through their minds…

"We simply are not related. Our DNA tests proved it. You know that project…"

"You mean, like one of you is adopted?"

"You nailed it. We need to tell you guys, 'cause you're our best friends and it's wrong to keep it from you. It was bound to come out at some point. The thing is, that was almost two years ago. We've had time to digest it, do some growing, and spend time together. I hope this doesn't freak you out, but Les and I have fallen for each other. I don't know what to say – we were in Banff, and being away from it all, all the boundaries, restrictions, everything – we discovered we were both having the same thoughts about each other."

Sean explains the scenario. Lydia's sister and husband's trip to Romania, Malcolm's affair, Malcolm and Marj taking both the kids.

There's a short silence when Mark says "Fuck it, you know what, you're the best two people I have ever known. I can totally see that happening – you two never really seemed to be related anyways. You have nothing to be ashamed of, and I'm for it. How can it be wrong? I mean, you never knew each other till a couple or so years ago, and here you find out you're not related… You guys love each other. Hey – look at me choking up…" He composes himself. "I suppose *some* people may have an issue with it, but that's their problem. This is your life. Live it the way it makes you happy. Cheers man." He raises his glass. Les replies "You're the best. Thanks." The tequila has loosened up Mark's tongue a fair bit.

Amy's turn.

"You know, with all the crap going on today thanks to greed, hate, jealousy, whatever – you've found out you're for each other. Funny circumstances if you ask me, but hey – this looks like the real thing, right? Something told me you guys were more than just good buddies."

"No question." Sean and Les speak at the same time.

"You got my vote. And mum's the word. Hey – will you be telling your parents about this some time?"

"Yes," says Leslie – "We're still trying to decide on a good time. Lydia thinks it should be sooner than later. We're just struggling with how everyone else will react. I mean, here we're supposedly cousins. Lydia thinks we should do some kind of 'reveal' thing on TV. I'm not sure about that. But one way or the other, we'll be together."

Amy interjects – "I'm remembering something here. It's funny this comes up now. My dad got an email a few months ago from people he knew growing up in the same neighborhood. They were from a 'blended' family before that word was even used, and they were totally unrelated. You know, the Brady Bunch thing. Anyways, my dad explained to me that they moved out of the house to go to college, and *they* ended up together. They're in India somewhere doing archeological work, and came to visit us just this past Christmas. Really cool people. So hey, maybe you have to become grave robbers and fly to the middle east!"

They all laugh.

Sean bows his head in humility – "Guys, I can't say how much Les and I appreciate this." Sean takes Les's hand as he continues. "We've been pulled through a knothole with all this and knowing you're behind us means lots. It's like a ton of weight is off my shoulders."

"Me too," sighs Leslie.

Mark raises his near-empty glass. "To the Hodges. And to all of us!"

"Hear hear!" They empty their glasses, then the bottle.

Just before they're about to leave and do the tourist thing, Sean suggests:

"Look, there's a restaurant across the street. I shouldn't drive, plus I'm hungry."

Everyone agrees. They lock up the van and head over to *El Cholo*.

Once inside and seated, Sean then suggests:

"Ya know what – everyone back home is dying to know what happens here. I say we phone them one by one and make the announcement. My cell has a speakerphone…"

Amy looks at Sean and Les's clenched hands and says, "Don't dial yet. Let me just say – I'm really glad you brought all this up. It took courage, you know? Plus, I could tell you weren't quite your-selves for the past little while. That's it – I'm done."

Sean dials – first the Hodges' home. Then Amy's. Then Mark's. All their parents are exuberant and congratulatory as they recount the experience with "The Doc."

"We'll be home the day after tomorrow as planned. We're painting the town red till then. See ya!"

"Where's our waiter? I'm starved."

"*God* yes…" agrees Amy.

"Nothing too heavy for me," asks Les. "My tummy doesn't feel up to par."

———————————

The airplane ride home is ridiculously upbeat. Rarely seen these days in the recording business, they signed a contract for a CD and a nation-wide six-month promotional tour. The compensation is good, though they're aware of the cut everyone gets: the producer, agent, distribution company… they all get a slice. But – talent this good out-of-the-box is also hard to come by, and The Doc heard it ten bars into the first song.

They're all enjoying the first-class seats, something Sean had pre-arranged – he wanted to spoil everyone whether they had a deal or not. They love the service and the free wine. Leslie excuses herself. *She looks kinda white in the face,* Sean thinks. *Maybe a bug.*

Chapter 22

Indigo Insight receive a hero's welcome when they return home to Grey Falls. Word spread like wildfire through the community shortly after Amy phoned her parents from LA with the news, so not surprisingly, there was a fair-sized entourage at the airport. As they walk through the doors about to go search for their baggage, they are totally surprised by the huge applause and 'Welcome Home Indigo Insight' signs.

"Wow, check that out," Sean says to Mark. "You'd think we were famous or something."

Other people in the terminal look around trying to figure out what all the fuss is about. The four of them aren't used to this kind of attention, so their faces go a bit red, but it doesn't stop Sean from acting the clown. He raises his arms overhead and does a celebratory "Woo hooooo!!!" Everyone responds. They didn't need to lift a finger once they located their luggage and instruments; the crowd of about thirty swarmed around them – "Hey – I got it" – "No it's alright, let me get that for you…" Sean sees Les struggling with her large suitcase – *She doesn't look too good. Maybe the food…*He has to remind himself about showing affection in public…

"Hey Les, you OK? You're looking kinda green around the edges."

"I don't know – I think it's air sickness." She slurs as her face turns white. In less than a second, she's headed for the floor. Sean hardly has enough time to grab her as she goes down. Friends notice and rush to her aid.

"Back off everybody!" Sean orders – "She needs air." He fans her face with his hand, unzipping her insulated jacket. Malcolm is there in a flash and helps Sean move her to a lower traffic area, out of the way. She starts to regain consciousness…

"Do we need an ambulance?" someone shouts.

"I don't think so – she just fainted. Les – Les… you OK?"

She stirs, opens her eyes, and is immediately embarrassed.

"I'll be OK. God it's warm – let me take my jacket off."

She's sitting up now; Sean and her dad help her up to a chair. Amy hands her a bottle of cold water someone handed her…

"Here Les – have a gulp."

The excitement is over, but everyone is treating her with extra attentiveness.

"C'mon, I'm not a cripple… I can walk on my own."

They start making their way to the parking lot.

"Just over this way," Malcolm points. The crowd starts dispersing, waving good bye, many reiterating their congratulations.

"Thanks everyone – you're great," waves Leslie.

"Let's get you home, young girl." Sean and Malcolm are on either side of her; Mark, Amy, and a few hangers-on are managing the luggage carts.

Marj organized a pot-luck at their house for the band and all their parents and families. The size of the meal means a bit of organizing, but this is a small occasion for her in comparison to others she's done. With possibly over fifteen people around the table, she gets Malcolm to put the leaf in the table, and sends Jake to the corner store for more coffee cream. She dotes on Leslie, telling her to put her feet up –

"Are you sure you're OK, honey?"

"I'm still a bit weak. I may go to bed right after supper if you don't mind."

"Anything sweetheart – whatever you feel."

The meal is a grand collection of everyone's specialties, from Asian to Mexican to Italian – there's more than enough for the upbeat crowd. Many toasts are made in honor of Indigo Insight, their parents, and families. Conversation evolves into questions directed to the stars of the show.

"You quitting your day job?"

"Where will you be touring?"

"How many CDs do they want?"

"When will you be on the radio?"

Everyone listens attentively as all four take turns fielding questions and answering them as best they can. After about 20 minutes of this, Leslie excuses herself and heads to her bedroom. People move out of the way, offering a hand.

"Thanks everyone, you've been great – I'm still feeling a bit woozy – think I'll lie down for a bit." She has to shimmy by Sean's chair, which is close to a wall… he leans forward to make room – no one notices the affectionate squeeze she gives his shoulder.

———————————

The various reactions displayed by each of their families are an interesting study in human behavior. Any parent of a child coming home with a guarantee of $100,000 over the next six months does tend to overlook past differences. "The royalties may be more," they all say.

Mark's step-dad takes him ice fishing for the first time in his life. He tells him of a car repair garage that just came up for sale, and how he always dreamed of running his own shop. He has old friends from high school he would hire to help them out; they have trouble finding work too.

"I love fixing cars, son. You know I'd help you out in the same way if I could."

Mark isn't so sure. He sees through his step-dad's greed, but sees his softer side as well. First time actually. They both land a couple of nice trout.

"Now there's a good lookin' supper if you ask me!" he exclaims.

Mark's step dad suggests they flip a coin to see who cleans them.

"Let's see if your recent good fortune helps you out here – I'll likely lose!"

And lose he does. He swears never to try *that* again.

I guess he can be kind of fun to hang out with, thinks Mark.

At Amy's house, her parents wag their fingers at her in a mocking style, saying: "We knew you were good!!! Just think – you can go to that college we were talking about."

"Well, I'm jazzed about the band, not some school thing right now. If things go good and our sales are up, we'll go on tour for who knows how long. But – I do have my sights on school in the long run."

Her folks are supportive of her in anything she pursues.

"We're behind you Amy – I wish I had your luck when our band was playing high school gigs." Her father has recounted – *many* times over in the past – the stories of his band's escapades throughout the seventies – "with our big hair, tight leather pants, and flying-V guitars."

Lydia reads a text message she received during a meeting: "record deal in the bag. possible tour coming up." She's astonished, proud, and can't wait to see her son in person. *I knew he had it in him, that charmer.* She responds "in Salt Lake till Saturday night. You and Les take the condo till then. Lunch next week."

Malcolm and Marj are in awe. They glow with pride for their children. *God must be rewarding us for some reason,* Marjorie thinks, but she has no explanation why. She has never really forgiven herself for their past. *I guess our pasts are forgiven and forgotten after all.*

The next few weeks sees the band practicing daily. Their original material is all they concentrate on in preparation for their first round of sessions at the end of April. The local television studio does a quick feel-good story on them for the tail end of the six o'clock news one evening, which draws more exposure. With their new celebrity status, they take many phone calls, one of which was Sean's old theater teacher suggesting they do a concert to raise funds for the band. Seldom do new bands get any kind of advance from a studio, and they were no exception.

"Mr. White – that's an awesome idea. We won't be getting any money coming in till April or May, so we could use an injection of cash. You know, we're really quite ready to record, but the studio is too busy – so, yes. Let's organize something."

Sean shares the news with the group, and they're all on board.

"We're back to our old jobs. I'll take care of the graphic art-work and printing. Les – see if your old high school friends want to help with putting up posters. Amy – your dad knows the TV people – maybe they can cover the concert itself. Mark – see if that old sound tech from WPCS still works on the side. I'm gonna see if Lydia can pull some strings and get us into the arena."

"Arena? Are you out of your mind?"

"I know it sounds crazy, but if we do this right, it'll be the perfect place. Their sound system is really good, so we'll only need our monitor setup. Lighting too – they got it covered. Let's do this!"

Sean gives them all a day off of practicing so they can all concentrate on their respective jobs. "Let's meet in two days, here – 1PM."

Chapter 23

The women's clinic gets busy around 8:30 every morning. On this particular Wednesday, there isn't an empty waiting-room chair to be found; a mother is on her knees with her 18-month-old over at the children's toy corner, and a lonely looking adolescent girl stands with her mother in another corner, both reading old *Cosmos*. Nurse Patrick enters the room with two folding chairs from another room.

"Here you are – they're a bit rickety, but it's better than standing."

Just then the front door opens and in walks Dr. Kao. After a quick survey of the room, he apologizes…

"Sorry I'm late everyone – car trouble. You'll be seeing me shortly."

Nurse Patrick flashes him a dirty look… *Car trouble my ass.*

He didn't get up at first alarm, and slept through the second. He just isn't the morning person Colleen thinks he should be.

With the crowd beginning to thin out a few hours later, Colleen returns to her desk and goes through the pile of phone messages left by the receptionist, Shirley.

"Midwest Mining – those morons."

The next one catches her eye, so just as she's about to lift the phone off its cradle, it rings.

"Line 3 for you, Nurse Patrick."

"Thanks, Shirley." She lifts the receiver and punches a button.

"Hello, Nurse Patrick speaking." The caller identifies herself, and Colleen's face lights up.

"It's been so long – I was just going to call you! How have you been?" The voice at the other end of the line sounds a bit down. They get through the weather talk very quickly when Colleen directs the conversation, asking for details. She listens for a good minute, with the occasional *Uh huh* and *OK* and finally *Oh dear…*

"I've got time this afternoon – I'll move some things around. 2:30 OK?"

"Thanks, Colleen. See you then." *Click*

Colleen flicks on her monitor. After entering her password, she navigates to the clinic's scheduling screen and blocks off exam room 3 from 2:30 to 3:00PM. She leaves the patient name blank, and enters her own name in the "Physician" field.

———————

It's 1:10 in the afternoon when Amy and Mark show up. They both report on their progress.

"Seems the TV station will at least be doing a short story on us, using the concert as a backdrop. They want interviews even!"

"Excellent, Amy. This keeps getting better. Mark?"

"The sound tech is gone from WPCS, but I did some digging and found out that the arena has a couple experienced guys they use for gigs like this. Should be OK."

"Good. And Les's high school friends are more than willing to put up posters. I talked to mom and we have the arena for the 10th – it's a Wednesday. I know a Saturday would be way better, but even the thirty-somethings like our stuff, so I say we should just commit to it right now."

"Let's do it."

Leslie is quiet, and Sean asks her if she'll be ready for the concert in two and a half weeks. She responds in the affirmative… "It's just a flu bug. I'll get over it."

———————

Malcolm is gathering garbage from around the house to put in the outside bins, and curses the day his ex-wife outsourced garbage pick-up. They've been coming quite early in the morning, so he puts it all out the night before. There's more than usual this week, as Marjorie is helping cater a social at the church. With two bags in each hand, Malcolm trips on the walkway at the rear of the house and deftly uses a bag to cushion his fall.

"Rats!" he says, looking at the split-open trash bag, with its contents all over the ground. "I better go get a shovel." And heads to the garage. The motion sensor at the corner of the house switches on two floodlights. Back with a shovel in his hand, something in the heap of trash catches his eye – a product package he's never seen before. Something clinical-looking. He picks it up and peers over his glasses –

"Quick Response Pregnancy Test," it reads. Huh? He reads it again, turns the box over and over...

"What the..."

His imagination spins, wondering whose it is, Marj or Les's. His instincts lead him to Leslie, but wonders about Marj too. *Les has been away a lot lately. She's been real quiet. I must speak to her in the morning.* Malcolm feels dread in his heart as he pockets the small box and tends to the mess in his yard.

———————

The scene the next morning is not pretty. Sean can't hear a thing, thanks to a bag full of weed he's been indulging in lately... he doesn't do mornings all that well when he smokes pot. Malcolm shows the package to Marjorie, and can tell from her reaction that it isn't hers, despite her red face. Then it turns white:

"Oh Malcolm, you don't think that... that Leslie is..." She can't finish her sentence. All the pride she felt from their success in LA vanishes. "Our past has come back to haunt us, Malcolm. Please be careful with her."

Malcolm makes his way to Leslie's bedroom. The door is open. He knocks on the door frame and approaches her computer desk; she turns around…

"Hey Les. I need to show you something," and pulls the box out of his shirt pocket, explaining how he found it.

"Is it yours? I saw it last night."

Her eyes fall to the floor. After a pause…

"Dad, why were you going through our garbage at eleven o'clock at night?"

"The bag split open. Finding this was an accident. I'd like to think this was your mom's, but we're not having any more children – I had a vasectomy five years ago. Les, I'm in shock – I mean…"

The anguish she feels in the pit of her gut leads to defensiveness. She looks at Malcolm, cocking her head. "You don't know *everything* about me and Sean. All you care about is how we make you look. Leave us alone! Get out of my bedroom please," she begs.

Malcolm is taken aback by her uncharacteristic reaction. *Wait a minute. What does Sean have to do with this?* His heart sinks to the floor… can it be??? Overwhelmed, the box slips out of his fingers, tumbling to the floor. His jaw drops while his eyes moisten – Leslie realizes what her father has now just clued into.

"What does Sean have to do with…" his voice trails off while Leslie turns her back to him in shame.

"Dad, yes, I'm expecting, but I can't keep it. It's all arranged. I know how you feel about this, but I have no choice. Dad, I'm sorry. Please leave my room. Please…"

He tries to object…

"*Please* dad…"

She pushes the door closed behind him.

Good thing Jake is at a weekend sleep over – Malcolm is near a breakdown. *She can't have an abortion – that's murder.*

Back in his own bedroom, Malcolm and Marjorie console each other. They hold hands while sitting on the edge of the bed. Malcolm's voice shakes as he speaks, trying to make sense of it all.

"Marj honey, she wants an abortion. That's just plain wrong – you know I'm not much of a church-goer, but I know how sacred a young fetus is… she should have the baby and give it up for adoption. Maybe we should all talk about this together."

Marj cautions him about his blood pressure – "Malcolm, go easy. We don't want you to hurt yourself. Or anyone else. Are you sure this is the right thing?"

"We have to get it out into the open, Marj, and resolve it as a family. You go get Les, I'll get Sean."

Malcolm gets Sean out of bed. "We're having a family meeting downstairs. Please make yourself decent and get down right away." He doesn't let on what he's found out. Sean doesn't like the sound of this – he overheard some harsh words coming from down the hall, but couldn't make anything out. He has a sense of impending doom, but then comforts himself. *Nah – there's no way they know.*

The living room is dead silent except for the ticking sound from the grandfather clock down the hall. With the four of them not saying a word, Malcolm breaks the uncomfortable silence by recounting the discovery he made last night. By the look on Sean's face, it was obviously not something Les shared with him. He holds his head in his hands… *Oh no-o-o-o…*

Les and Sean glance at each other, their hearts grasping for some kind of sanity. Tears fall from Leslie's face; Marj gets up and sits next to her, arm around her shoulder.

"There there – it's all going to be OK honey. I'm here for you, you know that, right?"

Les nods. Marj sends daggers from her eyes to Sean, but he's too overwhelmed to catch the uncharacteristic look from his step-mom. Malcolm takes the lead again.

"Leslie, you must have this child, no matter what you think. We can arrange for an adoption. There are thousands of couples looking for babies. You can't do this!"

"No dad, I can't have the baby. You don't understand."

Malcolm stands up and points his finger at Leslie. The holier-than-thou side of him surfaces as he raises his voice:

"*I* don't understand? What *I* understand here is that you're talking about an innocent baby!"

Marj loses it and rushes to the kitchen. Malcolm is torn between continuing his sermon, or attending to his wife – he chooses the latter. *Marj usually is stronger than this,* he thinks. This leaves Sean and Les alone for the first time since Sean found out. He looks at her, and throws his arms in the air, and whispers to her loudly:

"What the *fuck?!?* How come I don't know, and have to get it like this? Look, I know you're upset, but come on…"

"I was going to take care of it without anyone knowing. My school counselor friend did an ultrasound and found out that…" her sentence was interrupted by loud yelling from the kitchen.

"I'll stop this from happening if it's the last thing I do!" shouts Malcolm.

"Aw shit, now *they're* fighting. You still have a key to Lydia's condo?" They quickly vanish from the house without Malcolm and Marjorie hearing a thing.

Chapter 24

Church today is like any other Sunday. There's bible study in various classrooms throughout the building. Pastor Kenny teaches old testament prophecy for the adults. Then there's Paul's letters to the churches for teens, and the gospels for pre-schoolers, with visual aids such as coloring books and felt boards. At 9:45, the steeple bell signals the instructors to bring their lessons to an end, and announces to the surrounding neighborhood that church starts in 15 minutes. The congregation filters into the sanctuary; many people shaking hands, saying *hello, how's your health, what's new?*

In a flash, pastor Kenny is out into the foyer welcoming as many as he can, especially any new faces he's never seen before. Malcolm and Marj try to dodge him but aren't successful.

"Malcolm, nice to see you here – it's been a while!" He winks at Marj… "Mrs. Hodges – how are you? We're looking forward to the social this afternoon. The church greatly appreciates all the work you've put into this. You know, if it was up to me, we'd all starve, my cooking is so bad!"

"Thanks pastor. I made your favorite."

"Mmmm – can't wait," he says as he pats his little paunch. He loves her scalloped potatoes.

As they make their way inside, Malcolm points to a seat further back from where they usually sit. Marj complies.

At 10:00 sharp, the youth choir sings two selections from the hymn book just beautifully, thanks to the keen ear and friendly direction of Mrs. Tysdale, Malcolm's old music teacher from high school. There are announcements about the church social this afternoon, and a special treat for everyone: the missionary couple they've been sponsoring all these years in Africa will be home next month for a break. They will present a slide show of their church-planting experiences.

Then there are prayers for the sick and infirmed, and anyone feeling like they need support. With everyone's head bowed and eyes closed, the deacon asks if there's anyone in need of God's love and special attention this day – *just raise your hand. Take a step of faith...* Marj slowly raises her arm. Malcolm is displeased at her public show of weakness...

"Thank you sister, I see your hand. God is with you this day, rest assured."

Pastor Kenny delivers an exceptional sermon this Sunday. The church is usually rather staid, but there are two or three exclamations from the congregation:

"Amen!!!"

"Preach it brother!"

The outbursts startle both Malcolm and Marj; they're off in another world, rehashing the last twenty four hours over and over. *What can I do about all this?* ponders Malcolm.

The service ends, and the excitement in the crowd is obvious. This yearly social is a church favorite, and they all clear their time tables for it. Even if family is visiting from out of town, they drag them along for the great food, entertainment, and gossip. But the Hodges just aren't into it. Home life just blew up in their faces, the kids have left without saying a word, and there's all this food to bring into the church hall from the van. Though in her own funk, Marj doesn't like Malcolm's silence. He's usually more motivated and upbeat in the face of adversity.

After the service, Malcolm enlists the help of Toby, saying, "Hey Sparky, give me a hand with something. I could use some help bringing all the food in from my van."

"Sure thing Mac, lead the way."

Out in the parking lot, Toby says to Malcolm – "Hey Mac – you don't look so good today. Everything all right with you and the missus?"

"I've a lot on my mind, Toby. Our family is going through something right now, and I'm struggling with what to do about it. I can't share details."

Back and forth with bowls, trays, and plastic containers of cakes, salads, and cold cuts; every time they're alone, the conversation continues. Malcolm comes out of himself a bit.

"I know where you stand on the abortion issue, Toby; we've had many conversations about that. But – out of curiosity, how far do you think we should go to protect our families?"

Toby narrows his eyes – "Mac, I should tell you – I belong to something not many people know about. I'm new, but we talk about stuff like this. They're going to teach us how to protect righteousness and be a soldier in God's army. They told me to invite anyone I think has the same ideas. I know they'd approve you in no time. Why don't we meet them tonight? Nine o'clock is when we're getting together."

That's a puzzling response to my question, thinks Malcolm, but for some reason it makes both fear and adventure surge through his blood. He has suspected for some time that there was a secretive group operating in Grey Falls, and he connects the dots. *Maybe they're the same thing.* Nationally organized, they supposedly have groups in most mid-to-large cities. Their actions have been behind some headlines he read just this week regarding a women's health clinic in North Dakota.

The church social goes without a hitch, and Marjorie is bathed with complements from the congregation. She needs the distraction.

"Mrs. Hodges, those scalloped potatoes were your best yet," pastor Kenny says over the microphone. He mentions some other names; everyone claps. The pastor wraps the afternoon up with a prayer.

Afternoon passes to evening…

"There are leftovers in the fridge – I don't much feel like cooking tonight."

Malcolm acknowledges, and heads into the kitchen.

While finishing up his egg salad sandwich and pickle, he tells Marjorie there's a pressing work issue he has to go in for.

"At eight forty-five on a Sunday night?" Marj asks.

"Shouldn't be too long. There's a board meeting in the morning, and apparently some numbers aren't falling together like they should." Malcolm puts his jacket on to leave.

"Have you heard from the kids?" They've both been avoiding the subject all day.

"Nothing. Sean's cell goes right to voicemail. I have no idea, Malcolm… you shouldn't be leaving – I'm all alone…"

Malcolm sighs. "Sorry honey. Isn't Jake due home sometime soon?"

"Not till the morning."

Marj is still uneasy about Malcolm's demeanor. Something's not right. As her husband's car leaves the driveway, she sighs and goes back to her knitting, cordless phone close at hand. As the evening progresses, Marj gives in to her tiredness and retires.

———————————

Eight hours have passed since he left his house. Malcolm's rage and indignation have now found a channel and means of expression that feeds his resolve.

Malcolm is asked: "Please sir – turn off your cell phone; reception here is sketchy anyways."

His introduction to the Group was short – there was no small talk or idle chit chat – there is a battle to be fought. The soldier in him begins to stir.

Observing such an organized mix of men gathered in the basement of his own building was of no small surprise; yet what did overwhelm him was the military precision of the plan they all worked on together. The soldier in him his was now fully resurrected as they reviewed the schedule multiple times.

"I *will* stop this!" he hisses to the Group.

Finally, all notes and drawings are destroyed, then someone initiates a cleansing ceremony. Malcolm's first one.

Part Three
Chapter 25

Bill's alarm shocks him out of sleep. The clock radio comes alive with a hyperactive DJ telling the town of Grey Falls that it's time to start a new work week. *News and weather next.* Bill rolls over to give Colleen a shake, but she's already in the shower. He yawns, stretches, and sits on the edge of the bed. Another stretch.

Over at the window, he looks to the sky and mumbles something about not seeing the sun in three days. *Depresses me. I miss sunshine.* Movement catches his eye – he sees the birdbath already in use by two small sparrows.

"Good idea – let's clean up."

He steps into the shower with Colleen. He soaps up, then gives her a long slippery hug.

"Grrr. I see you're quite awake doctor. You got plans to use that?"

"You know how I like to work out in the morning…"

Thirty minutes later, they're both in the kitchen having breakfast. Colleen is scanning emails on her laptop while Bill reads the headlines.

"Oh no – Bill – another clinic was targeted on the weekend. *Shit.* No one hurt, but lots of fire damage. When are these moronic half-wits going to figure out it's a losing battle?"

Colleen belongs to a mailing list for clinic managers, and receives weekly updates on changing legislation, new R&D breakthroughs, and political items of interest to the medical community. The editor's pro-choice stance is reflected in the newsletter content, and is the main reason most subscribe.

"Where's the clinic?" asks Bill.

"A mid-size town in North Dakota – like ours."

A bit of a chill overtakes their conversation…

"You know, I detest having to keep looking over my shoulder."

Colleen comforts him. "Me too, sweetheart; I think we're through the worst of it though. No one's heard or seen anything suspicious in weeks, so maybe they're just giving up."

Avoiding the subject, Bill turns a page of the newspaper and a flyer drops out.

"Hey – check this out. Simpson's Electronics is having an inventory clearance sale – you know I've been eyeing that wide-screen for the lounge downstairs. I'd like to convert the room into a home theater – what say you?"

Colleen gives him a disapproving look…

"Get through that repair list and we'll see."

Bill is about 80 percent done the renovations he started over a year ago. He's pretty good with tools, but tends to procrastinate. Colleen keeps him motivated.

"I keep saying we can hire someone if you're not up to the challenge…"

"No no – I'll get to it. That bay window is supposed to be delivered this week some time. I have Steve coming over to help me install it."

He checks his watch.

"Time to go. We have an appointment first thing."

Colleen reminds him – "We'll have to take both cars. I have stuff in the trunk, and we both have running around to do in the afternoon."

"Right – I forgot about that. Yes – I'm seeing a new dentist today."

With that, they gather up the dishes, put things away in the fridge, and generally get the place ready for their house cleaner. In 5 minutes, Colleen is out the door.

"See you in ten."

"Yup – I'm right behind you" responds Bill. As he locks the front door of their house, he looks to the sky, and notices some dark rainclouds forming. He thinks, *Rain or snow? This is really dull weather for a spring day.*

Chapter 26

It's the morning of the big day. Prepping his old firearm means using liquid gun blue to protect the exterior of his .22 caliber rifle. Toby hates rust… makes his Remington look old. Well… it is old, but his gun kit keeps it shining. And thanks to a few drops of light oil here and there, it looks and handles as if it were brand new. As he savors the results of his efforts, the orange glint of the early morning sunrise off the scope's lens gives him pause. A new day. *Servants of Satan must be punished for all to see* he thinks to himself. But, daily devotions come first. His prayer time will help him focus, and distract him from the reality of today's mission.

The ride into town is a little different than usual; he doesn't normally drive this early Monday mornings, so traffic is sparse. "We should have this job done well before work starts," he says to his passenger. Today, they will exact judgment on a murderer of innocent life, and their reward is knowing that divine justice will be channeled through them.

———————————

The clinic door is locked. Leslie sits on the concrete steps, butting out her second cigarette since arriving ten minutes ago. She rarely smokes this heavily, but this morning is an exception. Her nervousness almost gets the better of her – she is just about to desert her appointment when two vehicles pull into the parking lot, one after the other. The first steers towards the sign that reads "Doctor" and the other over to a sign that reads "Employees". With a sense of relief also comes a fear of the unknown. *Will this hurt?*

A few hundred yards away sits an idling half-ton truck, with the passenger side window rolled half-way down, and a beanbag strangely perched on the edge of the glass… it's supporting the tip of a Remington .22 caliber rifle if you look close enough. "Why didn't he listen!" he whispers, peering through the scope. Letter after letter, the doctor was warned by an anonymous group to stop these pro-bono abortions on young girls – heck, they're not even in college yet. No money or medical coverage, and parents that won't listen, this doctor figures he is doing them and society a service. Why bring unwanted babies into the world?

Nurse Patrick waves at Leslie, walks to the back of her car, opens the trunk, and begins unloading the audio-visual equipment from last night's family planning seminar. Her presentations are an attempt to lobby for minors that need access to abortion without parental consent. "Equal access for all." That is her mission. Her day-dreaming is interrupted…

BLAM! The shot is precise. The .22 caliber jacketed hollow-point flies down the barrel at 1,750 feet per second, and instantly finds its way to the doctor's cerebellum. Stepping out of his SUV with briefcase in one hand and clinic keys in the other, he had no idea what hit him.

Colleen's back is turned, but she hears the crack of the rifle, tires squealing, and from her husband's vehicle – a tinkling sound. What catches her eye is someone running a couple of blocks away, then a set of keys skidding across the parking lot, stopping in front of her back left tire. She turns her head, and shock overtakes her perception of reality. *WHAT? Can I believe what I'm seeing right now?*

She runs to his side, watching literally quarts of blood cover the pavement, his arms and legs jerking as if a puppeteer was having a bad day. Hands shaking, it is all she can do to press the numbers on her mobile phone… 9-1-1. As she yells out the clinic's address, the doctor slips into unconsciousness.

Les has never seen this much blood before – knees shaking, she frees herself from the shock of disbelief and bolts towards the doctor, removes her hoodie, handing it to Colleen.

"Here's a pillow for the doctor – can I help?"… Colleen slowly looks up, tears streaming down her cheeks… "Thanks sweetheart, but I think it's too late."

———————————

In the dimly-lit basement of their usual meeting room, a small group of men are standing around their massive oval-shaped wooden table. Light from torches and candles barely illuminate the gargoyles and other night creatures carved into the large twisted pedestal leg. The men seem to be a little nervous at this present time… A figure from the shadows approaches the Group.

"For you, sir" he says, handing someone a mobile phone. The group leader quickly places the cell phone to his ear…

"Yes – yes – OK. No witnesses? I see… I'll pass that on. Well done, son."

He clears his throat, and in a low, booming voice exclaims:

"Gentlemen, it is done. We have conquered evil again. Our identities are safe. Brother Michael, please pour the wine."

"Yes, sir." Brother Michael walks around the table, pouring wine into everyone's chalice, then returns to his spot.

The leader raises his cup in the air as the others follow his lead.

"Death to evil!"

"Death to evil!" they all respond in unison, their voices echoing off the concrete walls.

———————————

This day in Grey Falls Utah, a contrived yet odd combination of pride, greed, fear, and love have entangled the lives of a middle-class family, their misguided father, a paranoid redneck, and a multi-national corporation. *All are changed from this day forward.*

Chapter 27

Like every other morning, Lydia has the morning news on during her morning workout. Then a coffee, a granola bar, a piece of toast. Her hangover begins to subside. She stayed up late with Sean and Leslie, consoling them and encouraging them to not go through with it, that is, until Les gave her all the details.

"I need to get drunk," Lydia said after hours of conversation. And that she did. *Regretting past mistakes is one thing, but having them slap you in the face like this is just too much for me.*

Sean and Les were gone in the morning, so she had the volume up high to hear the TV from her bedroom.

––––––––––––––––

A large white *Hummer* turns into the parking lot of WPCS's studios and finds a spot close to the building's entrance. The vehicle is basically a mobile billboard for the TV station with large, colorful logos and lettering on the sides, roof, and hood. The driver kills the ignition and grabs his satchel. As he walks up the first couple of steps, he hears what sounds like a firearm. Only one shot. He stops dead in his tracks as he turns around, looking in the general direction of the noise.

Backfire? No – too high pitched.

Then the scream. From the same direction as the women's health clinic, which isn't far away. He quickly pulls out his mobile and dials 9-1-1, hands trembling.

"Emergency services. How can I help you?"

"I – I – I'm pretty sure someone's been shot. Near the women's health clinic…"

"Yes, you're the second call on this, just seconds ago. Thank you, we are responding."

Shit, this is really happening! With that, he runs into the building screaming –

"Get outside with a camera crew. Someone's been shot at the clinic!!!"

Pandemonium breaks out. The morning news producer immediately shifts gears and yells at his side kick "I want the latest copy the *second* it comes in from the field." The announcer is halfway through the morning's script. Sports and weather are coming up really fast…

John Drew quickly has a handle on his staff, and begins orchestrating the coverage. "Susan – move your butt and get out there on scene – bring Jim with you; he's still got his camera in the microwave truck from last night's hockey game."

Off the two of them go, hauling Steve, the microwave tech, away from his desk. "My coffee's gonna get cold!" he protests. They explain the shooting… "Oh shit," Let's move!" Squealing out of the parking lot, Jim turns on the police scanner. It crackles and comes alive at 155 megahertz.

"This is officer McKinney at 7623 Broughton Avenue. I have a man down, non-responsive, massive blood loss. Looks like a sniper hit. Send a bus right away."

"Already on its way," responds dispatch. "Keep your head down, McKinney, we have no idea of the shooter's location. Secure the area; we've got air support on the way"

"Copy that."

"Floor it, Jim! We're only a block away!" They finally arrive and are met with an officer holding his hand up –

"No one allowed any closer. Stay put." Another officer is still yellow-taping the scene.

Susan and Jim are prepped and ready to broadcast in thirty seconds. Steve is still raising the microwave antenna. Susan thinks to herself – *Networks, here I come.*

———————————

Malcolm is breathless, his lungs bursting with pain. He curses himself for not staying in better shape as he negotiates another six foot high chain link fence. *Got to stay out of sight. Got to get home. I'm so scared – just a few more blocks.* Just then he hears a vehicle approach from behind; he quickly hides behind a dumpster, waiting for the vehicle to pass. Then another sound surprises him – something overhead. Malcolm's senses are working overtime as the adrenaline pumps through his muscles – he looks up and sees a low-flying police helicopter a few hundred yards away. He doesn't know what they are looking for exactly, but instead of chancing it, he eyes the road for vehicles then swiftly heads for a deep doorway just yards from the dumpster.

The pilot's headset squawks with more information.

"Sergeant Hicks, we're looking for a dark pick-up truck with a camper on the back, likely a three-quarter ton with a lift kit. Possibly headed south from the clinic. Over."

The pilot responds "Roger that sir. Is there anyone on foot I should be looking out for?"

"Negative. Find that truck!"

At that exact moment, the pilot's passenger points to his right…

"Hicks – look – three o'clock, five hundred yards!"

The pilot banks his R44 Raven chopper hard right while responding to his superior – "We've got a hot one here sir, he's speeding like a madman, and it fits the description."

Malcolm waits until the sound of the helicopter subsides, then he continues down another back alley towards home. As he crosses another intersection as nonchalantly as possible, a familiar car turns the corner, then begins to follow him east down White Boulevard. Malcolm uneasily slows down to see if the car does the same. As it does, he prepares to bolt in the opposite direction... the vehicle's passenger window rolls down under the control of the driver, who yells – "Get in. NOW!"

The breakfast show starts its closing theme music, but is strangely cut off. The host reappears and starts talking again, in a more high pitched, excited tone. *I've never heard that before* Lydia says to herself. She's zipping up her skirt while walking to the living room for a closer look.

"This just in. Moments ago, we received a report of a homicide at the women's health clinic on Broughton Avenue. Someone has been pronounced dead at the scene by the town coroner, but the police are not releasing any names. Police are combing the area for suspects as we speak. Our reporter Susan Philips is on scene. Susan, what can you tell us so far?"

"John, it appears the women's health clinic is the focus of yet another attack, this one fatal. Police officers agree it was the work of a sniper." She continues to report an unscripted story...

Lydia's eyes are glued to the TV. She can't believe what she's seeing... she quickly thinks of Leslie's safety. Just then, Les's face appears in the background, just over the reporter's shoulder while an ambulance attendant wraps a blanket over her shoulders.

Fumbling for the telephone, she dials Sean's cell, but it immediately goes to voicemail. *Either he's talking to someone, or his battery's dead.* She phones Malcolm's house, Marj answers.

"Marj. Turn on the TV. Is Malcolm at work yet?"

"What's wrong, Lydia?" They hardly ever talk to each other, but she perceives the immediacy in her tone. "I *think* he's at work. Why?"

"I can't get into the details Marj, but you should find Sean and get over to the women's health clinic on Broughton. Leslie is OK."

"Leslie is OK? – what *are* you talking about?"

Everyone knew where that clinic was. It was in the news more than once, with its pro-life protestors, police escorts into the building, the death threats…

"How do you know she's OK???"

"Turn on the damn television and watch the news!!!" Lydia says in a frustrated tone.

She does and also catches a glimpse of Leslie in the background, the handheld camera shaking as it pans the scene. The on-scene reporter continues.

"There is apparently only one casualty, and police are still on the lookout for a suspect. John, police are holding all spectators back including us as they question everyone on scene; I overheard an officer say they will bring all involved parties to police headquarters for further questioning."

The wheels start turning in Marj's head… *MALCOLM!!!!!! You Sonuvabitch… This better not be what I think it is…*

One hour passes. Lydia locates Sean at Mark's house and brings him to police headquarters where Leslie and Nurse Patrick are being questioned separately. Volunteer grief counselors are standing by. Out in the foyer, Sean is quiet, then turns to Lydia and asks…

"If you were to venture a guess, who do you think shot the Doc?"

She looks away, knowing what he's thinking.

"He didn't want Les to have an abortion – you know how religious-right he is, even after his Vietnam stint."

"Ya, I hated his preaching. I once shut him up for a while by reminding him of his affair with Marjorie. Didn't last long though."

"So, you suspect him?" Sean whispers.

"Sean, I can't judge. I haven't lived with him for a long time. C'mon. Give me a break." Just then Marjorie walks into the foyer, looking for a familiar face.

"Look" Sean says – "There's Marj." Sean rushes to his step-mom. They hug; Marjorie starts to sob...

"What happened to our family? One day, we're all happy, next I see my daughter on TV at a crime scene. At an abortion clinic no less." She sobs through the words. "I can't get a hold of your father, I think someone is covering for him at work. I'm suspecting the worst Sean... he never came home last night from a work problem he had to solve. I'm scared! The police asked me to come in for questioning. Do you know anything you're not telling? Please Sean, we all need to be honest."

Sean kisses her on the cheek and says – "It's time for another family meeting. I don't know where dad is, but it's better he's not there."

Marjorie looks puzzled, but is comforted by Sean's take-charge attitude.

"After we're done here, we'll head home. Lydia wants to come along for support. That OK?"

She looks over Sean's shoulder and notices her on the other side of the office, blowing her nose.

"Sean, it's wonderful how supportive she is, yes, I don't mind at all."

With that, they move back to the detective's desk who offers coffee and water.

"Sorry, we've nothing to eat. I can order in if you'd like. Looks like we'll be a while."

In the interrogation room, Leslie is being treated very respect-fully and with sympathy. A rep from the women's crisis center is in the room as well, holding her hand as the questions continue from detective Eileen Young, a career cop with twenty years on the force.

"Ms. Hodges, after the doctor fell to the ground, what else can you remember?"

Leslie describes in as much detail all she can remember: the quietness of the early morning, the sound of backfire, tires squealing, Nurse Patrick's screaming. It was all surreal past that. But she did kick into gear and offer help. She made no mention of the conversation at her parents' place earlier that weekend, or the fact she saw someone who looked like her father running like a madman across a back parking lot.

"Alright then Ms. Hodges, thanks for all your help. Carol here from the women's crisis center can chat with you if you wish."

Turning to the crisis counselor – "Thanks, but I have family here waiting for me. I appreciate the offer though."

"That's fine Leslie, you have my card. Please call the center any time, day or night – we're here for you."

In the hallway, Sean embraces Les for a long time. Marj embraces the two of them… Lydia watches at a distance. As they break up and head for the exit, they can hear Colleen Patrick sobbing down the hall.

Chapter 28

Back at the house, everyone's there but Malcolm. Sean initiates.

"OK everyone, it's obvious we all need a reality check. After this morning, it's time everyone knew *everything*. Les and I kept certain things to ourselves to protect you, mom. You and dad. I'm not trying to sound disrespectful, but you guys messed up, and now we're all paying for it. Well, it's time it all came out."

"Please don't do it like this Sean," pleads Lydia...

"It's too late," replies Sean. Marjorie's curiosity is piqued.

Big sigh. "Mom, as it turns out, Les and I aren't even related." Lydia nods for anyone wanting to look.

Sean continues. "The DNA project at school – remember that? It brought all this about, so we had to challenge Lydia to see if it was true.

"Lydia – er mum... you wanna kick in here?"

Lydia sighs and starts talking.

"Look, I know this should have been common knowledge a long time ago, but I was just trying to protect what we had. Sean's right, they aren't related. The reason is because Les was originally adopted by my sister in Romania. They obviously kept it a secret; I didn't have a clue till my mom sent me the papers."

Leslie jumps in.

"Think of what I went through. My parents die when I'm fourteen, and I come to Utah to live with family I've never met, who then divorce. So, after we go off to college for a year, and during that time discover we have feelings for each other... we end up sleeping together. Before you go all ballistic on us, consider how well we already know each other, how well we get along – then with that time to mull over the fact we're not even related... we eventually hook up.

We love each other. Then a week ago I find out I'm pregnant. As it turns out, the pregnancy is ectopic, in my fallopian tube." Marj gasps. "It had to be dealt with fairly soon, 'cause there was some bleeding. The nurse at the clinic recommended surgery as soon as possible. I would die if I tried to carry it all the way – but none of us could tell you or dad, 'cause you started fighting. I know we should have spilled everything, but we couldn't handle dad's preaching, so we crashed over at Lydia's. Now I feel guilty for everything that happened. If only dad knew why I was having the surgery…" A tear falls down her cheek.

Lydia continues. "You know, it's time this all came out. It's too late for it to do any harm to any of us, and maybe it gives Les and Sean license to be who they want with each other. I'm good with that. The last question is… where the *hell* is Malcolm, and what did he do???" Just then her cell rings. Very few people have her personal number. She scrambles to answer.

"Detective Young here, Ms. Forsythe. We have detained a suspect in the murder of Doctor Kao. Just thought you'd want to know."

"Who???"

"A man named Tobias Osborne. Heard of him?" Lydia mutes her phone.

"Anyone heard of a man named Tobias Osborne?"

Marjorie gasps. *Oh God. He's in on it too.* A knot forms in her stomach. She remembers how he and Malcolm hung out together so much at the social. She also knows something no one else knows about him: he consorts with some kind of secret group that is shrouded in mystery. How does she know this? She isn't ready to tell; there's enough coming to light today.

"Everyone listen!!!" she yells.

Whoa – Marj *never* loses her temper.

"I think I may know what happened."

Everyone listens as she describes bits and pieces of the last seventy two hours, including just enough about Toby that places him in high suspicion. An emotional discussion continues for twenty minutes, when they all decide that it's up to the police to handle everything. Marj just wants her husband back.

They all part ways. "I'm sure there'll be some kind of hearing," says Lydia. "Let's regroup when that happens." She then turns to Leslie:

"Girl, you get your ass down to that clinic as soon as the dust settles. They specialize in this. If you're spotting, then that means the embryo is damaging tissue, and you do in fact need surgery. Happened to my younger sister. Remember she couldn't have children?"

Leslie nods.

The basement is dark and damp, but Malcolm doesn't notice. Lives have been devastated, hearts broken. He knows life will never be the same for him or anyone in his family.

A fist slams down on the oval table, almost toppling the candelabra. "*What happened?* Dammit, I want every detail!"

Malcolm responds to the leader – "Sir, I had him in my scope as he pulled into the parking lot – I decided to wait till he got out of his car. My hands started shaking, I saw Leslie right there in the parking lot… I broke out in a sweat – my vision started to blur. I hate myself for that, but I ask all of you to understand – I've been overseas in battle decades ago; I guess the flashback was too much" he says as his voice drops.

"Continue, Brother Malcolm." says the leader in his low gravelly voice.

"I told Toby I couldn't do it. I handed the gun to him and bolted. I knew Toby finished the job when I heard the shot. I hear the police have him?"

"Don't worry about Toby. He'll not say a word."

"All I could think of doing was run. I took back alleys wherever I could – that's when Brother Gord saw me near my place and drove me here. I should get to my family."

"That would be a bad move right now – we must maintain your alibi – Brother Gord will go over it with you in a little while. But before that, we have a cleansing ceremony that I believe is very fitting for this occasion. Men…"

With that, they gather into a geometric formation around Malcolm, following a chalk outline someone drew on the floor earlier. One man ignites a clump of herbs in a stone vessel and waves the smoke into the air with large, exaggerated movements. The men chant something in a foreign language Malcolm has never heard before as they rotate around him. He begins to feel lightheaded, an effect of the ceremonial smoke.

———————————

It's mid-afternoon when Malcolm phones home. Marj has the cordless in her hand after one ring.

"Hello?"

"Honey, it's me. Someone told me to phone home – something's happened?"

"Oh Jesus Malcolm, where have you been all this time? I can't believe you waited this long to call. Your secretary wouldn't put my calls through – what's going on?"

"Marj, I'll tell you after you tell *me* what happened." Well handled.

"There was a shooting at the women's clinic – Les was there when it happened."

I *know.*

"They have Toby in custody – can you believe that?" She's fishing… A short silence. No nibbles.

Her voice turns stern. "Malcolm, there are other things going on in our family we need to talk about as well. I'm asking you to come home. Now. I don't care what you've been up to these past 18 hours."

Malcolm knows Marj well.

"She didn't even want to know what I was doing here all this time," Malcolm says to Gord, the Group's "handler."

"Tell you what. I come home with you, and you make the excuse you have to get a CD of last year's numbers from your safe. It melds with your original story. I make like your private delivery boy, running the CD back to the plant, where our supposed board meeting goes on forever."

"Excellent alibi. Let's go."

Marj is very kind when the two men enter the doorway. A quick peck on the cheek from Malcolm, and he says…

"Hon – I have to get something for Gordo here – it has to get back to the bean counters pronto." He disappears to his home office.

"Your husband – he's a hard working guy. Told me he was up all last night crunching numbers. I'm usually in before him, but there he was in the cafeteria making another pot of coffee for himself. He doesn't play baseball all that well, but he sure keeps that plant running smooth!"

"I heard that baseball remark!" Malcolm shouts from his office.

What a tag team, thinks Gord.

"Forgive my manners, Mrs. Hodges… how are you? I heard something happened today at the clinic or something?"

"Oh it was terrible – a shooting. My daughter was close by."

"That's awful – she OK?"

"A little shaken up, but otherwise she'll live."

Malcolm enters the hallway – "Here Gord – see this gets to the second floor board room – pronto!" He hands him a CD in a paper sleeve.

"Mrs. Hodges – good to see you," he says shaking her hand.

He's off in a flash.

"Hard worker, that man" says Malcolm.

"He says the same about you," Marj says. "Come, sit down."

Malcolm complies.

Marj recounts the day: the shooting, the fact that Toby is in custody.

"Did you not hear anything about all this? It's been all over television!"

"Marj, all I heard at work was something about a shooting. That's all. And Toby's a suspect? I know he's a redneck, but wow – that's hard to believe."

Marj leaves Toby out of the discussion for now. She begins to unravel an aspect of their family he had no clue about until today. She starts with Leslie's adoption.

"Lydia knew about it, but didn't want to make things more complicated than they already were by telling you. Besides, it all worked out, right?"

Then she explains the DNA test and the confirmation from the hospital that in fact, Sean and Les aren't related at all. Malcolm thinks back, straining his memory...

"The important thing is – well – think about Sean and Les being together. They've known for almost two years."

The light goes on. Malcolm's judgment of their "little tryst" fades. He leans forward in his chair... "Oh my God – all along none of us knew but Lydia that they weren't related. This really changes things."

"There's something else you need to know Malcolm..." He can't wait...

"Her pregnancy? Ectopic. She *must* have surgery. She was trying to tell us, but we were too involved in our own hurt." She watches his reaction as the blood rushes from his face. He lowers his head to hide the shame he feels.

Oh no. What have I done. Had I known that... His palms begin to sweat as his head rushes over the past two day's activities. He quickly seeks solace in knowing that although his personal reasons to have the doctor terminated were based on a false, or at least ill-informed piece of information, the fact remains he's terminated. He tries to recover quickly...

"Cripes Marj, I guess we *were* too hurt ourselves to listen. I mean, *really* listen. They should have been able to depend on us and we let them down. *I* let them down."

His false contriteness does seem to bring Marj around. She hates being accusatory.

She inquires – "Oh sweetheart, we were all having a tough time coping. Don't blame yourself. But – can I ask you a question? I want an honest answer – please be honest."

"Go ahead –"

"Malcolm – I feared the worst when I watched the news this morning. I saw you and Toby whispering together all afternoon at church… I heard rumors he's involved in some anti-abortion right-wing secret group. Is this true? Please Malcolm…"

"I haven't heard those rumours, Marj… I can't really say…"

And he *can't,* because he's not *allowed* to. Very good choice of words, in his mind anyways.

Malcolm feigns mild disgust… "You're thinking I had something to do with this? Marj – I can't *believe*…"

And she doesn't any more. Her doubts fade. She straightens up in her chair.

"Oh shush up, Malcolm. My imagination was working overtime, can't you see? The whole Sean and Les thing had me all upside down."

Malcolm plays the strong protector and takes her hand – "Marj, it's OK. I understand. Everything is going to be alright. Everything's in the open, and before you know it Grey Falls will forget what happened today."

They stand up and embrace for a while. Marj lets go and starts to sob quietly. Malcolm hands her his handkerchief.

———————

It's Tuesday, the day before the court decides on bail for Toby. He talks to his lawyer on the phone –

"But I handed *him* the rifle dammit! He ran like a chicken, so he left me with no choice but to finish the job," Toby exclaims in a stifled yell, hand cupped over the phone. He's still quite angry Malcolm abandoned him at the last second. His lawyer consoles him.

"I know, you explained that already. Anyway, it doesn't matter because they can't even find a weapon. There's possible motive and opportunity, but no evidence, Toby. Look – the grand jury will likely indict you – this is a high profile case, and the DA is a theatrical bonehead. In the meantime, don't even *breathe* a word about someone else being in the truck, or they'll be looking for an accessory. If you try and include anyone else in this, *then* you'll see the red tape pile up. Settle down Toby, I have this under control; you won't be in jail much longer. Hey – what did you do with the rifle anyways?"

"Secret compartment under the truck seat, thanks to you guys."

"And the empty shell?"

"As ordered: I swallowed it. Burned my tongue."

"Arraignment hearing is tomorrow. Once you're out, we have something special for you while we wait for trial. Something to look forward to. Sit tight Toby, we gotcha covered."

Toby hangs up the phone. The prison guard escorts him back to his cell.

––––––––––––

The Court Clerk hands the judge a folder.

"Docket number 7854, the People versus Tobias Osborne."

"What's the charge?"

"Murder in the first, Your Honor."

"Does your client have a plea, Mr. Combs?"

"Not guilty, Your Honor."

"The people request bail be set at one million," speaks the district attorney.

"Speak when spoken to, Mr. Biggs."

"Your Honor, that's outrageous. Mr. Osborne is not a flight risk, and he needs to keep working to provide for his family. That on top of the shaky evidence and lack of consistency in witness testimony."

"This isn't the grand jury, Mr. Combs," speaks the judge, viewing him over his reading glasses.

The judge clears his throat, hesitates, and exclaims – "Bail is set at $100,000." He slams down his gavel.

"Your *Honor…*" the DA protests indignantly…

"You heard me," He says to Biggs. "Next case!" He waves them off with his hand.

The Group already knew what bail was going to be. Seems the judge had his mind made up for him.

It's not often Grey Falls is the scene of a murder trial… they made *CNN* shortly after the live broadcast from the clinic, and a crew will be on site to cover the trial when it starts in a couple of months. Abortion clinic assassinations garner top billing on the news. The irony isn't lost on Malcolm Hodges or anyone else in the "Group."

———————————

A week goes by, and the Hodges' household is slowly recovering. Tough as nails, Sean and Leslie went through with their concert; Leslie had surgery and rested until the day of. The activity was a welcome distraction, even for Malcolm who volunteered at the gate. Marj brought ten pizzas for the crew… The after-party was a little subdued at first, but still upbeat. Everyone drank a bit too much, including Malcolm.

———————————

Toby, his wife, and their two large dogs are relaxing after a late lunch. Grease still under his fingernails from the morning's tune up and oil change, he pours his third cup of the day.

"Where's the remote dear?"

"Where you left it." She smirks, looking at his shirt.

"Aw geeze – I do this all the time."

He yanks it from a pocket in the bib of his dungarees and begins searching for his favourite fishing channel from the kitchen. One of the dogs perks his ears… the other barks…

"Well, what do we have here?" Toby eyes two vehicles lumbering down his long, uneven gravel driveway. The bigger one grabs his attention as he whistles… *That is some four-by-four.*

He steps out onto the veranda, coffee in hand. The two dogs circle the vehicles as they pull up in front of his house.

"Mindy! Ozzy! Get over here." They obey.

"Mr. Osborne. Toby Osborne?"

"Yer lookin' at him."

"Sir, we're here from Salt Lake City. We were given instructions to deliver this fine vehicle to your door," he says pointing to the pickup. "Kinda funny, we don't know who paid for all this, but they sure think something of *you.*"

Toby's mind is trying to digest the scenario. *Delivered to my door – huh?*

"Well then – who am *I* supposed to deliver it to?"

"No sir – what we're saying is the vehicle was bought for you. We're here to deliver it under orders of the dealership we work for back in Salt Lake." He describes the vehicle…

"400 horsepower V-eight, 20-inch wheels, all-wheel drive, lift kit. Seats five people." He tosses the keys to Toby, who reacts barely quick enough to grab them from the air.

Well I'll be… they told me somethin' was comin'. I never thought…

Toby's wife opens the door behind him – "Scoot forward – lemme out."

"Look at this baby – it's ours to keep. I don't believe this!!!"

"Believe it, Mr. Osborne. You'll find all the paperwork and the spare keys in he glove box. Enjoy your new truck, sir." They approach and shake both of their hands.

"Thank you. Thank you very much!!!" Toby sloshes his coffee.

The four of them chit chat for ten or so minutes. After circling the truck, he notices the license plate: *Tobias*. Toby pops the hood to look at the power plant of this behemoth on wheels. He has to stand on the bumper to even get a view. *V-eight is right. Holy moly…*

"I reckon I'll need to mortgage the house to fill this sucker up!"

Everyone laughs.

"Well, it's a long drive back to the Lake, so we'll be on our way."

Toby's wife is dumfounded, but not so much as to lose her manners… "Hey, we have coffee on, and there's iced tea… you guys hungry at all?"

"Thanks Mrs. Osborne, but that'll make us too late – we should get going."

"Here, at least let me fetch you a bottle of water each." She runs to the fridge. Toby thinks to himself – *Two bottles of water for a $40,000 truck. Good trade. I should go buy lottery tickets with this kinda luck.*

"Thank you, ma'am. You're very kind. Enjoy the new family toy!"

The two gentlemen enter the grey sedan and pull away from the house. The dogs follow them.

Toby's wife Jacquie loves trucks almost as much as he does. She can tell the difference between a half inch and 9/16" socket ten feet away, and is good at assisting Toby when vehicles are dropped off for their annual tune ups. But it isn't long before her excitement changes to suspicion.

"Toby, I'm afraid to ask what you did to get this." She's aware of his secret meetings and secret tasks and secret everything… lately he was doing a lot of target practice with his .22. But Toby hasn't let a thing slip. All he says is, "It's for the Lord, and he'll bless us. You'll see. Don't you go worrying that pretty little head of yours. I ain't worryin', so neither should you."

Chapter 29

Thinking that the investigators could only come up with a minimum of evidence, circumstantial at that, Toby's lawyer did not stand in the way of a speedy trial. The District Attorney's office knew it was a weak case even though the accused was indicted. The DA tried every trick in the book to intimidate Toby's lawyer to make a deal... he had to do *something* to justify his three months of sleuthing. He knows the presiding District Court judge to be a pragmatic, no-nonsense guy, so they have to walk the line.

Just before they enter court for what everyone thinks is to be a short trial (one to three days – tops), Biggs tries again.

"Hey, it's not too late – same deal is on the table."

"No chance Biggs, you're pulling at straws. You have *nothing* on my client, and you know it."

We'll see.

"All rise. This court is in session, Judge Williams presiding."

"Be seated."

The lawyers each present their opening statements. Standard fare for anyone who watches the Court Channel on cable, which many of the jurors did right after they were selected. Witnesses are called; Colleen Patrick is first on the stand.

"Ms. Patrick, please recount for us in your own words what happened the day your husband was gunned down at your clinic. Please take your time."

With precision, Colleen describes everything that transpired that Monday morning – pulling into the parking lot, waving at Leslie, and hearing what sounds like a firecracker a block or two away. Her attention is drawn to a tinkling sound behind her – she turns her head and sees her husband collapsing to the ground. She runs to help. It isn't until she sees blood that she realizes what has happened. Leslie hands her something for a pillow. A tear falls down her cheek as her voice drops off.

"Ms. Patrick, I realize this is difficult for you... is there anything else you remember from that day."

"Yes, I do remember hearing tires squeal, and I thought to myself that there's no way the police would be there that quick."

"Where did this sound come from?"

"North-east of the clinic."

"So, across the street and to the left?"

"That's correct, sir."

"Same direction as the firecracker?"

"Yes."

The lawyer unveils a large whiteboard with a map of the area drawn in black. He points to a parking lot behind a one-story building and addresses the jury:

"In this parking lot behind this building, our investigators found tire marks. Please examine the photo."

After it makes the rounds...

"Ladies and gentlemen, I present people's exhibit number one: A photograph taken by officer Daley the morning of the killing. It shows fresh tire marks left behind by someone hightailing it out of there... the remnants of rubber and spacing between the tires match the vehicle driven by the accused."

The crowd murmurs.

"Order!"

"Ms. Patrick, do you recollect seeing this vehicle?" He passes her a photo of Toby's pick-up.

"No sir, I do not." She had been groomed earlier. A *maybe* would have been better. Colleen thinks better of perjuring herself.

"I'm done, Your Honor."

"Mr. Combs, do you wish to cross examine the witness?"

"No, Your Honor." He leaves his thoughts for his closing statement.

"Ms. Patrick, you may step down," orders the judge.

"Next witness please."

Leslie, then the first officer on scene take the stand. Neither of them add much to the case... it's all fluff until a detective is called forward.

"Detective Philips, do you swear to tell the truth, the whole truth, and nothing but the truth, so help you God?"

"I do."

"Please be seated."

Biggs approaches the stand. "Mr. Philips, you coordinated the search of the suspect's vehicle following his arrest, did you not?"

"Correct, sir."

"Could you please describe to the court your findings."

"Yes sir. I have a pair of investigators that I assign to cases such as this, where a suspect is detained, but no initial evidence is retrieved. In some cases, a more thorough search will reveal a telltale sign that warrants more suspicion. I had a hunch on this one, so we went through the suspect's truck with a fine-toothed comb."

"What did you find sir?"

"A secret compartment under the seat. When opened, my men found a hunting rifle with a scope attached, the same caliber used to murder Dr. Kao."

"Objection! The caliber was described only as 'small' Your Honor. The exact size could not be determined."

"Sustained."

Again, the crowd starts murmuring.

"Order!!!"

The detective retracts his words…

"I stand corrected, Your Honor. It is correct that the coroner could not specify the exact caliber; only that it was small."

Biggs walks over to a table, opens a long narrow box and pulls out Toby's rifle with an identification tag hanging from the trigger shield. Toby's eyes bulge.

"People's exhibit number two, Your Honor."

Combs stays calm. He pats his assistant's hand as if to say, "Be cool..."

"Mr. Philips, please identify this object."

"It is the rifle my men found in the compartment under the bench seat of the vehicle owned by the accused."

The court recorder types away madly...

"Detective, what caliber is this rifle?"

".22."

"For the sake of the court Mr. Philips, is that considered a small caliber?"

"Definitely."

"Mr. Philips, is there anything else of significance you can add?"

"Yes. The rifle had fresh gunshot residue in the chamber, and the same GSR was found in the secret compartment, suggesting that it was fired, then immediately placed where we found it."

"Same residue?"

"That is correct, sir."

"Did you find this residue anywhere else?"

"Yes sir. Two places. First, spread across the truck's roof, inside."

"And the second place?"

"On the clothes and hands of the accused that morning he was stopped by police. That is why we searched the vehicle so thoroughly."

"Fingerprints?"

"They belong to the accused, sir. No others were found on the firearm."

Toby remembers the medical gloves Malcolm had on that day, and his anger gets the better of him... he stands to his feet and yells at the top of his lungs...

"I was killin' varmints on my land!!! I didn't shoot no doctor!!!"

The judge slams his gavel twice – "Mr. Combs, silence your client! Mr. Osborne, one more outburst and you will be removed from this courtroom. *Do you understand???"* he asks angrily.

"Yes, sir. Um. Yes Your Honor." He sits down, glaring at someone in the back row of the courtroom. Biggs picks up on his questioning.

"In your opinion, Mr. Philips, how long had it been since the rifle was fired?"

"There is no clear determining factor to tell how long GSR particles can remain in place. But my men did say it *smelled* fresh."

"Objection, Your Honor, calls for subjective speculation." Combs says, jumping to his feet.

"Overruled. These men are experts in their field. If it smelled fresh, it *was* fresh."

"So, we have a smoking gun, do we not?" Biggs asks the detective.

"Sir, I decline to answer that. I'm here to present the facts, not draw conclusions."

The crowd giggles a bit. *Damn, I like it when other people do my job for me* thinks Combs.

"I'm finished with this witness, Your Honor."

He doesn't need asking. Combs stands up, buttoning his jacket.

"Mr. Philips, in all your investigations in the months following the shooting, was there other evidence of any significance to this case that your men found, either on scene, or in Mr. Osborne's truck, or anywhere else for that matter?"

"None that we could find sir, other than what I've described so far."

"So let me understand this: we have a gun. We know it belongs to the accused. Mr. Philips, did your investigators, or anyone else, find the actual bullet that caused William Kao's death?"

"No, sir."

"How about the bullet's casing?"

"No, sir."

"No???" Combs says emphatically, drawing out the word, turning to the jury, then the court, then the judge. "Well *what* do you know!" Combs is never one to let such details escape his melodramatic attention…

"Mr. Philips, is it correct then to say that *this* rifle, including the gunshot residue, and the truck belonging to the accused, cannot in fact be placed at the scene of the crime, *even considering* the accuracy and range of such a weapon?"

"That is correct, sir."

"Thank you for your time Mr. Philips!"

He walks back to his desk. "No more questions Your Honor."

"You may step down, Mr. Philips."

The crowd's din raises. Judge Williams looks down at his schedule.

Combs whispers to his assistant –

"See? Nothing to worry about. It's all circumstantial."

"Then why did the grand jury indict?" she whispers with a puzzled look.

"Desperate I guess. And – Biggs can be really charismatic and convincing. You know, a verdict of innocence will sound echoes across the country – the pro-lifers will protest every clinic in the country, and the whole Roe v. Wade debate is rekindled. Fun stuff. Pays my bills – and your paycheck."

"Do the People have any more witnesses?" the judge asks Biggs.

"No, Your Honor."

"Defense?"

"No, Your Honor."

"Are we ready with our closing statements?"

Both lawyers respond in the affirmative.

"Very well. The court is in recess until 11 AM tomorrow morning."

He smacks his gavel on the sound block.

Combs gloats and leans over to his opponent – "Thanks to the DA's office, this may be the shortest murder trial on record for this county. I'll send you guys flowers."

"You know where *they* can go, Combs." answers Biggs as he exits the courtroom.

Toby asks his lawyer out loud –

"That was good, right? I mean, that it was a through-and-through?" referring to the missing bullet.

"*Dammit,* Toby, keep your bloody mouth shut," hisses Combs in a loud whisper.

———————

Judge Williams enters the courtroom. Before anyone has a chance to rise, he waves them down… "Be seated."

"Members of the jury, you now have all the evidence. We have three things yet to do: first, I will give you additional instructions for you to follow in deciding this case; second, the lawyers will give their closing arguments. The prosecutor goes first, then the defense. Because prosecution has the burden of proof, he may give a rebuttal. Lastly, you will go to the jury room to decide the case."

Judge Williams continues:

"Facts may be proven by either direct or circumstantial evidence. Before you can find the defendant guilty of any charge, there must be enough evidence – direct, circumstantial, or some of both. The defendant's guilt must be proven beyond a reasonable doubt. Thank you for your attention." He turns to the lawyers… "We will now hear the closing arguments. Biggs, you're up."

The judge knows where it's headed. Biggs' only hope is to hang the jury with his melodramatic rantings, and even possibly have the charges dismissed. Maybe another trial? Who knows… He doubts an appeal would go anywhere if they did find Toby innocent. *If they could only find that damned bullet.*

"Ladies and gentlemen. I appeal to you as a contributing member of this community. A community founded on hope, faith, friendship, and most of all trust. As we watch our precious city expand beyond our wildest imaginations, we have become plagued with the same problems larger cities have. Street gangs are organizing the drug trade, causing prostitution and other societal diseases to appear. We are becoming more and more godless – we're no longer able to say the Lord's Prayer in school. Nativity scenes are banned from city hall."

First, he plays the moderate right-wing, moral-majority card, trying not to inflame anyone who may be strongly pro-life. It's a fine line... He knows the political leanings of this state tend to be conservative, and there possibly could be one or two jurors who are closet supporters of Toby's alleged actions. He'll get to them shortly.

"It is intolerable to allow anyone with a sniper rifle to bring their brand of justice to our streets. We must make an example of anyone who thinks such a thing. Perhaps the accused thought he was doing the right thing, but ladies and gentlemen of the jury, if we let this man walk the streets, this town we call home will send a big message to the world that murder is tolerable. That anyone's brand of justice is defendable with a bullet. That murder in the name of religion can exist just as easily here as in the middle east. I say that we must find Grey Falls *no place* for anyone's holy war. Ever since that medical clinic was in business, we've all seen the controversy played out on the evening news – the protests, the threatening letters. The world is watching us. We need to send the right message. What message we send is up to you."

He takes a deep breath. *Now for the radical pro-lifers.* Excluded in his original closing argument that he finished typing just last night, he decides to go for the jugular. *And I know just how...*

"I know there is a small faction of society that is radically pro-life; those who believe their actions are justified. Shouldn't we feel very sorry for anyone who takes the law into their own hands, thinking they are so justified? These people are invariably religious extremists who are convinced they are acting on God's behalf. Members of the jury, we must raise a flag of sanity and condemn what is obviously very flawed logic. Taking a life to save another one is simply the most unloving, inhumane, and barbaric of all acts. Those pulling the trigger on medical doctors who work at such clinics – and there have been many – do they not thrive in a society of many advantages, freedoms, and rights? Are their lives *threatened* by the people they kill? The answer is no. And so should be the answer today: *no* – we the people will not tolerate such savagery!"

Biggs is impressed with himself. His booming voice and arm waving emphasizes all the right words. He turns slowly as he walks back to his chair.

"So as you deliberate, ladies and gentlemen of the jury, please be mindful of your community, your children, and your future. Please put this man where he belongs. Thank you." He sits down.

Combs approaches the jury…

"Thank you for those reminders, Mr. Biggs" he says in a condescending tone.

"Ladies and gentleman of the jury. Out of respect, I'll keep this short, because I believe that what we saw yesterday was, in my opinion, a waste of your time, my time, and the court's time. The people have not been able to produce anything of any real significance to convict my client. The small shred of circumstantial evidence is not enough to convict, and we all know it. To top it off, Mr. Osborne cannot be placed at the immediate scene. He was almost two miles from the clinic when the police stopped him.

Ladies and gentlemen of the jury, please do not be persuaded by Mr. Biggs's emotional plea. Yes, crime exists in Grey Falls, but would we not be part of the problem by using this court for our own needs? I beg you not to use Mr. Osborne as a literal scapegoat just because he owns a rifle; I *beg* you not to use him as an example to other murderers as Mr. Biggs suggests you do. I ask you to find the accused, Mr. Osborne, innocent of this charge. Thank you very much for your time."

One of my shortest. A slam-dunk and everyone knows it.

The judge declares: "Thank you, Mr. Biggs and Mr. Combs. The jury will deliberate until a unanimous verdict is reached. Good luck to you." His gavel dismisses the court.

It's almost lunch time, and everyone wants to stick around, knowing this won't be long. There are more hot dog stands around the courthouse than usual, and they're all swamped. These hustlers know when a big trial is scheduled...

"Good closing, Biggs. Emotional. *Manipulative.* I was ready to cry..." Combs's assistant reaches for the mustard. Biggs turns his head. *Oh you.*

"Well, ya gotta do what you gotta do. Like I always taught you, if you can't make it good, make it big." She worked in his office just before graduating. He was her mentor for a while.

Biggs continues — "So, how is it defending scum? You always liked the bad boys, eh?"

"More money. Lots more. You taught me that to win in this business, you can't have a soul no matter what side you're on. How am I doing?" She purposefully squeezes mustard onto his jacket. He doesn't notice till it's too late to say anything — *Yup, she did indeed learn...*

Three television networks are represented by their cube vans with satellite dishes pointed to the sky. Cameramen and reporters sip coffee and chat while their production managers back home wait for updates on their sat phones..

———————

The sheriff lays it all out for the jury. "Just knock on that door when you need anything. Like the judge said, you need to appoint a foreperson. If and when you reach a verdict, please fill in the verdict form. It has two blanks, one for 'guilty' and the other for 'not guilty'. The foreperson will fill in the blank to record your decision." With that, the eight men and four women file into the large room and find a place at the old table. Some of them are thinking – *I wonder how many other cases have been decided here.*

———————————

On the phone with his production manager, a news reporter voices his frustration. "We were told it was going to be a slam dunk. I mean dammit – this came from a reliable source. Weak evidence, she said."

"John, I know you have family stuff to get back to at home, but can you stick it out one more day? I'll send Wendy to spot you if you want."

No way. I'm covering this one.

"Nah, I just need to bitch. It's a nice town, the hotel is comfortable, and there's even a jazz club. Me and Rick have a competition going to see who gets the most phone numbers. I took one girl to see…" his boss interrupts…

"Spare me the details, John. Look, stay sharp and let me know when you go live."

"Will do, boss."

Deliberations take eight days in total. The vote kept changing throughout the week. Six to six. Seven to five. Then nine to three. It's been there for three days.

Combs's office is very tense. Combs himself can't concentrate, but the phone calls keep coming in for more work. *Take their number –*

we'll call back after this bloody trial is over, he tells his receptionist over and over.

He gets up to leave his office for a bite at the local greasy spoon and sees flowers on the front desk.

"Secret admirer?" he asks.

"No sir – they're for you actually."

"Oh! Let's see here" he says reading the card.

Short defense closings lead to long deliberations.
Law school 101. The DA's office thanks you.

Biggs.

"You rat bastard," he says under his breath. "Anne, get rid of these. I want them gone by the time I'm back from lunch."

During the week of deliberations, on-location reporters are feeding the news anchors back home as many sideline stories as they can dredge up. They heard from someone who heard from someone – who heard it from someone else – about an acquaintance of the accused who apparently went missing around the time of the murder. They chased it down to a gentleman who runs a window manufacturing company.

"OK – I'll go see him today," whispers the NBC reporter to himself.

"Now – let's look at this…"

The original footage of the murder scene is reviewed over and over.

"Who's that girl back there? We should see if we can find her."

Hardcopies of her out-of-focus face are printed... they hit the streets.

"Do you know who this is? Do you recognize her?"

Not me. Nope, never seen her. Oh, she looks familiar, but I'm not sure.

They get a hit an hour later when they visit the high school cafeteria.

"Leslie. Yes, she's in that band – Indigo Insight. They've been to LA to record an album. I think they're on tour though."

"What's her last name?"

"Sorry – dunno. Go to the office – they'll tell you."

Mr. Templeton is no push over. "Listen guys, unless you're the police with a warrant, no one gets any personal information about *anyone* from this high school, student, employee, graduate – doesn't matter. Go bug someone else."

Back at his hotel room, John from NBC decides to Google the band's name. *Bingo!* Their web site has a snail-mail address to send fan mail to, as well as their current tour schedule.

"Well, well – isn't this interesting. Greg – look – the girl in the background – Leslie Hodges. The guy missing for almost 24 hours... guess who?"

"Not a clue."

"Her *father*. This must mean something..."

Chapter 30

It's a typically hectic day at the plant, inside and out. Incoming trucks are delivering raw materials in the form of lumber, glass, nails, screws, and various other supplies, as the outgoing trucks deliver trusses, doors, and windows to various construction sites around the city and county. Inside, staff are busy about their jobs keeping the well-oiled machine spinning like a top, Malcolm included. He's on the phone with a supplier –

"Jerry, we're getting a little low on your glass, you know – the infra-red reflective product we started using last year. My purchaser is getting the run-around, so I thought I'd give you a call. Look into it if you could... Thanks." He hangs up the phone, when it rings again.

"Mr. Hodges, there's a gentleman from the media wanting to speak to you. Should I send him up?"

"Sure." Any refusal to speak only draws attention.

A minute later, and he's seated comfortably in Malcolm's large office, unpacking his notebook and voice recorder.

"Mr. Hodges, as you likely suspect, I'm here to chat about the Osborne trial. And as you know, the deliberations are taking much longer than many people expected. We're interviewing local business owners and community leaders to get their opinion as to why they think this is so."

Malcolm thinks for a second...

"It's hard to say. I can speculate I suppose – perhaps it's the demographics. We are in a conservative part of the country so perhaps that plays a part...?"

"I understand. The moral majority so-to-speak?"

"Yes."

"Are you part of that demographic Mr. Hodges?"

"I suppose so. I'm a God-fearing, church-going man. Went to bible college decades ago – so yes, I'd place myself there. Don't get me wrong – I do enjoy the odd drink with my wife or the boys after work, so I guess I'm sort of a moderate."

"Mr. Hodges, the accused – Tobias Osborne – rumor has it you are friends. Is that correct?"

So this is why he's here.

"Well, I know him from church. He cuts my lawn sometimes. I'm surprised frankly they thought there was enough to go to trial. He's a harmless guy, I can't see him pulling the trigger on another human being."

"I see. Thank you. I've another question sir."

"Go ahead."

"I heard a rumor that has to do with your activities around the time of the shooting. Apparently you were missing from Sunday night to Monday afternoon; that you couldn't be reached by anyone. Not to sound like a cop, but can anyone confirm your whereabouts for that period of time?"

"Well, you *do* sound like a cop, and yes – I *can* prove my whereabouts." He punches a button on his desk phone.

"Yes, Mr. Hodges."

"Page Gord and send him up here."

"Right away, sir."

"We'll settle this, then I have to get back to work" Malcolm states in an authoritative and dismissive tone.

"While we wait, what else did you want to ask me?"

"I don't suppose you'd want to talk about your daughter's involvement in all this. Her face in the original broadcast is all over town. People are asking questions."

Malcolm's instincts kick in full force.

"She's my niece, and if you come near her I'll strap a restraining order on you so fast, your head will spin. You can come in here

262

and question *me* all you want, but don't you *dare* fuck with my family, you got that?" Gord is at the door; Malcolm motions him in as he continues… "We've had enough of the media crawling around Grey Falls like we're some kind of freak show, looking for front-page stories. You must be one bored group of people to waste my time like this. Why don't you go bowling or join a local gym or something…"

He's out of his chair at this point, heading for the door.

"He's all yours. Gord – don't take any shit from this lowlife. Tell him where I was when Kao was shot, then escort his ass out of here."

———————————

Halfway up the block from the Hodges' home sits an idling car. One of the occupants speaks to the other through a mouthful of chocolate donut.

"She should be coming back from school soon."

"No, asshole, she's almost 20. We'll have to sit here till she decides to show her face to the world. God knows when that'll be."

"I wonder why John gave this address up so easily. Not like him."

"Who knows."

Two days of living in a car almost 24/7 takes its toll. "Damn, I feel like a low-life private investigator." He reaches for another donut when the front door opens.

"That's her!!! Hang on – let's see where she's going."

Inside the Hodges' home, the family was hunkered down for the length of the deliberations. With their first CD in full distribution, and a grueling tour schedule, they welcomed a two week break which happened to coincide with the trial date. Everyone was still adjusting to the new family dynamic, but Malcolm and Marj expressed their discomfort with the idea of Sean and Les sharing a bed, and decided that perhaps if they wanted to be together they should make their own arrangements.

"We love you both, don't get us wrong – you're always welcome here. But you're not married. Call us old fashioned – that's just the way we are."

No problem. We totally understand. After the tour, we'll figure something out.

"Hey mom – need anything at the store?" asks Leslie. "I could use the fresh air."

"Oh sure, sweetheart. We're almost out of bread. Oh – and your father would like some of that butterscotch ripple ice cream they have if you don't mind."

"OK – see you in a bit."

Leslie needs not only the fresh air, but some alone time as well. Half a block from her home, she didn't know what hit her. Seconds after walking past an idling car, she was accosted by someone with a microphone and another with a camera on his shoulder.

"Ms. Hodges, I'm Sandra Blake from CBS news. Do you have a moment?"

Les is annoyed. "Is this about the case? My dad told you to lay off…"

"Ms. Hodges, your face is recognizable from the Monday morning local broadcast when Dr. Kao was shot. Were you a passer-by? What was it you saw that morning?"

"Look – I can't talk about the case, you should know that. Any testimony I gave is evidence that can affect the case's outcome, so my lips are sealed."

Shit. Smart kid.

"Ms. Hodges, is there anything you *didn't* testify about that you could share?"

"Listen, I just happened to be there. Then it happened. The rest is history." She leans into the camera, saying sarcastically…

"Stay tuned for more on this station," wagging her head. She stomps away, giving them the finger. The cameraman zooms in on her hand. The bright red nail polish is a nice touch.

"Well, *that* was a waste of two days." Says the videographer.

Chapter 31

Now that Toby is in a holding cell for the duration of the trial, Colleen Patrick feels more at ease. It's a beautiful Saturday, and spring has melted away all signs of winter, save for the odd snow bank that never sees direct sunlight.

"Easter's almost here. I love chocolate." Colleen decides to take a drive by herself out in the country. Nowhere special. She finds herself on the I-15 headed south. After stopping for gas and a candy bar, she remembers about the land Bill bought. *Somewhere south. I think I remember the landmarks.*

Windows rolled down, she is enjoying her alone time immensely. She hasn't spent an hour on herself in months. No yoga. No romance novels. *Today is mine* she declares.

She recognizes the intersection a few minutes later, and the sign for Scipio.

"That's it. Not far now."

Seeing the grain bins off in the distance, she turns her Volvo onto the dirt road, heading west. She's looking for a fence post she remembers from the first time they visited. Finding it, she pulls the car over and kills the ignition.

She is taken by the quietness, so close to town, yet so far. Just some wind through the low brushes… A few birds. Stepping out of her car, she does a 360. No one for miles; the horizon is so far away.

Severed from a quarter section of land that hasn't grown anything in years, Colleen and Bill dreamed of one day retiring here to raise organic vegetables for the local farmer's market, perhaps keep a few goats and chickens, and lots of cats and dogs. She loves her pets. As she walks through the field that was to be their final and last place to call home, she lets her hands play with the tall grass.

Damn that mining company.

They dug three test pits. Two on the adjoining property, and one straddling the property line.

What a mess. No wonder Bill was pissed.

She closes her eyes and thinks of her husband.

What should I do with all this? Keep it? Sell it? What would you want?

Her mind wanders back to the funeral. The eulogies, the community support – it was all touching. The TV interviewers were appropriately sensitive. Phone calls from across the country bolstered her cause. But she was like a robot, going through the motions, not feeling a thing.

You're so strong. What can I do to help?

Even church people were willing to put their differences aside and help, *heck, she lives just down the street – how wrong it would be for me to ignore her.*

After the incident, she only spent a few days away from the clinic, returning to work the following Monday. Her employees and business partner were worried about the grieving she still needed to do. Stoic as ever, she replied that she wasn't going to let them win. Even though sleep was very elusive, she refused any medication.

Now in this field, totally alone with no one around for miles, it caves in on her. Married five years. No kids yet. A widow at thirty.

"Oh Jesus *no.......*" She falls to her knees sobbing, screaming, pounding the ground with her fist. "Why? WHY?" she yells at the sky. She slowly lies on the ground and forms into a fetal position, hand over her mouth, sobbing for what feels like hours and hours. The release wracks her body. Exhausted, sleep finally overtakes her consciousness. She has dreams of little children tugging at her dress asking for more cookies... her husband is out on his garden tractor tilling the ground... a large obese cat fills a window ledge, warming itself in the sun.

She must go collect the day's eggs. Leaving the house wearing tall rubber boots, a straw hat, and dirty jeans, she makes her way to the hen house. She walks inside and heads over to the light switch. As she does, the old rotten floor boards beneath her feet give way with a loud crack. *Shit! I'm falling!* She hits the bottom of what she thinks must be an old abandoned well. She can't get up. The rocks and stones beneath her are glowing in a purple, almost ultraviolet hue. Stay awake, she tells herself. *I have to get out of here.* But her eyes close for a time.

The sound of wind stirs her awareness. *I feel so cold. Did Bill find me down here?* The temperature has dropped from 60 to 40 degrees – the sun is about to set, and clouds are forming. Colleen's body has lost a lot of heat, and she begins to shake uncontrollably as her mind returns to the present. Raising her head, she looks at her watch. She feels the dampness through her coat as she stands. She's lost her sense of direction, but is finally able to retrace her steps back to the Volvo. Sitting in the driver's seat with the door still open for light, Colleen fumbles through her purse for keys when her cell phone rings. Call display shows it to be the District Attorney's office.

"Yes, yes – this is Colleen Patrick."

"Ms. Patrick, this is Judy Benshaw from the District Attorney's office. Court is back in session Monday morning."

A verdict. Finally.

Chapter 32

The crowd filters into judge Williams' courtroom. Leslie squeezes Nurse Patrick's shoulder as she and her family find a place to be seated just behind her. It won't be long before the courtroom is full. Toby's wife is right behind Combs' chair, asking him questions about sentencing. She is interrupted with…

"All rise."

The judge enters the courtroom and sits down. The crowd does so as well.

All eyes are on the jury, who are the first to be addressed.

"In the case of People versus Tobias Osborne, has the jury reached a verdict?"

The spokesperson rises.

"Your Honor, we have not. We've been at a stalemate for three days. Nine to three to acquit Your Honor."

Colleen's heart sinks. Biggs raises his eyebrows.

"Then I have no choice but to declare a mistrial."

The judge is not finished… the court is dead quiet.

"The evidence is, in my judgment, inadequate to retry the accused. Therefore, the charge of murder in the first brought against Tobias Osborne is hereby dismissed. Mr. Osborne, you are free to go." Toby's jaw drops. The crowd reacts. The judges slams his gavel, quieting the room. He turns to the jury:

"The court thanks the jury for their time. Your responsibilities have been fulfilled." He raises his gavel.

"This court is adjourned," he declares as he hammers the sound block one last time.

The roar is once again deafening. The two lawyers look at each other. Biggs' face is white.

Shit, I danced my best dance. What the...

Combs leans back in his chair – "Well, how's that for justice." He says to no one in particular, looking around the dazed courtroom puffing his chest out.

Within minutes, the generators are fired up and all the media trucks prepare for live broadcast. Headlines are written and texted all over the country. Satellite phones everywhere spring to life.

"Hung Jury. Osborne Free. Charges dismissed."

Colleen is surrounded by friends and family. She can't even stand up to leave she is so shocked. *Please let there be another trial. Another jury will be chosen,* they say to try and comfort her. She knows it's false hope. The DA cannot retry.

"I need a break. I'm going to my parents' in Florida. Can you handle the clinic?"

"Don't give it a second thought" replies Steve, Bill's partner and now sole practitioner at the clinic. "We've got it all covered."

The steps of the courthouse are full of people with microphones and cameras. John from NBC is in Malcolm's face once again...

"Mr. Hodges, why didn't your disappearance the night before the shooting raise suspicion? If I was a lawyer, I would have been all over that like a dirty shirt, being a friend of the accused, and all..."

"Well, I guess that's why you carry a microphone instead of a law degree," he spits back. "The detectives have testimony of two people who were with me at work... I simply was caught up with my job. But then, you knew that. I've nothing more to say – excuse me." Cameras point to John's fallen face; Malcolm ignores the other reporters and heads to his car.

Hah! Made him *look like chopped liver* Malcolm whispers to himself indignantly.

The reporters and cameramen clamor to hear from the lawyers, and Toby of course.

After finally getting them to hush up, Biggs addresses the crowd. There must be ten microphones in his face…

"Ladies and gentlemen, it is clear that the jury would not convict based on the available evidence. I would have preferred a guilty verdict of course, and may I suggest that if the trial had been held elsewhere, they may indeed have found Mr. Osborne guilty."

"So you'll try the case again? There'll be another trial?"

"No, the judge also thinks the evidence was too weak. That's his opinion, I suppose."

This was to be Combs's day. His gloating quickly turned to fear after the second day of deliberations. He was getting ready to tuck tail and steal out the back unnoticed.

"Mr. Combs, what is your reaction?"

"Well, my client is free, and we are very pleased to say the least. But – I *am* dumbfounded that a jury of 12 sane people could not see through the rantings of a madman. The so-called DA's office knew they only had a hope and a prayer, yet three of the jury fell prey to his sob story about crime in the streets."

"Are you saying the system is flawed?"

"No – *people* are flawed. My client should have been acquitted, that simple. He's free, so we are obviously overjoyed."

When questioned about his innocence, and how this case has changed his life, Toby's attempt at eloquence didn't help him much, with his stuttering problem showing itself for the first time in months.

"W-W-Well now, if those p-p-police officers hada been lookin' for those bad dope dealers instead of stickin' their noses into my business, all this never would have happened, now would it?"

The reporters are speechless.

Marj, Sean, and Leslie all exchange glances of relief. They answer a few questions from the press off to the side, such as *What has this trial done to the town,* and *did you know the doctor or the accused?*

They head back home with Malcolm. *No more publicity, please.*

The headlines on the front page of the Chronicle bring closure to a chapter of Grey Falls' history most would want to forget.

U.S. District Judge Williams declares mistrial when jurors report they were deadlocked after 8 days of deliberations in the case of Dr. William Kao's murder. "No retrial" says judge.

Chapter 33

In his north-facing corner office on the 43rd floor of a Manhattan office tower, Peter Underbridge has stayed after hours to take care of a phone call he'd rather put off until tomorrow. He fiddles with his fountain pen for a few seconds, then finally retrieves a satellite phone from his briefcase. As he wheels his chair close to the window for better reception, his fingers punch in a number he had committed to memory long ago. It rings twice when the other end picks up.

"Rudman here. That you Pete?" Few people have Greg Rudman's sat phone number.

"Yes Greg, I wanted to talk following our most recent victory. You didn't sound all that enthused during today's conference call."

Rudman weighs his words. "Pete, far be it from me to complain how things get done, so know that I'm on track with everything, but I do have to say…" Underbridge reads Rudman like a book. He interrupts.

"Look Greg – I know where this is going. What happened wasn't pretty. We had to respond to a threat, and we had the blessing of our boys here in New York; hell, it was their concocted plan. Before you go on, just know that there's something being cooked up in our group that is sounding more secretive than normal. I suspect something's up that certain ones of us are not part of, and this *only* happens when it's really shady. Keep your head low for now. I know enough about these men that I could be a threat, so I'm laying low too. And – for the record, I protested their plan that I fed you. Business is one thing, human lives are another. I'm re-thinking my membership."

Rudman is somewhat relieved, but is still stinging from the reality of his involvement in the Grey Falls fiasco. Underbridge finishes. "Let's hook up when you're back from Utah. That's Friday, right?"

"Correct, we're just about to land. See you then."

In a rare emotional exchange, Rudman continues...

"And... thanks for that. Good to know we're in the same corner."

"You got *that* right!" Underbridge responds as he terminates the call, wheeling back to his desk.

———————————

A rental pickup truck heads down the gravel road towards a private airstrip as the Learjet with a familiar logo on the side flies overhead, barely 200 feet off the ground. The driver looks up and flashes his headlights. The pilot does the same with his approach lights... a little game these two started months ago. Checking his watch, he confirms he's right on time. Greg Rudman is an impatient man, and the driver was late only once. *I'll never do that again.*

The countryside is very flat. At night, you can see the Milky Way and the amber glow of the city lights twelve miles north. The pilot checked wind direction a few hundred miles back and decided on a south approach. It's a perfect three-point landing.

The turbines wind down as the staircase lowers from the side of the aircraft. Floodlights from the hangar illuminate the tarmac as Mr. Rudman and his vice president disembark with briefcases in hand.

"Our suitcases are in the cargo hold," he orders the driver.

"Yes, sir."

The pilot, co-pilot, and flight attendant leave the plane to stretch their legs. One lights a smoke. It'll be another few hours back to New York.

"Good gig, didn't I say?" asks the co-pilot.

The flight attendant, a young 20-something blonde, wearing a black miniskirt and top that is too tight responds in a strong Asian accent…

"You didn't tell me he'd ogle me the whole way."

"That's why the big bucks. Better than stripping and lap dances, right?"

She looks away, dragging on her cigarette.

Ya, not bad for $85 an hour I suppose.

The driver retrieves a small box from the back of his pickup, then approaches the group on the tarmac. Everyone notices the radioactivity warning symbol and steps back. The driver comforts them…

"It's U-238. No worries – you can pretty well eat this stuff."

"More core samples I see. Expanding operations?"

"Yup."

"Cargo hold as usual. Strap it down good this time, OK?"

"Sure thing."

"OK, back on board folks," the pilot orders. "Gotta keep up with our flight plan."

The driver and his two arrivals are in the truck, heading north to the trailers. *HQ* the driver calls them. And headquarters they are – offices and sleeping quarters for engineers, truckers, crane operators, and the odd visiting executive. A small lab is directly opposite a larger double-wide serving as the cafeteria by day, and private tavern at night.

"It's late – but let's go for beers first."

The driver asks – "Mr. Rudman, it's none of my business, but is it true – the story went around for a while – that this property used to be owned by that doctor that was shot?"

Oh God, not again. More damage control.

"I know what the rumor mill is like – you can't believe everything you hear, you know. Now take us over to the cafeteria."

"Yes sir – here we are, just ahead." He turns a corner and pulls up to the cafeteria, placing the transmission into 'Park'. His two passengers head in for their nightcap.

"You know where each of our trailers are – just leave our luggage on the front step."

With that, the driver pulls away towards the residential area of the trailer camp.

"So, what *is* the story?" Maria asks.

Rudman sighs, then replies reluctantly –

"With her husband out of the way, his wife settled on market value and a generous donation to her cause. And between you and me, I'll never get my hands dirty like that again."

"What? You???"

"Confession's good for the soul. Forget you ever heard anything from me, OK? Look, there were other involved, so stop digging, or you might find yourself not sleeping at night, just like me."

They climb the six steps to the cafeteria's large front deck with its café tables and umbrellas. Looking inside they see their geologist sipping on a beer.

Rudman speaks – "Now if memory serves, it's your turn to buy."

Chapter 34
Three Years Later

Shortly after a 747 lands at LAX, a stretch limo pulls up to the arrivals area. The driver steps out and holds up a sign – "Mix'd Stuph." The next great Hip Hop band to hit the American music scene saunters through the arrivals crowd towards the exit sign, fending off photographers and news cameras. Roadies are there to pick up their suitcases. The band's lead singer spots the sign and pushes his way through the crowd. *Outa my way. I see our drive.*

"Make it to network television, and you're guaranteed a deal," promised their agent. The new hit reality show on Fox makes sure of that.

In another city 150 miles away, a jogger makes her way along a path just yards from the beach on her right, and a familiar house on the left, where she sees her friend and her friend's daughter through the expansive bay windows. The mother waves, and the jogger waves back. It's a lazy day for the mother, who is slowly enjoying a late breakfast. Her attention is diverted to the flat panel screen…

"Look at TV – that's them – Mix'd Stuph! Cuh-*ching!*"

"Mama… cookie. Mama…"

The mother looks back at her daughter.

"No, toast. This is *t-o-a-s-t.*" The mother pronounces it slowly so her daughter will mimic her. She spreads more organic strawberry jam on it.

"Here you are Mia."

Mia slowly reaches for the food

"Toaft. Toaft!" She giggles.

"Oh Mia, look!" she says, pointing at the large kite a young man is flying down at the water's edge. The large bay windows in their kitchen offer an expansive view of Mission Beach.

"High up! Look" as she points.

Mia squeals with excitement. Father walks into the kitchen, reaching for the coffee pot.

"Hey babe, what's up for today?"

"Not much. A day at the beach while we wait for these dudes on TV to record their demo in LA. They look OK, I suppose. Spoiled kids with moneyed parents. You leaving for there today?"

"No, Devon's got it handled. And hey – remember how *we* started? They pay the bills. So listen –" he says, changing the subject slightly – "there's a jam I want to go to downtown if you don't mind being alone with the kids. Some new names showing up. Good talent they say."

"Teresa's here today, so have fun – come back with more business cards!"

Being co-producers of new bands showing promise, Leslie and Sean Hodges found an interesting niche with the LA music crowd. *Send us your demo album, and we'll screen you and pick the top five bands. If you make it past that, we'll find you cheap recording time with professional background musicians. All on television nationwide.* Sean thought it would make a great reality show and pitched the idea to the TV execs a year ago. Now he's the executive producer. Twice a year, they find a promising band that "The Doc" then turns into stars. And the percentages are good.

"How long's it been since we performed?" asks Leslie.

"Oh, maybe 2 years. You missing it like me?"

"Think so. I'm feeling up to it now. Teresa is a great help with the kids, so we could conceivably promote her to 'nanny' so she can finally file taxes. Can you believe it? *Wanting* to file taxes? She just got her green card last week. Anyways, she's legit now so we can take her on our next trip to Romania. My family can finally meet Mia!"

Three years have passed very quickly. Proud parents of a boy and a girl, Sean and Leslie have a trust fund for each of them. Two platinum CDs and an Emmy can do that for people with talent and determination. That, and a sprawling waterfront bungalow in San Diego round things out quite nicely. Life is good.

———————

Mark and his step-dad are great buddies now – Mark built a car repair garage on their property where they work hard together during the week, then fish on weekends. They still flip a coin to see who cleans everything they catch.

Amy is in college, working on her law degree in Boston. She stays in touch with Les via email every few months. "I'm almost done second year. Woo hoo! Need a lawyer any time soon?"

"What do you know about the entertainment industry?" responded Les.

Lydia is in her second term as mayor, no thanks to the dirty antics of her opponent during the last campaign. A church attendee, it wasn't hard to find dirt on him thanks to one sharp and observant social coordinator... Marj was more than pleased to oblige.

Nurse Patrick sold her controlling interest in the clinic to Steve, Bill's old partner, and moved to California. Napa Valley in fact. There's something about growing things that she just can't get out of her head, and grapes fill the bill. Organic, no less.

Tobias Gregory Osborne still cleans yards, tunes up cars, and does odd jobs here and there. For some reason, no one wants to hire him full time. What he does enjoy most is the part-time outfitting company he and a friend started up. They guide out-of-town hunters to anywhere deer may be, or rent out quads, a GPS, and tents if they want to strike out on their own.

Malcolm expanded the plant just last year. At the expense of a baseball field out back, he doubled the square footage of the manufacturing floor, almost doubled profits, and took a sizable pay raise all at the same time. He keeps his association with "the Group" to a minimum. With just one child left at home, Malcolm and Marj host international students from Japan and elsewhere; Marj loves the stimulation from learning about other cultures first hand. She even picked up on how to cook a mean stir-fry, and the students love it. Malcolm and Marj still see Toby in church occasionally, but ever since the trial, they tend to sit on opposite sides of the sanctuary.

Specialis Ordo continue to create and manipulate so-called secret groups in North America, Europe, and the middle east. The members who do their dirty work are comprised mostly of religious extremists who think everything revolves around this or that god, with promises of eternal salvation, eternal rewards… something money could never buy, but something *Specialis Ordo* use as a means to an end. *Their* end.

At a recent meeting, the leader speaks:
"Gentlemen. We have a new player on the block. Her name is Ja'has Ibrahim-Hamdabagh, based in the Emirates. If you can believe it, she has princes eating out of her hand. She's eclipsing everything our newest member has done up to this point, so let's keep an eye on her. Last I heard, she bilked him out of 80 percent of his holdings. He claims he never saw it coming… happened in one fell swoop.

Thanks to Kirk over here, she's looking forward to meeting with some of us in a couple of weeks. Everyone please do their homework. First woman to perhaps enter our fold. Everyone ready for a shake-up?"

The End

Epilogue

Somewhere in a private lounge in Dubai, a cell phone hums. Expecting the call, she answers after one ring. "This is Ja'has." She extinguishes her cigarette.

"Underbridge here. Ready for the next move?"

"Divide and conquer as you say in your culture, correct? Yes my friend, everything is in place. I'm looking forward to the headlines."

"They won't know what hit them."

Ja'has comments: "Revenge is sweet, no? You will be hitting them right where it hurts."

"They went too far this time, Ja'has – they killed my daughter. I won't sleep at night until they're made to pay."

Underbridge pauses before striking the enter key of his laptop.

"This is going to cause a financial tsunami…"

Click

www.ingramcontent.com/pod-product-compliance
Lightning Source LLC
Chambersburg PA
CBHW071309200626
46813CB00015B/691